THE MARRIAGE
BETRAYAL

BOOKS BY SHALINI BOLAND

The Secret Mother
The Child Next Door
The Silent Sister
The Millionaire's Wife
The Perfect Family
The Best Friend
The Girl from the Sea

THE MARRIAGE BETRAYAL

SHALINI BOLAND

Bookouture

Published by Bookouture in 2019

An imprint of StoryFire Ltd.

Carmelite House
50 Victoria Embankment
London EC4Y 0DZ

www.bookouture.com

ISBN: 978-1-78681-736-5
eBook ISBN: 978-1-78681-735-8

For Natasha Harding, an editor in a million

PROLOGUE

She picks her way up the steep path as watery moonlight splashes down between the trees. Echoing strains of music and laughter floating up on the warm night air. The whispered hush and sigh of the waves in tune with her disappointment. She wishes she'd had more courage this evening. Why hadn't she been brave enough to speak to him? All that build-up to tonight… for nothing.

Her long strides turn into angry stomps. She'll be fifteen next week; she's not a child any more. So why does she feel so hopelessly young? So pathetically immature? The path narrows, and she ducks to avoid an overhanging branch. Blinks back frustrated tears and pushes her hair out of her eyes. She takes a breath, the familiar scent of sea salt and pine needles going some way to dampen her annoyance with herself.

A snapping twig makes her stop and cock her head to the side. She knows it's probably just a wild animal out hunting. Nevertheless, her breath hitches and her heart pumps a little harder. She's watched all the scary movies with her friends. She's seen the vampires and the zombies and the evil spirits that suck out teenage girls' souls. But it's the dark human characters who scare her the most. The ones who really do exist.

Still frozen in place, she wills herself to move once more. Lengthens her strides and quickens her pace. Not quite running. But almost.

Another cracking twig, a shuffle from behind. Sweat prickles on her back. Thoughts of soft lips and missed opportunities are pushed from her mind. Now, all she wants to do is reach the top of the cliff and race along the road. To get home and slam the door closed behind her. For her mum and dad to be angry that she's late back. For them to be furious that she walked home alone. For her to reassure them that she's fine. To roll her eyes and say, *It's okay, nothing happened.*

But now there's no mistaking the footsteps coming up the cliff path behind her. She reaches the stone steps and takes them two at a time, her wedge heels making a dull scrape and thud. The panic wanting to tear itself from her lips. She's only halfway up, and she won't be able to outrun whoever it is – not in these shoes. But there's no time to undo the straps and take them off.

Whoever it is, they're getting closer. She daren't turn around.

She times her next step wrong.

She trips.

Falls.

A hand reaches out to clasp her bare ankle.

She screams into the darkness.

CHAPTER ONE

NOW

The three-storey terraced house perches halfway up a steep cliff road, dramatically called Scar Point. It was described by the house-rental website as a handsome Gothic villa, but as we get closer my spirits drop a little as I note the peeling paint on the window frames, the mossy steps and rusted letterbox. I hope this isn't a taste of what's inside.

It's not just the look of the place that's put a dampener on everything – ever since we took the car-ferry to the Isle of Purbeck and we began winding our way to the sleepy seaside town of Swanage, I sensed my husband Jake's mood plummeting. This is obviously not the birthday surprise he was anticipating. He's been silent for the past half hour and I'm too nervous to ask him what's wrong, in case it descends into an argument.

'Is this our house?' Our seven-year-old son, Dylan, slides out of the car and stares doubtfully at the Victorian building looming above us, the setting sun reflected in its dark windows. He turns to look at me, his brown eyes brimming with accusation.

'Yes, it's going to be our lovely home for the week.' I heave a suitcase out of the car boot.

'So, we have to live here?' His voice wobbles.

'It'll be great,' I say brightly. 'We're right by the sea and, if you like, we can have ice creams tomorrow.'

Jake raises a dark eyebrow at my wanton use of bribery. I shrug apologetically – I hadn't expected to play the ice-cream card within seconds of arriving.

Tom and Lainy's Ford Focus pulls up behind our Nissan Qashqai. Lainy steps out of the passenger side, her biscuit-coloured hair pulled back in a ponytail, her skin pale, her eyes dark hollows. Lainy is my husband's younger sister, and she and Jake grew up in Swanage. They may be siblings, but they look nothing alike – Jake is tall and dark, while Lainy is slim and mousy.

It's Jake's birthday tomorrow, and so her husband Tom and I organised a nostalgic surprise week away for them – well, I say 'we' organised it, but actually it was purely my suggestion and legwork. Tom simply agreed that it was a great idea. But it looks as though our fabulous surprise has gone down like a ship with a cracked hull.

While Lainy bends down to usher their girls out of the car, Tom swings their suitcases out of the boot with ease and strides up the road to join us. He dumps the cases down, shades his eyes and gazes up at the house. 'This place is fantastic! It'll be like staying in a Hammer Horror movie.' He gives an evil laugh and grins at me. I sigh and avoid catching Jake's eye.

My little nieces, Annabel and Poppy, slip out of the car, yawning and rubbing their sleepy blue eyes, their clothes crumpled and their wavy blonde hair mussed up from the journey. Like a pair of well-played-with china dolls.

'They fell asleep about half an hour ago,' Lainy says, taking their hands. 'They'll probably be a bit cranky.'

I stop myself from adding, *Yes, along with everyone else.* Instead I lug one of our suitcases up the steps to the black front door and punch the code into the key safe on the wall. The metal hatch drops down and I draw out a thick iron key. Part of me wants to put the key back in the safe, jump in the car and drive all the way back home to London. But that's just my tiredness talking. We're here now. Whatever else lies on the other side of this door, we'll deal with it. I've spent weeks organising this getaway, so I'm not about to let everyone else's bad moods rub off on me.

The key slides into the lock effortlessly, and I push open the heavy wooden door. I was fully expecting it to give a theatrical creak, but it swings open noiselessly and I step inside the dim hallway.

'Smells a bit damp,' Jake grumbles, walking in behind me with Dylan.

'It'll be okay,' I reply, taking in the ornately tiled floor, dark wood panelling, sludge-green wallpaper, elegant, curved wooden staircase and impossibly high ceiling. Even Jake's six-foot-two frame is dwarfed by its height. 'We just need to open some windows, let some air in.'

'I don't like it, Mummy,' Dylan says. 'Can we go home?'

'Let's leave our suitcases in the hall and have our fish and chips,' I suggest, unwilling to brave the upstairs just yet. Worried in case it reveals more disappointment. 'Where's the kitchen?' We stopped off at the chippy in town on our way through, deciding that we're all too travel-weary to go out for dinner tonight, so we'll eat at the house and go exploring tomorrow. And now the salt-and-vinegar aroma is making my stomach gurgle.

Tom walks past me and starts opening doors, peering into gloomy rooms. 'Kitchen's back here!' he calls. 'It's… rustic.'

At least Tom is being upbeat. Lainy didn't look happy when she got out of the car. I hope she's okay.

'Good evening,' an unfamiliar voice calls out.

I jerk my head up to see an elegant woman walking down the stairs. She looks about my age, but that's where the similarity ends. She's tall, slim and blonde, wearing a tailored dress that manages to be demure and sexy at the same time. 'Uh, hello?' I stammer.

'Can we help you?' Jake says, stepping forward and extending his hand. 'Jake Townsend. Looks like there might have been a mix-up. Is it double booked?'

'Not that I'm aware of.' She gives him an amused smile, walks down the remaining stairs and shakes his hand. Holding on to it just a little too long for my liking. 'I'm Yasmin Belmont.'

The name triggers something in my mind. Where do I know that name from? And then it comes to me. 'Oh! Hello, Yasmin. You're the owner. We've emailed each other.'

'I am indeed. And so you must be Faye?' She turns her smile on me and I'm momentarily seduced. It feels like the sun has come out.

'Yes, I'm Faye, that's Jake, my husband, and this is our son Dylan. Nice to meet you. Is it okay that we let ourselves in? I didn't realise you'd be here. We did get the day right, didn't we?'

'Hello.' Tom reappears from the kitchen. And then Lainy and the girls come in through the front door.

'Goodness,' Yasmin says. 'There are a lot of you. What beautiful children!'

I detect the hint of an accent, but I can't place it. Maybe French, but I'm not sure.

'Well, welcome and hello, to you all. Apologies if I startled you – I always like to be here to greet guests on their first day. To introduce myself and answer any questions you may have. Please don't worry, I won't stay long.'

'No, it's fine,' Tom says. 'Stay for fish and chips, if you like?'

Lainy shoots him a look that makes him flush.

'You're so kind!' Yasmin replies with a laugh. 'But I'm sure you don't want me here longer than necessary. Is there anything you'd like to know about the house or the area while I'm here?'

'It's very kind of you, but I think we're okay. Jake and his sister know the area pretty well.'

'Okay.' She pouts. 'Well, let me at least tell you a bit about the house. My father bought it back in the nineties from an elderly couple who'd lived in it for almost fifty years! He bought up a lot of the property around here. Most of the houses are seasonal weekly lets, like this one, but we do also let them out for longer during the winter.'

I know she's probably trying to be helpful and interesting, but quite honestly, I wish she would go and leave us to it. We're all tired and a bit irritable and could really do with food and an early night. It's also a little bit strange that she's been waiting here in the house for us. We never told her what time we'd be arriving. It was available any time after noon, which was hours ago. Does that mean she's been here all that time? With most holiday rentals, you're just given a key and the place is yours for a week. I realise she's still talking, but I must have zoned out, so I nod and smile, stifling a yawn.

'Okay, so if you have any questions or problems, please don't hesitate to get in touch. I only live up the road, so it's no trouble to pop down if you need me. Faye, you have my number?'

'I do.'

'Thank you,' Jake says. 'Everything seems really great. It's a wonderful old house.'

I wonder if she heard his 'damp' comment when he first walked in.

'It certainly has a lot of character. A bit like this handsome chap.' Yasmin bends and squeezes Dylan's cheek affectionately.

'Ow!' My son puts a hand to his cheek and looks at me, outraged.

Yasmin doesn't seem to notice. 'Okay, well. I'll get out of your hair now. Have a wonderful stay. And, like I said, any problems just shout.'

We say our goodbyes and she sashays through the hall and out of the front door, closing it firmly behind her.

'Well. That was a bit weird,' Lainy says.

'I thought it was quite a nice thing to do,' Tom says. 'To welcome us. It *is* her house after all.'

Lainy gives him a look and then frowns. 'She looks really familiar. I'm trying to think where I've seen her before.'

Dylan tugs at my arm. 'She pinched me, Mummy, did you see?'

I smile down at him. 'I don't think she meant to hurt you, Dyls.'

He scowls and takes his hand away from his cheek, and I see that she's left quite a livid red mark. 'Oh, Dyls, are you okay?'

'He's fine, Faye,' Jake says. 'Don't mollycoddle him.'

Jake has a point. It was just an overfriendly gesture. I probably shouldn't fuss so much.

We pile into the kitchen. It's clean at least, if a bit dated. And Jake was right earlier – it definitely smells a bit mildewy in here. I ease up one of the sash windows overlooking the forlorn back garden, walled on all sides. Tom unlocks the back door and props it open with a stone planter. A shaft of evening sunlight spills onto the grey kitchen flagstones, and a breeze stirs the discordant wind chimes hanging by the back door.

'Okay, plates…' I open one of the kitchen cupboards but find mugs and glasses instead.

Lainy and I bustle about the kitchen finding plates and cutlery, while Jake unwraps the fish and chips.

'It's strange to be back in Swanage,' he murmurs.

'How long's it been?' Toms asks. Five-year-old Annabel clambers onto his lap, sticks her thumb in her mouth and closes her eyes.

'Don't let her fall asleep again!' Lainy says. 'She'll be awake all night. Hey, Annabel, sweetie, do you want some juice?'

'Yes please.' She nods sleepily, burrowing deeper into Tom's lap, like a hibernating dormouse.

Jake starts portioning out the food. 'We haven't been back here for… must be seventeen years, right, Lainy?'

'About that,' Lainy agrees. 'I wonder if it's changed much down in the town.'

Jake shrugs and his face closes down again. My stomach knots. Coming here has definitely unsettled my husband. I was looking forward to supper a few moments ago, but my appetite is rapidly waning.

I pick at my fish, trying to think of a way to lift the mood.

'Where are the onion rings?' Dylan asks.

I glance around the table, just in time to see Poppy eat the last one.

'Oh, Poppy!' Lainy says. 'Those were Dylan's.'

Seven-year-old Poppy frowns. 'But I like onion rings too.'

'Yes, but you asked for cod and chips. Dylan asked for onion rings.'

'It's fine,' I say. 'Dylan doesn't mind, do you, Dyl?' I give him a look to let him know he shouldn't kick up a fuss.

'Aren't there any left?' he asks, his voice perilously high.

'We'll get some more tomorrow.' I'm desperately thinking of a way to change the subject. The last thing we need is for one or more of the kids to have a meltdown.

'But that's not fair!'

'You can have some of Poppy's chips,' Tom says, grabbing a handful off his daughter's plate and plonking them onto Dylan's.

'Daddy!' Poppy cries. 'You had an onion ring too. So did Annabel.'

'Tell you what,' I say, attempting to make myself heard above the escalating squabble, 'after supper, we'll go and choose our bedrooms. What do you think about that?' I'm hoping that after a good night's sleep, things will improve.

'What's my bedroom like?' Poppy asks. 'Can it be yellow? Yellow's my favourite colour.'

'I don't know, sweetie, we'll have to take a look.' I turn to Lainy. 'I thought the girls could share a room? And Dylan, you can have your own room if you like?'

My son doesn't reply, his arms folded across his chest in full-on sulk mode, which isn't like him at all. He's normally so sunny and easy-going.

'Want to choose your own room?' I ask once more.

He shrugs.

I suddenly realise he might be nervous about sleeping on his own in a strange house. And he'll be too embarrassed to admit it in front of everyone. 'How about when we've finished eating we go upstairs and take a look? Maybe you could share with your cousins?'

'Okay,' he replies, looking a little less cross.

Lainy comes upstairs with me and the children while Jake and Tom stay to clear the table. With all thoughts of their earlier argument forgotten, the three kids eventually settle into one of the huge bedrooms, which has two sets of rickety-looking bunk beds. I leave a nightlight on, kiss them good night and then let Lainy choose which bedroom she and Tom would like. She doesn't seem too fussed, taking the first one she sees, next to the kids' room.

This leaves me with a choice of three other bedrooms. I decide to ignore the top floor and take the remaining room on this floor. It's large and square with lumpy-looking woodchip on the walls, an ornate fireplace and a huge bay window overlooking the road below. The sun has already dropped behind the houses opposite. I guess, in the daytime, we'll be able to glimpse the ocean beyond. But, for now, all is shrouded in darkness apart from the warm pools of yellow light cast by the Victorian-style street lamps. I glance at my watch, surprised to see it's nearly ten o'clock already. No wonder the children were so cranky.

'You okay?' Lainy asks, tucking her mousy hair behind her ears and following me into what will be mine and Jake's bedroom.

'I was about to ask you the same thing.' I sit down heavily on the double bed. But my backside hits a hard ridge, and I realise it's two singles pushed together. I shift over.

'It feels a bit weird to be back.' She wanders over to the window.

Guilt tugs at my chest. 'We shouldn't have come—'

'No, no, it's fine. I just… didn't expect to feel like this.'

'Like…?'

She shrugs.

'Don't you have any happy memories of the place at all?'

'I suppose I have a few. We had some nice family beach days.' She gives a thin smile. 'I remember one day, Dad's deckchair folded up while he was still sitting in it. At first, Jake and I couldn't stop laughing. But then we realised Dad was furious. He strode off to get his money back from the deckchair guy and then we all had to pack up and go home.' Lainy's eyes take on a faraway look.

'Would you rather we hadn't come?'

'No, course not. I'll be fine. Just tired.'

This downbeat withdrawal is very out of character for Lainy, who's normally the one to take charge. She's a primary school teacher and possesses the kind of commanding confidence that's a necessity for wrangling a class of thirty bouncy kids.

Footsteps on the stairs summon her out of the room. It sounds like Tom and Jake are coming up.

Jake pushes open the door enquiringly. 'Is this our room?'

'If you like. There are other rooms upstairs but—'

'No, this is fine.' He casts his eyes unenthusiastically around the space.

'Sorry the place is a bit run-down. It looked much nicer in the photos.'

'It's fine, don't worry about it.'

'I guess all those glowing website reviews were left by friends and family.' I smile, hoping to engage him in some light-hearted banter, but my husband doesn't want to join in. 'It's your birthday tomorrow.' I try to elicit at least a small smile.

'Don't remind me. Thirty-four years old! How did that happen?'

'You don't look it,' I reply, wrapping my arms around him and pressing my head into his chest. His heart beats against my ear and he strokes my hair. Kisses the top of my head.

'Sorry I've been grumpy,' he murmurs.

'You haven't been grumpy,' I lie. 'I just feel bad for springing this surprise on you when it's obvious you're not happy about being here. I'm an insensitive idiot.'

'Your heart was in the right place. It's just… I don't really have great memories of this town.'

'I remember you saying earlier this year that you miss the smell of the sea. So I thought that meant you missed your childhood home. That's the reason—'

'Let's go to bed,' he says, abruptly changing the subject. I stare up at him, into his dark eyes, and he gives me a cheeky grin. 'Just let me brush my teeth and wash the journey off. I'll be back in a minute.'

While he's gone, I start unpacking our case, hanging my long summery dresses and Jake's cotton shirts in the massive wooden wardrobe. A wailing car alarm draws me to the window and I peer down. It's not one of ours, but a vehicle parked further down the street. There's a bleep and it stops. I shift my gaze across to the gap between the two houses opposite. The moon comes out from behind a cloud, shining onto the rippling ocean below. It's magical. Like something out of a fairy story. I take it all in for a few moments and then I notice a silhouette on the opposite side of the road.

Someone is standing just beyond the street light, staring up at the house. Staring up at the window.

Staring at *me*.

CHAPTER TWO

It's a muggy night and the street is quiet. He's standing in the warm shadows, in the black space that hovers between the ornate Victorian street lights. He's been here for a while now, staring up at the house, contemplating its latest occupants. Wondering what he's even doing here. He didn't intend to come out. He just… well, he just ended up here somehow.

And now she's at the window, illuminated behind the glass like a living doll in a box. Staring off into the distance, over the rooftops towards the sea. He takes a breath, but doesn't bow his head, or move away. Will she spot him down here?

Yes!

She sees him. And instead of feeling caught in the act, he feels… what? Somehow pleased. He continues staring at her. Maybe she'll be reassured by his presence.

But he knows he shouldn't linger. With regret, he realises that it was a mistake.

He should leave. Disappear back into the shadows.

For now, at least.

CHAPTER THREE

I step back from the window, my heart hammering in my chest. Why is that man looking up at me? I peer down again. It looks like Jake! But I thought Jake was in the bathroom. What on earth is he doing outside? I look again and see I was wrong, it isn't Jake at all. He's still staring up at the house, but he's in shadow so I can't get a good look at him. What does he want? With a shiver, I pull the curtains closed and wrap my arms around myself.

'What's wrong?'

I jump at the sound of my husband's voice. 'You scared the life out of me!'

'Who else did you think it would be?'

'No one. I just… I didn't hear you come in.' I draw back the curtains a little and stare down at the road again. But the man has gone. Did I imagine him?

'Faye?' Jake comes over to where I'm standing. 'What's the matter? You look like you've seen a ghost.'

'Nothing. Just tired.'

He gives me a strange look but doesn't ask any more questions. I take his hand. 'Come on, let's go to bed.'

It's only nine thirty but the sun is already high in the sky, lasering into my skull like a blow torch. The children have been slathered in sunscreen, hats wedged tight onto their fair little heads. I had to give myself the same treatment – covering my arms and head – as pale skin and red hair are not the best combination to have during a heatwave. But at least there's a soft breeze blowing in off the ocean as we make our way along the ridgeline at Durlston Head, the winding clifftop walk that leads to Anvil Point Lighthouse.

Jake and I had sex last night and I put more of myself into it than usual, wanting to ease my guilt. Trying to get him to relax. To start enjoying our time away together. He murmured my name, his fingers gripping my hips. His body less tense afterwards. Relaxing into sleep almost immediately. I envied him in that moment.

I slept fitfully, still worrying about whether this trip is a giant mistake. At least I didn't have any nightmares, which is unusual for me. Most nights I suffer from what can only be described as night terrors – extreme fear where I wake up sweating and gasping for breath. Jake is a deep sleeper, so he rarely witnesses these episodes. And when he does, he's always shocked. Last night's absence of fear makes me think that planning this holiday was the right thing to do... for *me* at least.

When I awoke this morning, I hoped that Jake would be in a more positive frame of mind, but he is still quiet and withdrawn. Almost sullen. All I can do is to make the most of being here. To continue on with the plan for a day out at the country park, followed by a birthday cream tea for Jake at Durlston Castle. Hoping that a lovely family outing will put Jake in a better mood. It hasn't so far...

'Mummy, can we go inside the caves?' Dylan asks, his fists gripping a set of rusted metal gates looped over with a chain and padlock. He rattles them noisily and we're given disapproving looks by a group of passing hikers wearing bright shorts and expensive walking boots.

'No, Dyl. They're not safe.' I'm surprised Dylan would even want to go into the caves. The entrance looks absolutely terrifying, closed off with two sets of gates, bramble bushes and a keep out sign. Tom and I peer down at the information board.

'It says here the Tilly Whim caves were eighteenth-century quarries – where you dig out stone to make things with,' Tom explains to Dylan. 'But then they were closed and only smugglers used them.'

'What's smugglers?' Dylan asks. 'Is it like pirates?'

'Kind of,' Tom says. 'Smugglers used to hide illegal things in the caves. Things they didn't want the government to take away.'

'Like knives?' Dylan says. 'Or bombs?'

Poppy rolls her eyes and shakes her head. 'Daddy means things like whisky and wine. We did a project at school.' I often forget that Poppy is the same age as Dylan – she always seems so much older.

'So can we go in the caves or not?' Dylan asks, pretending to hold a sword and slice off his cousin's head. She shoots him with an imaginary gun.

'Not,' I reply.

'They used to be open to the public,' Lainy says quietly. 'But there was a rockfall in the seventies, so they closed them again.'

'That's not fair,' Dylan says. 'I wish we could go in.'

'They're not safe, Dyl,' I reply, peering down at the overgrown entrance. Giving a shiver at the thought of the dark dankness beyond.

'We could wear those yellow builders' hats,' Poppy says. 'Then we'd be okay.'

'Sorry, guys, you're still not allowed. Even with hard hats,' Tom says. 'But how about we try to spot some seals instead.'

'Or dolphins,' I add. 'There's supposed to be a dolphin-watching station up here somewhere.'

Jake has been lagging behind, but he's catching up now and Dylan bounds up to him as he draws near. 'Daddy, we're going to look out for dolphins. Do you want to help?'

'Sure, bud. We should have brought binoculars though.'

'Can we go back and get some?' Dylan asks.

'I think there's a pair in the glove box,' I say.

'Really?' Jake frowns. 'I don't remember there being any—'

'I bought some for the holiday,' I reply. 'I read up about the place beforehand and it mentioned all the wildlife.'

'It's too far to go back for them now,' Jake says.

'Maybe you could bring Dyl up here tomorrow morning,' I suggest. 'Bring the binoculars with you.' I turn to our son. 'Bet you anything you'll spot some dolphins if you come early enough.'

'Really?' Dylan bounces from foot to foot, and my heart blooms with love for his wide-eyed excitement. 'Can we, Daddy?'

Jake shrugs. 'Sure, why not.'

'Mummy, can you come too?'

'Why don't you make it a boys' thing?' I suggest.

'I don't think Mummy wants to get up that early,' Jake says. 'You know she likes her lie-ins.'

'Please, Mummy!'

'We'll see,' I reply, wondering how I can get out of it. In any case, my husband's spot on about me not being a morning person. I never have been.

I can tell from Jake's demeanour that something is still not right. He doesn't want to be here, and his discomfort is making me anxious. It's also making me sound too bright – injecting a perkiness into my voice that's irritating even to my own ears. Like I'm trying too hard. But I can't seem to stop myself. I want to make everything perfect today.

I met my husband almost a decade ago, when a mutual friend recommended me to design the graphics for Jake's new web design business. Although we met in London, we found we had a lot in common. He grew up in Swanage, and I grew up not too far away in Dorchester. We were both small-town Dorset kids who had found ourselves in the big city… and we loved the freedom and anonymity of it. Taking advantage of all the cultural events, the theatres, bars, restaurants, galleries. We spent hours just walking the busy streets, people-watching and enjoying one another's company.

Intoxicated by such abundance after the limitations of nothing but a single high street and an out-of-town cinema complex.

'Guys, guys, look!' Tom points out to sea. 'Is that a seal?'

We all swivel our heads around and crowd over to where Tom is standing. Lainy lifts Annabel up and points. I follow Tom's line of sight to see a small dark shape bobbing in the blue-green water below.

'It looks like a dog, Mummy!' Dylan cries.

Sure enough, its dark fur and black nose do look very dog-like. Irrationally, I have the sensation that this sea creature is staring right at me, its dark eyes boring into mine, warning me of something. And then, suddenly, it's gone. Disappeared beneath the waves.

'Where is it?' Poppy asks. 'I can't see it any more.'

'She's gone back to her family,' Tom replies.

'Does she have a mummy and daddy?'

'Yes, and probably brothers and sisters too.'

After the seal sighting, the children are excited, making up stories about seals, dolphins, mermaids and other sea creatures, real and imagined. We continue on up to the lighthouse, gripping their small hands as we traverse the trickier parts of the trail – uneven rocks, steep winding steps and loose gravel pathways. At least there's a low wall along this particular part of cliff edge. Nevertheless, we're mindful to keep the children on the inside of the trail, away from the ocean side.

'Did you guys used to come here when you were kids?' Tom reaches out his hand to help Lainy over a particularly challenging group of rocks. 'Must have been amazing to have had all this on your doorstep. Bit different to growing up in Croydon.' He laughs.

'Not very often,' Lainy replies. 'We mainly hung out in each other's houses. But I guess we sometimes went to the caves and the beaches.'

'The caves?' I reply. 'I thought they were all closed down.'

'Yeah, well, kids have a way of finding themselves in places they shouldn't be,' Lainy says.

'I hope our kids don't!' Tom says. 'If they do, I'll know who the bad influence is.'

Lainy gives a short laugh. I notice Jake hasn't joined in the conversation, but I don't want to push it, so I leave him be.

Finally, we clamber to the top of the cliff, and reach the flat, grassy headland around the lighthouse. To my disappointment, the white tower is surrounded by a drystone wall and a gate, meaning we can't get close to it.

'Can't we go inside?' Dylan asks, peering through the gate.

'It looks private to me,' Tom says.

'Maybe we could ask the lighthouse keeper,' I say, turning to Jake.

My husband shakes his head. 'There isn't one.'

'No lighthouse keeper?' Tom says. 'How do you know that?'

'It's been automated for years. Even when we were kids it was automated.'

We wander around the perimeter wall, finally deciding on a grassy spot to have our picnic. The sky above is blue but there are black clouds on the horizon and a sudden breeze shivers the grass as seagulls wheel and hover around us. Out on the glittering sea, white sailing boats bob about like toys, while more dark cliffs stand firm in the distance.

The atmosphere between us all is strained, but at least we have the children here to inject a bit of normality, their chatter breaking up the awkward silences and stilted conversation. Jake wolfs down his food, but Lainy hardly touches a thing, her normally smiling face pale and drawn, her eyes dull. Both she and Jake barely say a word, only answering when they're spoken to, or interjecting to admonish one of the children.

Tom and I keep throwing one another glances, silently commiserating that our surprise holiday has so far been a spectacular disaster. Once again, I stare at my husband's troubled face, searching for clues to his state of mind. But he doesn't even glance in my direction. His thoughts are hidden from me. And I daren't ask about them, for fear of what he might say.

CHAPTER FOUR

THEN

It's dark in the cave, and the flickering light from the fire makes it difficult to tell, but Lainy is pretty sure that Owen is checking her out. Trouble is, every time she looks over to catch his eye, he looks away. Or maybe she's just imagining it. Yeah, she's obviously got it totally wrong. And anyway, he's in the year above so he probably doesn't even know she exists. Plus, he's sitting next to Rose, who's totally beautiful with her strawberry-blonde hair and cute freckles.

Lainy's only here with all the cool kids because her older brother Jake is supposed to keep an eye on her during the half-term break while Mum and Dad are at work. To be fair to her brother, he doesn't complain about her tagging along. But she's careful not to annoy him, staying quiet and keeping herself to herself. Content to watch from the sidelines.

The irony is, her parents could easily leave her on her own. Lainy always gets her homework done on time, meets her curfew and keeps her room tidy. She has no interest in being a rebellious teenager. She's far more sensible than her older brother and is perfectly capable of looking after herself. She's fourteen, not four. Although these ghost stories are definitely starting to freak her out. She's trying not to listen too hard to her brother's best friend Mark's creepy urban myth about a woman lured from her car by an axe murderer. But snippets of the story keep penetrating her brain. She's probably going to have nightmares later. Her mum says she has an overactive imagination.

The only bad thing Lainy's ever done is coming here. The caves are supposed to be a totally out-of-bounds place. All the local kids grew up with strict instructions never to go in them, their parents warning about the perils of rockfalls and dangerous tides and a million and one other disasters waiting to happen. I mean, if they were so worried, why did they even live in such a treacherous place? Lainy's sure her parents must have snuck into the caves when they were young, so, if you ask her, it's hypocritical of them to keep going on about it. And it's not like there's anything else to do around here. But all the same, she can't help imagining the horror of what it would be like to get trapped in here by a rockfall or an incoming tide. She'll probably breathe easier once she's back out in the open air.

Instead of listening to Mark's story, Lainy lets her mind drift. Cath, from the year above, is sitting opposite, and she definitely has a crush on Mark. She keeps touching his arm and thrusting her huge boobs in his direction. Lainy can only dream of having boobs like that. Her own meagre chest barely fills out a training bra. She can't tell if Mark likes Cath back. But, then again, boys are so hard to read.

Mark must have reached the punchline of his story because Kayla – also in her brother's year – suddenly grabs hold of Lainy's arm and gives a squeal. For a small person, Kayla's grip is surprisingly firm, and Lainy flinches. The cavern is filled with screams and squeals. The boys' delighted laughter echoes around the dark chamber. Lainy's glad she didn't listen to the awful story. She shifts and re-crosses her legs, the hard rock floor becoming uncomfortable.

'You okay, Lainy?' Cath asks, her voice carrying above the laughter.

Everyone turns to look at Lainy, who flushes, embarrassed to be the focus of everyone's attention.

'Weren't you freaked out by that story?' Cath asks. 'You didn't even jump.'

'I wasn't really listening.'

Cath gives her an odd look and Lainy realises she should have pretended to be scared. Now everyone will think she's weird.

'I was thinking about the summer holidays,' Lainy mumbles.

'Oh yeah, summer holidays!' Cath glances around the small circle of friends, her eyes shining. 'We should have an end-of-year party down at Smugglers' Cove!'

This suggestion is met with murmurs of excitement, and suggestions for when to hold it and who to invite. Smugglers' Cove is a small sandy beach at the base of the cliffs. Lainy and her family often go there, as it's the closest beach to their house, accessed by a steep, little-known path. Most tourists don't know about it, so it's become a locals' well-kept secret. Lainy hopes her parents will let her go to the party. She'll have to get Jake to plead her case.

She twists a strand of hair around her little finger and finally catches Owen's eye. He smiles, and Lainy swears it's a smile of promise. A smile of what's to come…

CHAPTER FIVE

NOW

After a somewhat disappointing day, including a lacklustre rendition of 'Happy Birthday' in Durlston Castle and the unexpected arrival of torrential rain, I drag everyone down to a pub in town for Jake's birthday dinner. I would have booked a posh restaurant, but we wouldn't have been able to relax with the kids in tow, so the Jolly Sailor is the next best thing. The menu is good and the place is jammed, its windows steamed up and the rain still bucketing down outside. It's lucky I booked a table. I'm hoping a few glasses of wine will cheer everyone up. I haven't smoked for years – not since college – but I'd kill for a cigarette right now. Even a hit of second-hand smoke would be better than nothing. Something to quell this jittery feeling.

Having ordered our food at the bar, I make my way back to the table with a tray of drinks. Our little group is seated by the front window, at two dark-wood tables pushed together. Anyone looking would see two young families having a relaxed evening out. They wouldn't see the discomfort, the anxiety, the resentment. They might even be envious. Two handsome men, two well-dressed women, three beautiful children… but looks can be deceiving. Nothing is ever as it seems. And we are all as far from relaxed as it's possible to be. Miles out of our comfort zones. Pretending to be enjoying ourselves.

I should probably ask Jake what's wrong. In fact, he's probably *waiting* for me to ask. For me to be concerned. To apologise once more for bringing him back to his childhood home. But I don't want to risk an argument this evening. I already want to relegate this trip to history.

'The food will take about half an hour,' I say, sliding back into my seat between Lainy and Dylan.

'That's ages!' Dylan cries. 'I'm sooo hungry.'

'They're bringing bread,' I reply. 'But I don't see how you can be hungry. You haven't stopped eating all day.' I poke Dylan's tummy, making him giggle.

As it turns out, the food arrives quite quickly and we tuck into our traditional pub fare – lasagnes, sausages and chips, fish pie. I can tell it's good, not because I'm enjoying it – I'm too keyed up for that – but rather because I'm experiencing it on a detached level. Like a wine-taster or food technician who might appreciate the quality of something without dwelling on it. Jake and I give one another polite smiles. His mouth is drawn into a taut line and the skin around his eyes is strained. We're pulling apart, like a frayed piece of elastic.

'Hey, guys,' Tom says, holding up one of his chips, 'why did the chip cross the road?'

'I don't know,' Poppy replies with a giggle.

'Because he saw a fork up ahead.'

Poppy and Dylan groan, but Annabel doesn't understand, so Lainy starts explaining what a fork in the road is.

Tom catches my eye and shrugs. It was a terrible joke, and Tom knows it, but at least he's trying to jolly everyone along.

Much like earlier in the day, our evening revolves around the children. Focusing on them stops us focusing on ourselves. Checking if they've eaten enough, if their hands are too sticky, if they're being too noisy, if they're having fun… Suddenly, I'm desperate to get back to the house. To slip into bed and pull the covers over my head. To not have to pretend we're all having such a wonderful time. But it's Jake's birthday, I need to pull myself together and be happy for his sake – even though he's not himself either. Normally, when we're in company, he's confident, sociable, upbeat. Not today.

The meal is soon finished, a generous tip left on the tray, and we vacate our table, much to the excitement of another hovering family who pounce on our seats before we've even gathered our belongings.

Outside, the evening is warm and drizzly – a small respite after the sticky heat of the pub. With Dylan's hand in his, Jake turns to head back up the hill.

'It's only eight thirty,' Lainy says. 'We can't go back yet. It's your birthday, Jake, we should go somewhere, do something.'

Jake stops and turns around. 'I'm not that big on birthdays, guys. And anyway, the kids are yawning and the weather's vile. We should probably get them into bed.'

'The kids will be fine, mate.' Tom claps Jake on the shoulder. 'If they have a late night we might even get a lie-in tomorrow. We're on holiday. Come on!'

Jake hesitates. I can tell he wants to go back, but at the same time, he doesn't want to offend Tom. 'What do you suggest? Pretty sure my clubbing days are over, and anyway, where can we go with the children in tow?'

'Look.' Lainy points down the street. 'There's an art gallery down there. Looks like they're having an exhibition. Why don't we all take a look and get out of the rain? Then we can see what we feel like doing afterwards.'

Poppy pulls at Jake's hand. 'Can we go to the art place, Uncle Jake? For your birthday?'

Jake always manages to be won over by his nieces. He sighs. 'Sure, Poppy. Okay, why not.'

We troop down the road to the gallery, where visitors are spilling out onto the pavement, taking shelter under a sky-blue canopy, glasses of fizz in hand. A damp-looking dog has been tied up outside and it lies on the pavement beneath the canopy, forlorn, its nose between its front paws.

'Aw, a doggy!' Poppy cries. 'Can we stroke him?'

'Better not,' Tom replies. 'We don't know if he's friendly. Come on, let's go inside.'

It appears to be an exhibition of local artists – landscapes and seascapes of the surrounding area. My heart gives a little tug as we walk into the gallery, the chatter and buzz embracing us in its warmth. The atmosphere is friendly and inviting, welcoming smiles aimed in our direction.

The girls pull Tom and Jake across the room to a striking mermaid watercolour.

'Lainy, look.' I nudge her with my elbow.

She follows my line of sight to see a blonde woman walk across the room towards Jake. 'It's the woman who owns our holiday home.'

'Yasmin Belmont.'

Her blonde hair is pulled up into an artful knot that looks like something out of a style magazine.

'I think she fancies Jake.' I roll my eyes.

'Do you want to go over there?' Lainy asks.

I shake my head. 'He's with the children. What's she going to do, force her tongue down his throat?'

'She might. She looks the type.' Lainy gives me a quick grin to show she's joking, and then cries, '*I've got it!*'

'Got what?'

'I've remembered where I know her from.'

I'm only half listening, watching Jake laugh at something Yasmin has said. He hasn't shown half as much interest in *me* this holiday. Unless you count the routine sex we had last night.

'Faye, are you listening?'

'Sorry, what?'

'I said I've remembered where I know her from – Yasmin. She grew up around here. Only I never knew her full name back then.'

'Did she go to your school?'

'No, she lived at the top of the cliff in this massive house. Went to a private school outside town. She was always being chauffeured around in this huge, shiny black car. Thought she was better than everyone else because her family was loaded. We thought she was a bit of a stuck-up bitch. I never realised she was French, or whatever that accent is.'

'Maybe she wasn't stuck up. Maybe she was just… rich.'

'Perhaps. But you saw what she was like when she met us at the house.'

'Hmm.' I don't want to speak badly about someone I've only just met. But I have to admit, I didn't take to the woman. Mainly because she pinched Dylan's cheek so hard. 'She certainly seems to like Jake.'

'Don't worry about my brother,' Lainy replies. 'Where's the alcohol? That's what I want to know.' She glances around, her forehead wrinkling.

'Over there.' I point to a table on our right. We link arms, walk over and help ourselves to a glass of bubbly. 'Do you think we need to pay someone for these?'

'No one's here asking for cash,' Lainy says. 'I think it must be complementary.'

'Nice.' I take a sip; it's a little warm and a little flat, but still tastes pretty good.

'Do you miss it?' Lainy asks, touching my arm. 'Your art?'

I flinch. It's a straightforward question, but one that I'm not sure how to answer. The truth is, I try not to think about what might have been. Art has always been in my blood. A way to lose myself. To work through the feelings of losing my mother to cancer when I was ten years old. A way to deal with having a grieving father who was unable to cope with his distraught, angry daughter. I lost myself in the images I created. Painted away my pain. Exorcised demons.

Eight years ago, I won a coveted award from the London art college I attended. At my graduation show, I sold all my paintings to several well-known collectors. I was also offered representation by two prestigious galleries. But then, a week later, I discovered I was pregnant. I suppose I could have continued down both paths, having a child while continuing to pursue my career – plenty of people do. But I was in a relationship with Jake. I was in love. Infatuated. And everything else seemed pale by comparison. I had this image of the three of us making a wonderful little family without any outside distractions – creating a family to replace the one I lost. I would paint in the evenings while our baby slept. My inspiration would be limitless. So, I foolishly let those early offers of representation fall by the wayside, assuming there would be plenty more opportunities in the future. I was wrong. After Dylan was born, there was no more interest. No more offers.

But I wasn't unhappy about it. I didn't regret my choice. Instead, I threw myself into motherhood and helping Jake with his web design business. He likes me working for him – says it makes more sense for me to use my artistic talents for his clients. Plus it helps with the tax side of things. I missed having my own income though, so now I do a bit of freelance illustrating on the side – children's books and personalised kids' art for a little extra. It's not the big, shiny career I was primed for, but at least it's creative. At least, that's what I tell myself.

Yet a part of me misses the raw creativity that comes with painting for pleasure. The release of letting the paint fall on canvas without thinking about clients or money. The sheer freedom of it.

People occasionally ask why I don't start painting again. Now that Dylan is at school, I could make time. Make space. But the truth is I don't want to. Or rather, I'm scared. What if I can't do it? What if I've lost that spark? What if I can't regain that feeling that my art once gave me? If it's gone forever, I think I would rather not know. Which is why I never usually walk into galleries. They remind me too much of what I left behind. Of what I'm too insecure to return to.

'Faye?' Lainy prompts me to answer her question.

'Do I miss it?' I pretend to consider her question, like it's something I've never thought about before. 'Not really. Too busy with Dylan and the business. You know what it's like. Real life takes over.'

'Tell me about it. In my case, my life is all about planning and marking.'

'Don't forget the nice long teachers' holidays,' I add.

'True,' Lainy replies with a smile. Her eyes suddenly narrow, and she nods her head towards the rear of the gallery.

I look across to see Dylan chatting animatedly to a dark-haired man. 'Back in a mo,' I say, already heading over to my son.

'So, are you an artist, young man?' the man asks Dylan, his voice gravelly, with a faint Dorset accent.

'My mummy is,' Dylan says with pride in his voice.

'If only that were true,' I interject.

'You *are!*' Dylan looks up, cross with me for playing down my status. 'She's done pictures in books and on websites too.'

'Is that right?' He gives me an appraising look and holds out his hand. 'Louis Michael.' He pronounces his name without the 's'.

'Faye Townsend, and this is Dylan.' We shake. His hand is firm and calloused.

'Are you an artist too?' Dylan asks.

'Sort of. I'm a stonemason.'

'What's a stone basin?'

'*Mason.* I make things out of stone. Local Purbeck stone. You can come up to the quarry if you like. Have a go yourself. It's good fun, chipping away at bits of rock.'

I clear my throat.

'With your mum of course. The more the merrier. I sell my work, maybe you'd like a piece for your garden? A stone bench, a bird bath, or maybe something more interesting like a lion?'

'A lion?' Dylan's eyes widen. 'Can we, Mummy?'

'We'll see. Thanks for the invitation, Louis.'

'My pleasure.'

'Faye?'

I jump at the sound of my husband's deep voice behind me. Put a hand to my chest. 'Jake! You startled me.'

'Who's this you're talking to?'

'Oh!' I'm still flustered. 'Dylan was chatting to this stonemason – *Louis*, is that right?'

The man nods and gives me a smile.

'Louis works locally, and Dylan was saying he'd like to go to the quarry to see some of his work.'

'Sounds interesting, but I doubt we'll have the time.' Jake looks regretful. 'We're here on holiday. Only staying for a few days.'

'That's a shame,' Louis says. 'Your son tells me your wife's an artist.'

Jake nods. 'She illustrates and designs web pages for my company.'

'Very nice.'

'Well, we should be getting back.' Jake takes hold of my hand and rubs his thumb across my palm.

'Nice to meet you,' Louis says. 'Enjoy the rest of your stay.'

'Thank you.' Jake nods.

'Bye, Louis!' Dylan waves enthusiastically.

'Bye, Dylan.' Louis gives him a wink.

The three of us walk back to the others, weaving our way through the crowded gallery. Suddenly, everything feels too hot. Too bright. Too loud.

'You look a bit peaky,' Jake says, frowning. 'Are you okay?'

I nod and give him an automatic smile. But I really don't think I am.

CHAPTER SIX

The kids are tucked up in bed and the four of us are seated around the kitchen table while Tom pours four measures of brandy into cheap glass tumblers.

'When did you get that?' Lainy nods her head at the bottle.

'This evening. I was inspired by the smugglers,' he explains with a grin, doling them out to each of us and then raising his glass. 'Happy birthday, Jake.'

We raise our glasses in a birthday toast. 'Happy birthday, Jake.'

'Cheers, guys.' Jake takes a healthy gulp. 'Mm, this is good.'

'So…' Tom says, drumming his fingers on the table, 'are we all having a shit time, or what?'

Lainy chokes on her drink, and I manage a small laugh at Tom's outspokenness.

Jake shakes his head and grins at his brother-in-law. 'Tell it like it is, why don't you? I thought we were too British for that. Surely we're supposed to smile and pretend everything's great.'

'Yeah, I don't think you've quite got the hang of the *smiling* part.' Tom cocks his head. 'So everything *isn't* great, then?'

Jake shrugs and knocks back the rest of his brandy.

Lainy places a warning hand on Tom's arm, but he misconstrues her meaning, taking her hand and kissing it.

I know Tom is trying to break the uncomfortable atmosphere, but I really wish he wouldn't. He doesn't know what he'll unleash. And I'm too tired, my emotions too on the edge to cope with a soul-baring session. It's taken me weeks to organise this trip. And that on top of finishing off an illustration commission and getting Jake's bookkeeping up to date. Plus managing Dylan's school life, his crazy amount of homework and end-of-year school projects and shows. For a seven-year old, his diary is fuller than most adults'.

'So, what's up with you two?' Tom ploughs on, looking from Jake to Lainy. 'Not happy to be back in your childhood home, is that it? Did Faye and I make a mistake booking this holiday? Should we all pack up and go home?'

'Go home?' I splutter. 'It's not that bad, is it?'

'Personally, I think it's great here,' Tom replies. 'But it's not just up to me. This was supposed to be a nice surprise, a chilled holiday, but it's not panning out that way, so…'

'I'm happy to do whatever everyone else wants.' Jake reaches across the table for the brandy bottle and pours himself a large measure.

This conversation is in danger of getting out of control fast, and I don't want to contribute to it. I know Tom means well, but we're all tired and becoming a little drunk.

'Lainy?' Tom prompts.

'What?'

'You haven't been yourself since we got here.'

'Haven't I?'

'You know you haven't.'

Lainy stares into her barely touched drink, running her finger around the rim. 'It's just strange… being back in Swanage. It feels different, but exactly the same, if that makes sense. And random memories keep popping into my head without any warning. It's just a bit unsettling, that's all.'

'Yeah.' Jake nods. 'Like Lainy says, it's unsettling.'

'So, are we staying, or shall we call it a day? Go back to London?' Tom asks.

No one answers so I break the awkward silence. '*Really?* We only just got here. It's the only holiday we've had in three years. We won't get a refund, you know.'

'Sorry, Faye,' Jake says, not catching my eye. 'But I'd rather go home, if that's okay with everyone else. And you have to admit, the weather's pretty bad.'

'But…' I exhale, thinking about everything I have planned.

'I know you meant well, and I'm grateful, but—'

'Fine. Okay. If that's what everyone wants, we'll pack up and go home,' I say. 'But can you at least take Dylan dolphin watching tomorrow? He's so excited about it.'

'Of course,' Jake says, his face relaxing. 'It's already arranged so I'm not about to disappoint him. Gonna get up early and head up there with the binoculars and bacon butties. I take it you're not coming with us?'

'I will if you want, but it would be nice for the two of you to have some time on your own.'

'Yeah. Okay.' He takes a large swig of brandy.

'And the girls want to go to the beach for a sandcastle building competition,' Lainy adds. 'I checked the forecast, and it's supposed to be sunny tomorrow. Although who knows with the British weather.'

'Okay. So… how about we aim to head home late afternoon?' I say.

Jake frowns. 'Lunchtime would be better. Otherwise we'll be driving all evening.'

'That's cutting it a bit fine. We'll need to pack up,' I reply, feeling like everything is unravelling. 'And if the girls want to go to the beach in the morning…'

'Fine.' Jake says with a scowl. 'We'll head back in the afternoon then.'

I pick up my drink and down it. The burn in my throat makes my eyes water. Or at least, I think that's why they're watering. I was going to ask Jake what he was talking to Yasmin about earlier at the gallery, but I don't want him to take my question the wrong way, so I bite back the urge.

We all look up as the kitchen door opens and Dylan shuffles in clutching his threadbare rabbit. 'Mummy, I can't sleep. I keep thinking of horrible things.'

I open my arms wide and he comes and sits on my lap, his small body warm, his dark hair all messed up. 'Are your cousins awake too?'

'No. I tried to wake them up, but they kept on sleeping.'

'Well, you need to go to sleep or you'll be too tired to go dolphin watching tomorrow.'

'But it's scary in that room. It's not like at home.'

'You slept okay last night,' I say.

He doesn't reply. Just leans into me and bows his head.

'Do you want me to come up with you?'

Dylan nods and yawns. He slides off my lap and I take his hand. Everyone wishes him good night as we leave the kitchen.

I hope he'll be okay. I kiss the top of his head and we head up the creaky stairs. I'll lie with him until he falls asleep. Perhaps I'll fall asleep too. That way, I won't have to talk to Jake.

CHAPTER SEVEN

THEN

'No,' Lainy's dad says, putting another dandelion plant in the bucket. 'Absolutely not. You're too young.'

'But Jen's going.' Lainy lays her trowel on the grass and wipes her hands on her jeans. She's been helping her dad weed the front garden of their small terraced house for the past half hour, trying to judge the best time to ask him if she can go to the leavers' beach party next weekend.

'Jennifer's going?' Her dad turns to look at her. 'Are you sure?'

'Mmhm.' Lainy nods, knowing she's hit the bullseye. Her parents adore her best friend Jennifer Walton. Jen's parents are both doctors and they live in a posh house further up the hill. Jennifer always gets good grades and she's always super-polite to Lainy's parents, knowing just what to say to get them relaxed and laughing. It's like she has this magical power over them.

'I can't imagine Dr Walton allowing his daughter to go to an unsupervised party.'

'It's not really a party, Dad, and anyway, you know everyone who'll be there. It's just the usual lot from Jake's year and a few friends from my year.' This is a slight stretching of the truth. It's a leavers' party for Jake's year and the event is all round school and beyond. Everyone who's anyone will be going. Not that

Lainy's bothered about everyone else. There's only one person she's interested in.

A black car cruises past their front garden, spraying windscreen wash as it passes by, wipers swishing across its dusty windscreen.

'Bloody idiot,' Lainy's dad mutters. 'They'll have sprayed detergent all over the roses.'

'It's that girl who lives at the top of the cliff. She comes back from her posh school every summer.' Lainy stares after the car, wondering what it must be like to be super-rich and be driven around by a chauffeur. Not that she's bothered by all that stuff. She'd be happy to be poor all her life, as long as she can be with the person she loves. That's all she asks for. And that's why it's so important that she's allowed to go to this party. *He* is going to be there. Owen Pearson. Her pulse races even thinking about him. And she has this excited but nervous feeling in her throat and stomach.

Jake said he didn't mind her tagging along with him if their parents said it was all right. So she got Jen to get the okay from her parents first. That part was easy. Jen's mum and dad let her do pretty much anything she wants.

But, strangely, now that Lainy's on the verge of getting permission, part of her wants her dad to forbid it. To stop her from going, because, really, she's more nervous than excited. Nervous about boys and parties and all that stuff. The other girls in her year seem far more experienced. They talk about boys all the time. About who's kissed who, and who's gone further. And there are a couple of girls who are supposed to have gone all the way. She and Jennifer are both virgins. Neither of them has even kissed a boy, although they both say they want to. And Lainy wants to. At least, she thinks she does. She's not sure. So if her dad says no, she'll be upset and she'll probably sulk, but maybe she'll also be a little relieved.

'What does your mother have to say about it?' her dad asks, getting to his feet and picking up the almost-full bucket of weeds.

'She said to ask you.'

He sighs and scratches his cheek.

Lainy takes the bucket from him. 'I'll empty it, Dad. And then I'll put the kettle on. Make you a cup of tea.'

'You wouldn't be trying to get round me would you, Lainy Townsend?'

She feels her cheeks redden. 'No, Dad. Course not.'

'Because if I do let you go to this shindig, it won't be because you've made me tea or helped with the chores, love. It'll be because I think you're old enough and responsible enough to attend, all right?'

She presses her lips together and nods. Waiting for him to give her an answer. Not quite sure what she wants that answer to be.

CHAPTER EIGHT

NOW

My eyes fly open. The night terrors cling to me in the shape of cold sweat and a racing heart. That unnamed fear constricting my breathing, making me gasp and claw at my throat. The white glare of morning doesn't comfort or calm me. *Where am I?*

I pull the sticky sheets from my slick body and realise I'm still wearing yesterday's clothes. I'm in the kids' bedroom. In Dylan's bed. I must have fallen asleep while trying to soothe him. But Dylan's not here. And then I remember. Jake has taken him dolphin spotting this morning. They must have left already. Jake said they would walk up to the clifftop rather than drive. I sit up in bed, the bunk above bearing down oppressively, hemming me in.

My nieces aren't in here either. I hear the distant chatter of their voices downstairs, easing me into the day, away from the darkness of my nightmare. But still remnants of it cling to me, an anxious twisting in my belly and an itching on my skin. A heaviness in my head that has nothing to do with last night's brandy.

I need a drink of water and a shower.

A couple of hours later, we bustle out of the local supermarket with carrier bags containing far too much food for our picnic lunch. It was one of those situations where we had no shopping list, so were all piling things into the basket. As we're supposed to be leaving Swanage later, Tom thought it wouldn't hurt to have extra foodie treats for lunch to make up for cutting our holiday short.

After enjoying the cool air of the store's chiller cabinets, the heat outside feels thick and heavy. The rain has gone, but the air is still hazy. Everything looks slightly surreal, with a muffled texture, like I'm still trapped inside my dreams.

'What time will Jake and Dylan be back?' Tom asks.

'Not sure,' I reply, pressing myself flat against a shop front while a woman with a double buggy manoeuvres past.

'Shall we head straight down to the beach?' he asks. 'I'm dying to get in the sea and cool down. We can text Jake. Let him know whereabouts we are. Then they can join us once they're back.'

'Good idea,' Lainy replies. 'Keep hold of your sister's hand, Poppy! It's busy and I don't want either of you getting lost.'

'Lainy? Lainy Townsend?'

I turn to see a petite, dark-haired woman striding down the road towards us. Her face a dark cloud of anger.

'Shit,' Lainy murmurs under her breath.

'Who's that?' Tom asks.

'Hi, Kayla,' Lainy says quietly, ignoring Tom for the moment.

'What are you doing back in Swanage?' Kayla snaps, her eyes darting from Lainy to me and Tom. She makes no attempt at friendliness.

'We're just here on holiday, that's all.' Lainy's face is colourless and her voice doesn't sound like her own.

'I can't believe you came back,' Kayla hisses. 'Are you an idiot, or what?'

'Keep your voice down, my children are—'

'You brought your kids with you? I hope you're not here to do anything stupid, because—'

'Kayla, calm down.'

'You don't know what it's been like, trying not to think about what—'

'Kayla, please!' Lainy turns away from us, puts her hand on Kayla's back and tries to usher her away. But Kayla isn't budging.

I take hold of Poppy and Annabel's hands and lead them a little way down the road, away from the altercation. I keep glancing back, my ears flapping trying to catch the rest of the conversation.

'Don't worry. We're leaving today,' Lainy says.

'Good. Because I don't want any trouble.'

'You won't get any from me.' Lainy raises her hands in a gesture of surrender.

Seconds later, the angry woman shoulders her way past me and marches off down the road.

'That lady was rude,' Annabel says. 'She shouted at Mummy and bashed into you, Aunty Faye.'

'Yes, she *was* rude,' I reply, unsure whether to go back to my sister-in-law or keep walking to give her some space. I dither for a moment, and then we turn back towards her and Tom.

'Who was that?' Tom asks, his hand on Lainy's shoulder.

'No one.'

'Lainy…'

'Just someone I fell out with at school… over a boy. It was nothing. I think she must have become a bit unhinged.' Lainy gives a short, unconvincing laugh.

'Are you okay?' Tom sets down the shopping and tries to give Lainy a hug, but she steps back, bumping into a young woman who swears at her.

'Being back here… makes me feel like a teenager again,' Lainy says, her facade dropping, 'and not in a good way.'

Tom tries to hug her once again, but she extricates herself and takes a step back. 'Don't be nice to me, Tom. I can't take anyone being nice to me.' Her voice breaks.

'Lainy…' he says with a stricken expression.

'I'm fine, I'm fine. It's just memories, that's all.'

'Do you want to—'

'Just leave it, Tom, please.'

While Tom and Lainy continue talking, I take the girls across the busy road to peer into the window of an old-fashioned sweet shop. 'Wow, look at all these different types of fudge!'

'Can we get some of that pink and white one, Aunty Faye?' Annabel asks. 'I've got my birthday money.'

'I think that one's coconut ice,' I say, looking across at Lainy and Tom, who are still whispering furiously together.

'I don't like coconut,' Annabel says, her shoulders slumping.

'I'm saving my money,' Poppy says, 'for something better than sweets.'

'Good idea,' I reply.

'Who was that lady, and why is Mummy cross with Daddy?' Poppy asks.

'She's not cross, darling. She's just explaining something.'

'I want to go home,' Annabel says, her voice wobbling. 'I mean our proper home, not that smelly one.'

At this precise moment, I want to go home too, but I can't let my nieces see how disconcerted I am by everything.

Annabel's face is growing redder, a sure-fire sign of an impending meltdown.

'Tell you what –' I crouch down so I'm at their level – 'why don't we go to the beach for our picnic?'

'Can we swim in the sea?' Poppy asks.

'Absolutely!' I reply. 'And we can have a sandcastle-building competition.'

Annabel's eyes light up at this prospect. 'Can I use the red bucket and spade?'

'Of course.'

'Can Dylan come too?' Poppy asks.

I check my watch. It's almost eleven. 'Yes. He and Uncle Jake should be back soon. I'll message them to meet us there.'

'Yippee, a picnic!' Poppy says, taking her younger sister's hand and jumping up and down. Thankfully, Annabel joins in with her sister's excitement and the two of them squeal together with glee. *Phew.* Tantrum averted. Poppy gives me a complicit look over the top of Annabel's head, and I wipe my brow in exaggerated relief. She grins and then gets back to the business of keeping her sister happy.

I throw a worried glance over my shoulder at my sister-in-law. Somehow I don't think it's going to be as straightforward to fix the grown-ups.

CHAPTER NINE

He enters the trailer with Scout at his heels, quickly showers, washes his hair and changes into his running gear. He hardly ever runs – not unless he needs to – but people tend not to pay attention to joggers and runners, especially in the early morning.

'Sorry, boy,' he says as he heads out of the bedroom and into the lounge area. 'You'll have to stay here for now.' Scout's tail goes down and he takes himself off to his basket in the corner, sinking into it with a heavy grunt.

Hooking a baseball cap off the corner of a dining chair and ramming it onto his head, he checks that Scout's water bowl is full, then leaves via the front door. His battered Citroën is parked around the side and he gets in, the interior already warm from the rising August sun.

The back roads are quiet, and he doesn't pass anyone he recognises, just a couple of caravans and a cyclist. He parks in an off-road layby behind the woods, having decided to approach the cliffs via a woodland path rather than alongside the castle.

Beneath the trees it's cool and fresh, the damp scent of loamy soil in his nostrils, reminding him of another forest in another place. Scout would have enjoyed this run. After a few minutes of steady jogging, the path opens onto an area of tinder-dry heathland. A few minutes more and he's on the cliff path, the deep, foaming sea below him. He takes in a lungful of briny air, scans left to right and back again. There's no sign of human activity.

Perfect.

CHAPTER TEN

'Are you okay?' I ask Lainy.

She nods, but her eyes are filmy and her face closes down. She takes the girls' hands from my own and starts walking down the road with them. 'Right, little misses, who's going to help me build the biggest sandcastle in the universe?' she cries, pretending to be cheerful for her daughters.

'Me!'

'Me as well!'

They put their hands up in the air and dance around her.

I glance at Tom, walking by my side laden down with carrier bags, but he just shrugs and shakes his head. I don't want to make things worse, so I decide not to ask about the altercation with Kayla. It doesn't look like he knows anyway. Instead, I take one of the bags from him and we walk in silence.

Poor Tom. He's been fairly upbeat until this moment, but now his whole body sags. As a paramedic, Tom's used to facing uncomfortable and stressful situations. I've never really seen anything faze him. But he worships Lainy and I can see how much her distress is upsetting him. I'm beginning to feel like some kind of holiday-camp leader, trying to keep everybody happy. It's exhausting.

After a few moments, we round the corner. Before us lies Swanage Bay – a beautiful beach that none of us is truly able to appreciate today. It has a wide promenade, a curved strip of golden sand, a long, low jetty and an azure sea, framed by a lush, green headland on each side. The beach itself is traditional, with striped deckchairs, windbreaks and an ice-cream kiosk, like a scene from a 1950s postcard. Families and couples have already started to stake out their spots on the beach. It's busier than I thought it would be.

'Looks like we should have got here earlier,' Tom says.

'Let's keep walking,' I reply. 'I'm sure we'll find a spare bit of sand somewhere.'

We quicken our pace to keep up with Lainy, who's being dragged down onto the beach by Poppy and Annabel. Eventually we come to a less crowded part, near to some colourful beach huts and a striped Punch and Judy tent with a sign that says the next show is at 2 p.m. We spend the next few minutes spreading out the rug, putting up the parasol and getting the girls into their swimming costumes. I text Jake to let him know whereabouts on the beach we're sitting.

Tom glances down at my phone. 'Any idea what time Jake and Dylan will be back?' he asks.

'I just texted, but they haven't replied yet.'

'Phone signal's non-existent up there,' Lainy says. 'They won't get your message until they leave the headland.'

'Hopefully, they'll be back in time for lunch.' Tom rubs his belly. 'I'm starving, I could probably dig into that picnic right away.'

'Let's at least wait until twelve,' Lainy says, her voice steadier now.

I give her arm a squeeze, pleased she seems to be recovering from her recent encounter.

'Right!' Tom cries, stripping off his T-shirt. 'If we can't eat yet, who's coming into the sea with me? Last one in is a rotten banana!'

The girls squeal and run the short distance to the shoreline with their dad. He loses the race on purpose and they splash at him with glee, taking great delight in calling him a rotten banana.

While Tom and the girls swim, Lainy puts on her sunglasses and starts reading on her phone. I don't try to make conversation. I know what it's like when you don't want to talk. Instead,

I sit cross-legged on the rug and stare at the sea, beyond the holidaymakers splashing in the shallows and out to the horizon. My gaze shifts round to the headland, to the green hills that give the illusion of having been created just for us, to provide a pretty backdrop. But the truth is that whatever is going on in our lives here today, the sea and the hills will just keep on existing. They will watch all this human drama without opinion or judgement. All our trivialities mean nothing to the landscape. Our hopes and fears, our holidays and night terrors. None of it will endure. But that isn't of any comfort.

'You okay?' Lainy asks, easing me from my thoughts.

'Me? Yeah. How about you?'

'I haven't seen Kayla for years,' Lainy says. 'She was so angry.' She massages her forehead with her fingertips. 'It shook me up a bit.'

'I can imagine. She didn't seem very happy to see you.'

'Well, you know what she—'

'Mummy! Aunty Faye! I did a handstand in the sea for ten seconds.' Poppy comes racing up to us, her eyes bright, hair dripping. 'Do you want to see?'

'Definitely!' Lainy says, standing up and wriggling out of her shorts.

'I'll keep an eye on everything. You go,' I volunteer.

While they swim, I call my husband. My call goes straight through to his voicemail, so I leave a message:

'Hey. Just calling to see how you're getting on. Did you spot any dolphins? Send me photos. Anyway, we're going to have lunch in about an hour. We're at the beach, about halfway along by the Punch and Judy tent. See you in a bit. Love you guys!'

The sun has moved round, so I shift further under the parasol. Even though I'm wearing a long-sleeved shirt and linen trousers, I'm paranoid about sun exposure. My mum died from skin cancer not much older than I am now, so I always make sure Dylan and I cover up well in the summer. Jake is a sun worshipper and never listens to me when I ask him to put sunscreen on, so I've given up trying.

Eventually, the others return from the sea, grab towels from Tom's rucksack and begin drying off, spraying sand everywhere and chattering excitedly about what fun it was.

'Was the water warm?' I ask.

'Refreshing,' Tom replies.

'Is that a nice way of saying freezing?'

'No, honestly, it was a nice temperature,' he says with a pretend shiver. 'Are you going in?'

I rub at my arms self-consciously. 'Maybe later.'

'Aren't you hot?' Tom asks. 'You should go in. Cool down.'

'Leave her be, Tom,' Lainy says, trying to dry off a squirming, wriggling Annabel. 'Faye said she doesn't want to go in. Poppy, lay your towel flat and it will dry out quicker.'

'Sorry,' Tom replies. 'Just trying to help.'

'I know.' Lainy leans over, kisses his cheek and they smile at one another.

I stand abruptly. 'Maybe I will have a little paddle.'

'See,' Tom says to Lainy.

She gives him a gentle shove.

'Any news from the boys?' Tom asks.

'Not yet. I left a voicemail letting them know where we are, so keep an eye out.'

'Will do.'

I pick my way across the sand, past other families and a group of laughing teens. Was I ever that young and bright-eyed? It seems a world away from the person I am now. At the shoreline, I hitch up my trousers and let the waves roll over my toes. There's more of a breeze here and it's pleasant to stand and let the water cool me, to let my mind go blank for a few minutes. The lapping of the ocean is soothing. I can see how people enjoy living by the beach, but I've become a city girl. I like the hustle and bustle. The sense of purpose everyone has in London. If I lived here, I would have too much time to think. I would feel adrift. Wouldn't I? I try to imagine what it might be like – the slower pace, the countryside and ocean – but I can't seem to picture it. Not as my everyday life. It's too far removed from what I know. But maybe that's not such a bad thing.

Lunchtime rolls around, and there's still no word from Jake or Dylan. We decide to eat without them, figuring that they must have decided to grab something in the castle café. After lunch, the area around us starts to become even more crowded.

'The Punch and Judy show is starting in a few minutes,' Tom says. 'Shall we stay and watch, or should we head back and start packing?'

'Stay and watch! Stay and watch!' the girls cry.

'Okay.' Tom closes the parasol and we shuffle around to face the brightly painted puppet theatre, feeling quite smug that we managed to bag a spot so close to the entertainment.

After what feels like an interminable wait, the show finally opens with Judy asking where the baby is and Punch replying that she accidentally fell out of the window. At this, Judy starts bashing Punch over the head with a wooden spoon. The children all start laughing their little heads off.

'Have you seen one of these shows before?' Lainy asks me.

'When I was a kid. Can't remember much about it though.' I turn back to the puppet show, where Punch is now telling Judy he's going to teach her a lesson. He hits her repeatedly with a stick, crying, 'That's the way to do it!' Judy is whacking him back with the spoon. The children in the audience are laughing so hard, they can barely breathe.

'Er, okay, girls,' Lainy says quietly, 'I don't think this is appropriate, let's start packing our things away.'

'Noooo, we want to stay,' Annabel cries, through squeals of laughter. 'It's funny!'

'Mr Punch isn't very nice.' Poppy's eyes are wide.

'It's just a bit of fun,' Tom says, 'and anyway, Judy's giving as good as she's getting.'

Lainy glares at him with her best cross-teacher look. 'Really?'

Tom drops his smile and nods. 'Fine, you're right. It's probably a bit, er, sixteenth century.'

We gather our belongings and leave the puppet show and the beach, making our way back along the promenade, Mr Punch's squeaky words reverberating in my ears.

'Any word from Jake?' Tom asks as we walk.

I check my phone, but there are no texts and no voice messages. 'Not yet.'

'What time did they leave this morning?' he asks.

'Not sure. I was still asleep. I think Jake said they were going to leave at six.'

'That was eight hours ago,' Tom says with a frown.

'No, it's not that long ago; it's only…' I do a quick calculation on my fingers, but realise Tom's right. 'That's too long, isn't it? Something must have happened.'

'Not necessarily,' Tom backtracks. 'Maybe they're just enjoying themselves. Lost track of time…'

'Do you think so?'

'Yeah, of course. Could be any number of reasons why they're late back.'

But I note Tom's grim expression, and I wonder if he thinks something's happened. Something bad.

CHAPTER ELEVEN

THEN

Lainy takes the clear glass bottle from her brother's friend and takes a swig of the vodka. It tastes bitter and disgusting, and it burns her throat, but he's watching her closely so she's trying not to grimace. It's the last day of the summer term today, and tonight is the Year Eleven leavers' party at Smugglers' Cove. After repeated begging, her parents had let her come. But, honestly, she now wishes she hadn't bothered.

She thought that once she was here she would finally get to talk to Owen Pearson. If she's honest, she's thought of nothing else since she knew this party was happening. Imagining what they might say to one another. She pictured herself playing it cool, and then Owen would make her laugh, and they would talk all night. Maybe even kiss. But she hasn't managed to speak one word to him all evening. He's been hanging out with his mates by the shoreline, mucking about and laughing. He hasn't paid her any attention. And she doesn't have anywhere near enough courage to go over there and make the first move. Instead, creepy Mark Tamworth has been following her around all evening. It's obvious he fancies her, but she wouldn't go out with him if you paid her, even though her brother keeps trying to set the two of them up.

Talking of her brother, he hasn't spoken to her all night either. She glances over to where he's sitting on the rocks talking to Rose.

Lainy catches his eye and he smiles approvingly at her, tilting his head in Mark's direction. She scowls at Jake and shakes her head, turning her back on him, wondering how she can evade Mark without annoying or upsetting either of them. She's fed up with her brother trying to meddle in her life. She'll be pleased when he leaves home and goes off to uni. But that won't be for another couple of years. Until then, she'll just have to make the best of things.

Lainy went to Jen's house before the party and they spent hours getting ready, trying on clothes, doing each other's hair and make-up. It was probably the most fun part of the whole evening. Listening to music and having a laugh, gossiping about how the evening would pan out. So far it looks like Jen's evening is turning out just the way she imagined.

She and Jen were supposed to look out for one another tonight, but right at this moment Jen is snogging the face off her crush, Luke Bayswater, and she isn't looking out for anyone other than herself. Not that Lainy blames her. Jen has fancied Luke for ages. If Owen had shown Lainy the slightest bit of interest, she'd probably have ditched her friend too. No, Lainy's just jealous that Jen has snared the boy she likes, yet here Lainy is, stuck with Mark flipping Tamworth. And now her best friend has moved into a different league.

Lainy sighs. She must be the only girl left in her year who's never kissed a boy. How humiliating. For a moment she wonders whether she should kiss Mark, just to say she's done it. But then she looks at him, with his arrogant expression and self-satisfied smile, and she knows she could never let him touch her. The thought of it makes her shudder.

CHAPTER TWELVE

NOW

Back at the house, Poppy and Annabel thunder up the stairs to their room, repeating Mr Punch's words with abandoned glee: 'That's the way to do it!' while Tom, Lainy and I head into the kitchen. Lainy puts the kettle on, but we're all so warm and sticky, I can't imagine any of us will actually drink boiling hot tea. I fan myself with a local takeaway flyer while checking my phone for messages. The knot of anxiety in my chest is tightening.

'Still no word?' Tom asks.

I shake my head.

'Don't worry, I'll go out and have a look for them.' He stands abruptly, his chair making a loud scrape across the floor.

'Thanks. I think I'll come too.' My voice sounds far away.

'Lainy –' Tom picks his keys up off the table – 'are you okay to stay with the girls while Faye and I go up to the clifftop?'

She turns and leans back against the countertop. 'Of course. I'll text if they show up here while you're out, although the signal's pretty ropey up there, isn't it? Do you want tea before you go?'

'No thanks.' I get to my feet and slide my phone back into my handbag.

'We'll have tea when we get back,' Tom replies.

'Or maybe we'll need a shot of that brandy – if there's any left.' I pour myself a large glass of water and down a couple of paracetamol.

'You okay?' Lainy asks.

'Bit too much sun. Just having some tablets to take the edge off.'

'You should have said. We could have come home earlier. Your cheeks do look a bit pink. Are you going to be okay to go back out? Do you want to stay here with the girls?' She straightens up. 'I can go instead…'

'No, it's okay, I want to go. I'll wear a hat and drink lots of water.'

She gives me a quick hug. 'Don't worry. Dylan will be fine.'

I nod, not trusting myself to speak. Panic bubbling up, threatening to spill over.

'Yeah, we'll find them,' Tom says. 'In an hour, we'll all be back here wondering what we were getting so stressed about.' He kisses Lainy and follows me back down the cool hall and out into the blazing afternoon.

'I'll drive,' he offers. 'We can go slowly while you keep a look out, in case they're wandering back.'

'Okay. Good idea.'

His car unlocks with a beep, and we get in, the seat leather hot even through my trousers. I'm glad I'm not wearing shorts like Tom.

'Air con!' he says, turning the dial up. He drives slowly up the hill while I scan the street. There are plenty of people walking down towards the town, laden with beach bags, cool boxes and other seaside paraphernalia. I'm glad we're going in this direction, as there's a never-ending line of cars snaking down the hill, all trying to get to the seafront.

'They'll be lucky to get a parking space down there,' Tom observes.

We reach Durlston Head car park without spotting Jake or Dylan and manage to nab a space as someone is just leaving. I get us a ticket and Tom takes a large green bag out of the boot.

'What's that?' I ask.

'My medical kit.'

'What! Why?'

'Don't worry. I'm sure I won't need it. But it's better to bring it with me, just in case.' He slings it over his shoulder and we make our way down to the castle.

'I suppose we should take a look inside,' Tom says.

'Good idea. I'll scout around the café, you check the loos.'

We spend the next ten minutes peering into all the rooms. There's a photography exhibition on, but it's empty, as most people are out enjoying the sunshine.

Back outside, we walk down past the castle, past the stone globe, and onto the cliff path. It's fresher up here, a warm sea breeze ruffling my shirt and pulling at my hair. I can't help peering over the wall, down the cliffside at the silvery foam swirling against the rocks.

'They'll be fine,' Tom keeps saying. 'Don't worry.' But he has this tight look in his eyes, like he doesn't really believe that. And I'm not sure how long I can keep myself together. How long I can keep pretending that everything's okay. As we walk along the cliff path where Jake and Dylan came earlier this morning, I'm on the verge of losing it. I dig my fingernails into my palms and breathe deeply, willing myself not to have a panic attack. I try to pretend we're just out for an afternoon walk. But my legs are shaky and my brain feels as though it's floating free in my skull.

'Do you want to sit down for a minute?' Tom asks, drawing me to the side of the path so another couple can pass. 'You don't look well, Faye. You should have stayed at home. I can drop you back. I'll come and look for them on my own.'

'No, I'm fine. Maybe… just… have you got any water?'

Tom reaches into his bag and pulls out a metal flask. He unscrews the top and passes it to me. I take a few sips of the cool liquid and feel my head clear a little, the world coming back into focus. I press the cold metal to my forehead.

'Better?'

I nod and hand him back the flask.

'Look, the dolphin-watch hut is up there. Let's go and have a look. You can sit inside for a bit. Get some shade.'

I glance up at the plain-looking wooden structure set up above the path, with its two viewing windows. I wonder if Jake and Dylan were in there earlier, peering out, gazing at the ocean below.

We shuffle inside. My eyes take a few moments to adjust to the gloom. It actually feels hotter in here than outside. My nose and throat clog with the musty scent of wood and dust.

'Look!' Tom cries, pointing at a clipboard on one of the ledges.

I peer down and see it's a record of marine sightings. The second-to-last entry is in Jake's handwriting:

23/8 – 6.45 – Two groups in the bay. One dolphin jumping – Dylan Townsend (age 7)

'They were here,' Tom says. 'And they saw dolphins.'

'But that was hours ago.' Suddenly my legs can't take my weight and I squat down on the floor, using my hands to help me balance. Tom goes all serious and paramedic-ish, reaching for his bag. But I put out a hand to stop him. 'I'll be fine. Just give me a moment.'

'Nice slow breaths,' he says, crouching down in front of me. 'You're having a bit of a panic attack, but it will pass.'

'I just… it's just…'

'Shhh. Nice steady breaths. Don't talk for a moment. Everything's going to be okay.'

I do as he says and breathe in and out, slowly, trying not to let my imagination race away.

'Now,' he says, 'I'm going to suggest that you stay here while I have a scout along the cliff path.' I shake my head but he holds out his hand to stop my silent protest. 'Faye, it'll be quicker if I go on my own. I won't be long, okay?'

'What if something's happened to them? What if they're in trouble? If they've fallen down a cliff?'

'If I can't find them, we'll call the authorities, okay?'

I nod.

Tom gets to his feet and shoulders his bag. As he turns to go, I feel the air leave my lungs and the hut seems to grow darker. It's as though I'm trapped in one of my night terrors. I don't want him to leave me here on my own, so I manage to suck in a lungful of air. To pull myself together and stop the darkness from taking hold.

'Wait!' I cry.

He stops and turns. His broad frame silhouetted in the doorway.

I stand up shakily and force my voice to sound normal. 'I feel much better. I'm coming with you.'

'Faye—'

'Honestly, I'm okay.' To prove my point, I walk past him and stride back down to the path, squinting at the brightness, pushing all panicky thoughts from my mind.

We walk the rest of the path together, peering up the hillside and down the cliffside, looking for any sign of them. I still don't feel a hundred per cent, but I'm determined to continue the search with Tom.

'Something's happened to them, hasn't it?' I say.

'We don't know that. And even if it has, it might not be something terrible. Maybe Jake's sprained his ankle or something. There could be any number of harmless reasons.'

'But we're almost at the lighthouse and they're not here.'

'Maybe they're having a picnic up there and lost track of time.'

'But Jake wanted to go back to London today. He would've come back by now. He would have wanted to get on the road.'

'Let's try to stay calm until we've at least had a look, yeah?' Tom takes my hand to help me over some loose rocks.

'You're right,' I say. 'Sorry.'

'Don't apologise. I'd be exactly the same if it were Lainy and the girls.'

'Somehow I doubt that,' I say. 'I can't imagine you having panic attacks and wobbly legs.'

'I'll have you know my legs can be extremely wobbly in the right circumstances.'

I muster a wry smile. 'Good to know.'

Tom stops walking for a moment and turns to me. 'We will find them, you know.'

'I know there has to be a reasonable explanation for their disappearance, but I can't help thinking the worst.'

'Of course. But it's only been a few hours.'

'This was supposed to be a lovely family holiday. A wonderful birthday surprise.' I give a bitter laugh. 'But so far, it's been a disaster.'

'I wouldn't say that.' Tom sits on a boulder and looks up at me.

'I can't help blaming myself for bringing everyone here. I know Jake's always been wary of surprises, but I really did think he would have loved to revisit his childhood home. Was that naive of me?'

Tom shakes his head. 'You can't blame yourself. It wasn't just *you* who thought it was a good idea. I agreed with you. And anyway, it's been okay. We've had a couple of nice days out, a pub dinner, a visit to a gallery. And let's not forget Punch and Judy.' He grins.

I give Tom a look. 'Actually, if I'm honest, I find it a bit odd that Jake never wants to talk about his childhood. Maybe I came here for selfish reasons. To find out more about him.'

'I know what you mean. Lainy's the same. Whenever I mention things from my childhood, she listens, but never really reciprocates. She always says, *what's the point of focusing on the past?* I just thought she was being very Zen and living in the moment. Maybe there's more to it than that.'

'You don't think…' I shake my head. 'No.'

'What?' Tom prompts.

'No. Nothing.'

'Go on. What were you going to say?'

'Well…' I sit precariously on a jagged rock. 'You don't think he's stayed out on purpose because he's annoyed with me? To… I don't know… make a point or something?'

'That would be a very childish and irresponsible thing to do,' Tom says. 'And I don't think Jake's like that, is he?'

'No. You're right. It's probably just my brain making stupid assumptions.'

'Like I said before, I think the most likely thing is that one of them has hurt an ankle or something and they're waiting for help.' Tom stands. 'The best thing is for us to keep looking. And if we can't find them, we'll call for help.'

'You mean the police?'

'Let's not think about that yet. Come on, the quicker we find them the quicker we can all relax.'

Finally, we reach the grassy headland and the walled lighthouse. There are a few families and couples dotted about having picnics or just enjoying the view, but no sign of Jake or Dylan.

'Have you got any photos of them on your phone?' Tom asks.

My screensaver is a picture of the three of us in a restaurant. It was taken last Christmas, so isn't that old. I pass him the phone and we walk over to a young family who are sitting on a rug, their kids looking down at their phone screens.

'Excuse me,' Tom says.

The woman looks up with a smile and shades her eyes. The man nods warily.

'I don't suppose you've seen this man and child up here today, have you?'

The woman takes the phone and has a closer look, showing it to the man.

'Dylan would have been wearing a red baseball cap,' I say. 'That's my son. He's seven.'

'Have you lost them?' the woman asks, getting to her feet. 'Kids, have you seen this lady's son?'

I blink a few times and take a breath. 'My husband and son came up here this morning, to look for dolphins. But they haven't come home yet and my husband isn't answering his phone.' As I say the words, I start understanding how serious this is. And how this might be about to turn into something life-changing. I'm not sure if I'm strong enough to deal with it. But I have to be. I can't fall apart now.

CHAPTER THIRTEEN

It's 5 p.m. – around the time we had arranged to leave Swanage to drive back home to London. Instead, Tom and I get out of his car on the narrow, unassuming road where Swanage Police Station is situated. The air is still warm, but the sun has lost its intensity now, dipping out of sight behind the buildings.

'We should have called the police hours ago.' As I say the words, I understand that it's too long for my family to have been out of contact. Too long to assume that everything is okay with them.

I stare across the road at the stone building. You wouldn't even realise it was a police station if you didn't know. Apart from the blue metal hand railings outside, it looks like nothing more than a characterful stone house. Following Tom across the road, I feel dishevelled and sweaty. My mouth is sour and dry, my head thumping. I want to go home. And not to our holiday home, but back to London. At this moment, I wish we'd never come to this pretty seaside town. I wish my plans had stayed unplanned. As I follow Tom up the gentle slope, my heart thumps painfully and my left leg trembles.

'It'll be okay,' Tom says as I hesitate outside the door. 'The sooner we report this, the sooner they'll be able to locate them.'

I nod, not trusting myself to speak right at this moment.

Tom has already phoned Lainy to let her know what's going on. To tell her that we'll be home later than planned. I wonder what she's thinking right now. As well as being my husband, Jake is also her brother. This must be equally upsetting for her.

My stomach lurches at all the what-ifs going through my mind, but I have to trust that everything will be all right. I can't let my overactive imagination take over. Imagination is an artist's blessing but a mother's curse.

We walk straight up to the front desk, where a youngish desk officer with sandy hair looks up and gives us a professional smile.

'Afternoon,' he says. 'Can I help you?'

'I'd like to report two missing people,' I say, my voice remarkably calm. 'My husband and my son.'

'Okay. Can I take your name?'

'Faye. Faye Townsend.'

'Thanks.' He picks up a pen and starts writing on the pad in front of him. 'How long have they been missing for?'

'They went up to Durlston Head at six this morning. So, it's been eleven hours.'

'How old is your son?' he asks.

'He's only seven. My husband isn't answering his phone. It's not like him. I think… I think something must have happened to them.' My voice cracks and the officer gives me a sympathetic look. He must have to use that expression a lot in his line of work.

'We went to look for them this afternoon,' Tom adds. 'Up along the cliffs. And we asked around if anyone had seen them. But there was no sign. We're here on holiday.'

'And you are?'

'My name's Tom Ellis. I'm the brother-in-law.'

'Okay, if you can both take a seat, I'll see if anyone's free to take a statement.'

We sit in the waiting area, but Tom stands up again, nodding in the direction of a vending machine. 'Want anything?' He puts a hand in his pocket and pulls out a handful of loose change.

I shake my head. 'Not hungry.' Although my stomach feels empty, there's a lump in my throat. I don't think I'd be able to swallow anything down.

'A drink?'

'No thanks.'

Disappointed, he sits back down.

'You get something, though,' I urge.

'No, I'm fine.'

So we wait. And time seems to stretch out like a piece of chewing gum. Taut and thin. Ready to snap. I read the posters on the wall without really taking in what they actually say. And then, finally, my name is called.

I look up to see a slim, dark-haired woman in a light grey suit. I get to my feet. Tom stands with me and we walk over to her.

'Hi, I'm Detective Sergeant Lisa Nash.' Her voice is firm with a faint Dorset burr.

Tom sticks out his hand. 'Hi, I'm Tom Ellis, and this is my sister-in-law Faye Townsend.'

She shakes his hand and then mine. 'You're here to report missing persons?'

'Yes. My husband and son.'

'Shall we go and sit down, and I can take some details?'

We follow her down a corridor and into a bland room with cream walls and a wooden desk. She sits on one side and we sit on the other and I launch into an explanation of what's happened while DS Nash listens and takes notes.

'Can you give me their ages, and a description of what they were wearing? A photo would also be helpful.'

'Dylan's seven and Jake's thirty-four. It was Jake's birthday yesterday,' I add. 'I'm not sure what they were wearing because they left before I woke up this morning. But probably jeans and T-shirts. I'll check when I get back to the house, if that's okay? But Dylan would have been wearing his red baseball cap.'

'That's fine. The sooner you can get me those clothing descriptions the better.'

'I have some photos on my phone.'

She slides a card across the table. 'If you text them to this number that would be great.'

I pull out my mobile, scrolling through my photos until I find a clear, recent shot of Dylan.

'Are either of them on any medication?' she asks.

'What?' I look up from my phone screen. 'No. No medication.'

'Does your husband suffer from depression? Could he have been drinking?'

I feel Tom's gaze on me. He's worried by the implication of her questions. I shake my head quickly. 'No, no. Nothing like that,' I reply, typing Nash's mobile number into my phone and pressing send. Next, I find a photo of Jake and send that one through too. Then I send the screensaver picture of the three of us.

'Was their trip planned?' Nash asks. 'I mean, did you know they were going beforehand, or did they leave you a note?'

'No,' I say. 'There was no note. We knew about it. They arranged it yesterday. A bit of father–son bonding.'

'And did they give you a time when they'd be home?'

'Er, no, not as such. But, I mean, it was early morning dolphin watching. We just assumed they'd be back by lunchtime at the latest. Especially as we'd just decided to go home this afternoon.'

'Decided?' she asks. 'Are you going home sooner than planned?'

'Uh… well, yes, but…'

'It's a bit complicated,' Tom says, coming to my rescue. 'Faye and I planned this holiday as a surprise for our spouses – they grew up here. But, well, it turns out they weren't wild about being back. Jake was the one who wanted to leave early.'

'I see.' DS Nash raises her eyebrows.

'It's nothing sinister,' Tom says. 'I just think it felt a bit odd for them, coming back after so many years.'

'I've sent you the photos,' I say, replacing my phone in my bag and sliding Nash's card into the side pocket.

'Thank you. Do you have any other children?' the DS asks.

'No, just Dylan.' I clench my hands into fists, trying not to cry.
'And your husband, is he Dylan's biological father?'

'Yes.'

'Apart from your disagreement over the holiday, have you and he argued about anything recently?'

'Argued? No. And we didn't really have a disagreement about the holiday. It was just a birthday surprise that didn't turn out so well.'

'Do you have any reason to believe your husband might have taken Dylan deliberately?'

'Taken him? You mean, as in an *abduction*? No! Absolutely not.'

'That's okay, I just have to ask these questions. Establish what we're dealing with. Eliminate possibilities.'

'Yes, of course. Sorry.' I take a breath. 'It's just… this is all so… I can't get my head around it. I'm freaking out.'

'Don't worry, Faye, it'll be okay.' Tom briefly rubs my shoulder.

'So you're Mrs Townsend's brother-in-law?' DC Nash asks Tom. 'You're married to Jake's sister, is that right?'

'Yes – Lainy.'

'And where is Lainy now?'

'She's back at the holiday home with our two young daughters.'

'Can I have the address?'

I pull up the details on my phone and pass them across to her.

'Very nice,' she says, looking at the website photo. 'I love those old Victorian terraces.'

'We're worried they may have hurt themselves on the cliffs,' Tom says, bringing her back to the matter in hand.

'Okay. Yes, you were right to come and report it. We'll send some officers up there to take a look,' she says. 'And I'm also going to alert the coastguard. Jake and Dylan will be easier to spot from the helicopter.'

'Oh. Right. Okay.' My head swims at the seriousness of everything. At the thought of all the people who will be called into action to search for my family.

DS Nash frowns. 'My greatest concern is that there are only a few hours of daylight left, so we need to act quickly. It'll be far easier to locate them in the light. Okay. Can you wait here while I go and make a few calls?' She gets to her feet. 'I'll be ten minutes or so. There's a vending machine and some loos out the front in case you need anything.'

'Thanks,' Tom replies.

DS Nash leaves the room, taking an air of security and calm with her. Now she's gone I feel untethered. My mind skitters across all the possibilities of what will happen. Will the helicopter find them? Is Dylan all right, or is he anxious… scared even? Will everything be okay? Or is my life about to come crashing down like a landslide?

CHAPTER FOURTEEN

THEN

Jake takes a sip of his warm beer and shifts his position on the rock so he can edge a little closer to Rose. She smells amazing – like strawberries and cream – and her hair hangs straight down like a red-gold curtain shining in the moonlight.

Tonight is almost perfect. The only minor worry is Lainy. Mark is keeping an eye on her, but Jake has seen Owen Pearson eyeing her up. Every time Jake looks at the twat, he's staring at his sister and it's getting on his nerves. He'd better not try anything on with Lainy. Jake toys with the idea of going over to his sister and warning her not to speak to Owen. Of telling Mark to keep Lainy away from him. Owen thinks he's all that, just because he's in a band and plays the guitar. Jake knows it's all an act just so he can get the girls' attention. It's obvious what the guy's about.

Jake has despised Owen ever since Year Nine, when he moved to Swanage and slotted into their school with such ease, making friends and getting all the top grades. Walking around with that irritating swagger. Owen didn't grow up here, so why should he act like he owns the place? It's so annoying. And he's always so condescending and arrogant.

'You okay, Jake?' Rose asks, her voice pure and concerned.

'Yeah.' Jake's voice cracks, so he clears his throat and speaks again, trying to make his voice as deep as he can. 'Yeah, just keeping an eye on my sister.'

'Aw, you're so sweet. There's not many boys in our year who'd be so thoughtful. Most of them are really immature. It's nice talking to you.'

Jake feels his cheeks warm under the compliment. He gazes down at the sand, wondering when he should make his move. He really thinks he might actually get to kiss Rose tonight. If he does, he won't hang around, he'll ask her to be his girlfriend straight away. He doesn't want to come across as too keen, but he's wanted this to happen for the past two years. And now it looks like he's actually got a real shot.

Rose takes a swig from her bottle of beer and gazes at him from under her lashes, her green eyes flashing with promise. Jake swallows and pictures himself taking the bottle from her hand and leaning in to kiss her soft, pink lips. But he's nervous. He's never fancied anyone this much before. It's like a physical ache in his gut. He doesn't want to mess it up.

He tells himself not to be such a coward. It's just a kiss. What can go wrong?

CHAPTER FIFTEEN

NOW

After a few more questions and promises from DS Nash that she'll do everything she can to help locate Jake and Dylan, Tom and I leave the police station and return to the house. Lainy pounces on us as soon as we walk through the door.

'Hey.' Tom kisses Lainy and tucks a loose strand of her hair behind an ear. A tender gesture which almost finishes me. 'Have you been cooking?' he asks.

The smell of bubbling tomato sauce and garlic sets my stomach growling as well as heaving. I have to breathe through my mouth for a moment to stop myself from throwing up.

'I couldn't just wait around doing nothing, so I made spag bol. Thought you guys might be hungry.' She turns to me, her eyes wide with concern. 'How did you get on?'

I shake my head. We've been updating her with texts, but she naturally wants the full details now we're back.

'Come and sit down.' She's babbling, out of breath. Her emotions on the surface. 'Tell me everything. Supper's ready, I just have to grate some cheese. The girls have already had theirs. I put them to bed early so we could talk.'

'Thanks, Lainy. Let me just go and wash my face.' I walk over to the staircase and take a breath, gripping the bannister.

She comes over and hugs me. 'It'll be okay, I'm sure it will,' she says with an extra squeeze, which I return. But the tone of her voice suggests it will be far from okay.

I don't trust myself to reply, so I nod and take myself upstairs. Up on the landing I hear the low murmur of their voices – snatches of words relating to how I'm feeling and what happened at the station. As I go into the dank and dated bathroom, I wonder how on earth I'm going to get through this. How I'm not going to fall apart. I turn on the tap. It squeaks, and the pipes judder before a stream of cold water finally rushes out. I wash my hands with the small bar of complementary soap and then splash running water onto my face. I keep splashing and splashing and splashing. Trying to turn my brain off for a moment. To let everything go blank.

An insistent banging rises above the gush of the water. I turn off the tap and straighten up. Someone's knocking at the bathroom door.

'Faye?' It's Lainy. 'Are you okay?'

I wipe my face with the hand towel and open the door.

'Just wanted to see how you're doing.' She gives me a piercing look, but if I start talking about my feelings, I'll crumble.

'Just freshening up.' I cut off her concern. 'Shall we go and eat? It smells lovely.'

'Faye, you must be going out of your mind with worry. I know *I* am—'

'Please, Lainy. Can we not talk about how I feel? I've been interviewed by the police for the past hour and I feel like the only way I can keep it together is to be practical and logical rather than dwell on my emotions. Do you know what I mean? Focus on what we're going to do next…'

'Yes, sure. Of course. Sorry.'

'No, don't apologise. Look, Jake's your brother. You must be freaking out too. But let's just eat, and then we can talk about what we're going to do next, okay?'

'Yeah, you're right. Of course you're right. It'll be okay.'

We go back downstairs, and I try to force a few mouthfuls of supper down as Tom tells Lainy exactly what happened at the police station in fine detail. I don't contribute much. It's as though my mind has gone into lockdown, refusing to process anything more. My gaze flits from Tom to Lainy, their features distorting and reforming. Am I losing my mind? Perhaps I'm in shock. Outside dusk is falling and the night is encroaching. Dylan is out there without me. Is he all right? Is he scared? What was I thinking, booking this trip?

'Faye... Faye?' Tom is speaking.

I lay my fork back down and push my virtually untouched food away.

'Maybe you should have an early night,' he suggests. 'You look exhausted. I'll wake you if the police get in contact. I'm sure they'll call any minute with good news.'

He's crazy if he thinks I'm going to get any sleep at all tonight. Vivid images keep popping into my mind – of my husband lying dead and my son terrified and sobbing. My palms itch and the skin on my face feel like it's on fire. I suppose it could be mild sunburn, but whenever I'm stressed, I get this tingling, burning sensation on my skin. I'm guessing this must be stress-related, so I tell myself not to worry about it. It's a symptom, that's all.

'Faye?' he persists.

'I'm fine.'

They're both staring at me as though I've turned into an alien.

'Honestly, I'm fine. I just think I need to do something. Actually, do you know what, I'm going to head into town and see if anyone's seen them.'

'What do you mean?' Lainy asks, raising her eyebrows.

'You know... I'm going to show their photos to people. Like Tom and I did earlier up on the clifftop.'

'But aren't the police out looking for them? It might be upsetting for you, speaking to strangers.'

'Not as upsetting as sitting around doing nothing and waiting for news that might never come.'

'Okay, that's actually a good idea,' Tom says. 'I'll come with you.'

'Tom,' Lainy says, 'would you mind if I went with Faye instead? I feel like I need to do something too. I've been at home all afternoon with the girls and I'm going a bit stir crazy.'

Tom looks taken aback. 'Uh, yeah, sure.'

'Thanks.'

'Be careful, though. It's Friday night and you'll be talking to strangers. Stay in public spaces.'

Lainy huffs. 'I have been out on my own before.'

'I know, I know, I'm just being concerned, that's all. I'm allowed to worry about you both, aren't I?'

'Yes, but we're quite capable of looking after ourselves without a big, strong man.' She flashes him a brief smile to let him know she's not cross with him. But Tom's jaw tightens briefly before giving a tense smile back. The situation is getting to all of us.

'Okay. Text me to let me know how you get on,' he says.

Lainy and I both start clearing the dishes from the table.

'Leave it.' Tom waves us away. 'I'll do that when you've gone.'

'You sure?' Lainy asks.

'Yeah. Go.'

Lainy and I walk down the hill, frantically stopping people as we go and showing them images of Jake and Dylan on our phones. Everyone we meet is tanned and dressed up for a fun evening out, but they're friendly, shocked and sympathetic when we tell them about our family. I can almost hear their thoughts – thanking God it isn't their loved ones who have gone missing. I feel like such a harbinger of doom, ruining their carefree night out with our shocking news.

Although it's after seven, most of the independent shops are still open, making the most of tourist season before the lull of autumn arrives. Lainy takes one side of the high street and I take the other, but we agree that we'll go into the pubs and bars together once we've tried the shops. Forty minutes later and neither of us has had any joy in the shops. I've been met with blank-eyed stares from young shop assistants, hurried excuses from people who think I'm trying to sell them something, or sympathy from families and couples who are in town for a relaxed evening out. No one has seen Jake or Dylan. Or if they have, they can't remember.

I meet up with Lainy at the quieter end of the street as the shops peter out, making way for terraced houses and flats.

'I need a quick drink,' Lainy declares. 'Let's go in there.' She points to a stone-fronted pub we passed a few moments ago. The blackboard outside advertises Curry Night and Sky Sports. It doesn't look like the mellowest of places, but I'm not in any frame of mind to be picky.

Inside, it's brighter than I expected. A semi-circular bar dominates the lounge area, with stools ranged around and a few tables and chairs all angled towards the mega-sized flatscreen on the wall, blaring out an ad for a bookmaker. The place is a little under half full, but we don't draw any attention as we head across the sticky, patterned carpet to the bar.

'Evening, ladies,' the skinny barman says, trying to sound older than he looks, which, by the way, is about twelve years old.

'Hello,' Lainy says.

'You here to watch the big one?' he asks.

'No. Football's not really our thing,' Lainy says. 'Can we have two vodka tonics with lime?'

'Not football. Boxing. It's the big fight tonight at nine.'

'No. We just need a couple of drinks, please.'

'No problem.' I can tell he's put out by Lainy's abruptness and unwillingness to engage in conversation, but I can't worry about that.

'Have you seen either of these people?' I ask, holding my phone screen out. 'My husband and son. They're missing.'

'Let's have a look.' He takes my phone and stares hard at the image before shaking his head and handing it back. 'Sorry, no. How long they been missing?'

'Since this morning.'

'Ah, that's not long. My old man's been known to do a disappearing act for days at a time.'

'Well, this is a seven-year-old boy we're talking about,' Lainy snaps.

'Oh, well, yeah. Sorry, I haven't seen them. You local?'

'No, we're here on holiday,' I say. 'But my husband grew up here.'

'Lainy!'

We both look up at the same time to see a thick-set woman who's just walked out of a door marked 'private' behind the bar. She's wearing blue overalls and carrying a crate of fresh glasses.

'It is you, isn't it?' She squints hard.

I look at Lainy, but she's showing no sign of recognition on her face. Instead, she grips the counter top and presses her lips together.

'It's me – Cath. From school? I haven't seen you for years, but you look exactly the same – like a scared little mouse.' The woman laughs, a loud, raucous chuckle, dumps the crate a little too hard on the bar and comes around to give Lainy a huge bear hug.

'Cath?' Lainy says, stepping out of her arms. 'Cath Lawrenson?'

'One and the same. You didn't recognise me, did you? Not surprised. I've got three kids now and one divorce under my belt. Got fat and old, haven't I?'

'Not at all,' Lainy says. 'You look great.'

'Liar.' Cath grins and runs a hand through her greasy blonde hair. 'I can't believe it's you! How's that hunky brother of yours? *Jake.*' She gets a dreamy look in her eyes. 'I had a right crush on him when I was younger. Way out of my league though. That's why I went for his best friend, Mark. More fool me.'

'This is his wife, Faye.' Lainy gives me an apologetic look.

'Well, aren't you the lucky one,' Cath chortles, unembarrassed, and gives me a wink.

'Thing is,' Lainy starts to explain, 'that's kind of the reason we're here.'

'Oh?'

'We're trying to find him.'

'*Find* him? Done a runner has he? Sounds like my ex. Useless waste of space.'

'It's a bit more than that,' Lainy says.

'Hang on,' Cath interrupts and turns to the barman. 'Going on my break, Si. Bring their drinks over, will you? And add on a Diet Coke for me.'

'We can't stop.' I panic that we're going to get delayed talking to this person. That she's going to expect to spend the evening catching up with Lainy. 'We're just going to have these drinks and go.'

'You can spare two minutes,' Cath says, giving me a hurt look. 'I haven't seen this one for years.'

I don't think her version of 'two minutes' is going to be quite the same as mine. She guides us over to a table at the opposite end of the room, further away from the TV speakers. 'Can't hear myself think in here.' She carries on talking without drawing breath. 'Yeah, my Mark left me in the lurch a few years ago when the little 'uns were tiny. I rent a place just outside town. It's a dump, mind, but I don't get any maintenance, so it's all I can afford.'

'You don't mean Mark Tamworth, do you?' Lainy asks.

'Yeah, your brother's best mate. I think he had a soft spot for you back in the day.'

'Me? No.' Lainy's face turns crimson. 'Look, Cath, we really can't stay long. We're having a bit of a nightmare at the moment. Jake took his and Faye's son up to Durlston this morning, but they never came back. They're missing. We're asking around town in case anyone's seen them.'

'Missing? *Oh no*. Why didn't you say? There's me wittering on about my problems and you're going through a trauma. No wonder you want to get back out there. What can I do?'

'Here's a photo of them.' Lainy passes her phone to Cath.

Si brings our drinks over. 'That's eight pounds forty-five.'

'These are on me,' Cath says.

'No, no, that's okay.' I pull a ten-pound note out of my purse and hand it to Si. 'Keep the change.'

'Ta.' He pockets it.

'Put that change in the tips jar, Si,' Cath says with a stern look.

He smirks and walks off with a swagger.

Cath takes a sip of her Coke and studies the phone screen. 'He's bloody gorgeous. And your kid's a beauty too.'

I pick up my drink and take a large gulp.

'Afraid I don't remember seeing either of them,' she says. 'I'm so sorry. But they'll turn up, surely. What do you think might have happened? An accident at the cliffs?'

At Cath's words, a wave of nausea hits and my hand starts to tremble. I clamp it extra hard around my glass, but now my glass is shaking so I put it back on the table and shove my hands between my thighs to still them.

'We don't know what happened,' Lainy replies. 'The police are out looking for them now. Along with the coastguard.'

'Well,' Cath says. 'I know me and Mark have split up and there ain't no love lost, but if you want to know what's going on around here, he's the person to ask. He knows everyone and anyone. I'd go and have a word with him, if I were you. Not saying he gets up to anything dodgy –' she rolls her eyes at this – 'but he always keeps his ear to the ground. If anything untoward has happened, he's bound to know about it.'

'Why would he know about it?' A seed of worry starts to bloom in my chest.

'Not saying he'll definitely know,' Cath says, backtracking a little. 'Just that he's well connected locally.'

'Okay,' I reply, still uneasy. 'So where can we find him?'

'He lives up at the Grey Dolphin,' Cath says.

'The Grey Dolphin? What's that?'

'A caravan park,' Lainy explains.

'Yeah, he's their maintenance guy. Lives and works there. You can find him in Block C, caravan number forty-two.'

'Will he be there now?' I ask.

'Maybe. He might be home with his fancy piece – twenty-one she is. It's pathetic. He's almost old enough to be her father. Either that, or he'll be drinking at the club bar.'

'Okay,' I reply, downing the rest of my vodka, experiencing a swirl in my brain as I stand. 'Thanks, Cath.'

'No problem.' She turns to Lainy. 'You married? Got kids?'

'Yes, I'm married. We've got two young daughters – Poppy and Annabel.'

'Lovely,' Cath says. 'Well, if you need me to mind your girls during the day while you're looking for your brother and nephew, just say the word. Where are you staying?'

'Scar Point,' Lainy replies. 'Number seventy-one.'

'Very nice. Okay, well, I'll give you my number and then I better get back to work.' Cath gives Lainy her mobile phone number before making her way back to the bar.

Lainy stays seated, holding her phone, her eyes trained on her empty glass.

'So are you coming with me?' I ask. 'To this Grey Dolphin place?'

'I'm sorry,' she replies dully. 'I can't. Not to see Mark.'

CHAPTER SIXTEEN

He parks up and waits the few seconds required for the unit door to open. Scout sits next to him in the passenger seat. 'Good boy,' he praises. As soon as the door is high enough, he eases the truck underneath, drives to the far end and kills the engine. Now all he can hear is the soft whirr of the unit door closing behind him, blocking out the sound of birdsong and the sharp rays of the morning sun. Until, finally, there's the satisfying rattle and click as the door auto-locks, plunging him into an inky darkness.

Slipping out of the truck, he carefully makes his way over to the wall, where he presses the light switch. The temperamental strip light buzzes, deciding eventually to illuminate the cavernous space. He walks around to the flatbed at the rear of the truck, Scout at his heels, and unzips the bulky canvas bag that lies on top. As the bag falls open, he gazes at the unconscious face of the gagged and bound man.

He feels no remorse, only regret that he wasn't able to do this sooner.

CHAPTER SEVENTEEN

'Look, I really am sorry that I don't want to see Mark,' Lainy says as we leave the pub and step back out into the high street. 'I feel like I'm letting you down.'

'Why don't you want to see him?' I ask, stopping on the pavement, turning to her, my eyes narrowing slightly.

'I just can't. I don't like being back here, Faye. I don't want to talk to anyone that I knew back then.' Lainy's eyes skirt away from me, her gaze falling to the floor. 'I mean, Cath seems lovely and friendly, but being back in Swanage… it all just makes me feel—'

'Okay,' I say gently, guiltily. 'Don't worry. Of course you don't have to come. We'll go back to the house and I'll drive to the caravan park myself.'

'No, I don't think you should go up there on your own.'

'I'll be fine. This Mark guy is a father of three. What's he going to do? Although it was a bit strange that Cath seemed to think he might know what's happened.'

'I don't think she meant anything by that. I just think she meant that he knows a lot of people so he might be able to put out feelers.'

'Well, either way, it's worth going up there to see if he knows anything. Or if he's heard anyone talking about… anything.'

'No! Please, Faye. It's not a nice place to go. And anyway, I don't think there's much point. I mean, do you really think some bloke in a caravan park will have heard about Jake and Dylan going missing? It seems a bit random.'

'Yes, but if there's the smallest chance he knows anything about this, then of course I have to speak to him.'

Her shoulders drop. 'At least take Tom with you. The Grey Dolphin isn't the nicest place in the world. It's full of all sorts – at least it used to be. It's not safe.'

'Okay. Well, if Tom doesn't mind…'

'He won't mind. He'll want to go. Or maybe…' She chews her lip.

'What?'

'Maybe you should leave it until tomorrow. Or maybe, like I said, you shouldn't go at all.'

I bite back a snap of frustration. 'I have to go *now*, if there's any chance he knows anything.'

'You're right,' she says. 'Of course you're right.' She twists her fingers. 'I'm sorry I'm not up to coming. I really do feel like I'm letting you down.'

'Stop saying that. You're not letting me down.' I give her a brief hug and we start walking. 'This Mark guy,' I begin, 'did he do or say something to you back then?'

'What? No.' She exhales. 'Can we not talk about it right now? Would you mind? I'm feeling a bit… overwhelmed by everything. Coming back here, it's thrown me.'

'Yes, sure. Don't worry. Look, we'll go back to the house, okay?' Actually, it suits me not to talk. My brain is churning.

Lainy and I walk the rest of the way in silence. The vodka coupled with the fresh air, stress and lack of food has made me feel quite light-headed and I have to concentrate on putting one foot in front of the other. The pavement blurs and then clears. I focus on my breathing to stop myself from either breaking down in tears or throwing up. It's incredible how much a person can keep inside without letting any of the turmoil show. Perhaps someone who was skilled in reading body language could look at me and instantly recognise the signs of traumatic stress – an involuntary fluttering eyelid, a hand tremor. But at this moment, I feel rigid and taut, like a Tupperware container housing a volatile substance that could blow the lid off at any moment.

Lainy texts as we walk. 'Tom says that's fine. He'll drive you there when we get back.'

'Great. Thank you.' Although I'm not sure if it *is* great. I'm not sure if I shouldn't just be waiting at home while the police continue their search. Is driving up to this caravan park going to be helpful? Or am I just wasting my energy? I feel as though I have no choice. My body is antsy, twitchy. I can't sit around waiting for the police. I have to keep searching, keep moving. Not allow myself to think.

Half an hour later, Tom and I arrive at the caravan park. He pulls up outside the clubhouse and we exit the car. We walk across to the reception building – a fake log cabin with a faded metal sign swinging from its entrance depicting a smiling, leaping grey dolphin.

'Shall we just go straight to the caravan?' I ask. 'Seeing as we have the number and everything.'

'If you like,' Tom replies. 'But it might be worth asking about Jake and Dylan at reception too.'

'Good point. Let's speak to Mark first, and we can drop by reception on our way back.'

We start walking towards the rows of static caravans, leaving the brightly lit entrance area. I duck and cry out as a black shape flits past my head. Surely it's too late in the evening for birds to be flying around.

'Bats.' Tom points up at the inky sky, where the little creatures rise and fall like puppets being pulled about on a piece of string.

'Wow,' I say, without enthusiasm. Ordinarily, I'd be thrilled to see them. They're not the kinds of creatures I ever see back home in our London suburb. We regularly glimpse foxes, and occasionally hedgehogs. Once we even spotted a cuckoo on our back fence. At least *I* thought it was a cuckoo, but Jake said it was a jay. I wish Dylan were with me now. He'd really get a kick out of seeing these bats. But he isn't here. He's somewhere out there, without me, in the dark night. My heart twists and I walk a little faster.

The Grey Dolphin Caravan Park seems mainly given over to holiday lets with a few residential chalets. The place itself is situated on the hills high above Swanage, set back from the cliffs on a vast, sprawling plot. I'm assuming it must have been pretty once upon a time – a cheap and cheerful holiday destination – but time and the elements have rusted the fences and flaked the paint, soured the drains and pitted the pathways. Nowadays it's more prison camp than holiday camp. The whole place retains an air of neglect, and subtle menace. It's not somewhere I'd willingly pay money to visit.

The way is intermittently lit with unevenly spaced lamp posts. Tom and I navigate the gravelly road, our feet crunching past rows of evenly spaced caravans. Some are dark shapes bathed in darkness, others are illuminated from within and I spy the various occupants, sitting watching TV, or getting ready for a night out, oblivious to my prying eyes. I briefly wonder which of these people live here permanently, and which of them are here on holiday. I wonder if they're happy.

'Thanks for coming with me.' I realise Lainy was right. I wouldn't have felt safe arriving here on my own at night. Walking along these semi-deserted pathways alone.

'No worries,' Tom replies. 'Did you say it was Block C?' He points to a metal sign up ahead with the letter C and an arrow pointing left, illuminated by a dirty street light. Someone has written three more letters after the C in black permanent marker.

'Yes, Block C, number forty-two.'

We pause at the sign, double checking which road to take, as the path splits off into four.

'There.' I point to the furthest path, where caravan number forty sits. We trudge past forty and forty-one, both of which appear to be empty. I give a start as, ahead of us, I make out the dark shape of a man in profile, wearing a baseball cap. He's standing outside the door to number forty-two. The light from the street lamp doesn't reach this far down the path, but he's shining a torch at the caravan door. This must be Mark Tamworth, Cath's ex-husband. He looks up as we approach, eyes wide beneath the cap, startled, his face illuminated in the torchlight.

'Hi,' Tom says. 'Mark?'

'I didn't do anything,' the man grunts before the torchlight disappears, swallowing him into darkness. There's a sharp crunch of gravel and then the dull thud of disappearing footsteps.

'Hello?' I call out, my eyes adjusting to the darkness. 'Mark!'

'I think he's just run off,' Tom says, surprised.

'I think you're right,' I cry, my heart thumping. 'Why did he run away? Why did he say he didn't do anything? Do you think that means he *did* do something? We should go after him!'

'It's too dark to go chasing around here,' Tom interrupts my worries, putting a restraining hand on my arm. 'We'll never find him. We've got no torch and we don't know the layout. And anyway, what would we even do if we caught up to him?'

'Hey!' I cry out into the dark. 'Mark! We just want to talk!' I have a strong urge to run after the man, but Tom is right – I can barely see in front of my hand, so goodness knows how I'd catch up to him. I wish we'd thought to bring torches.

Tom strides across to the caravan and looks through the window.

'What are you doing?' I go over to join him.

'Trying to see inside.' He tuts, and cups his hands around his face as he peers through the glass. 'It's too dark. I can't see a thing.'

I stand next to my brother-in-law, peering through the adjacent window.

'I wonder why he ran away,' Tom muses.

'Do you think he could be trying to hide something?'

'What if…'

'What?' I step back and turn to face him. 'What if *what*?'

'Mark saying that he didn't do anything has got me worried. What if he actually is something to do with Jake and Dylan's disappearance? Lainy said Mark and Jake used to be best friends. Maybe they had a falling out. What if Jake and Dylan are in the caravan?'

My pulse begins to race. I peer harder through the window, but I still can't see anything, so I give up and turn to face Tom. 'Do you really think they might be?'

'I don't know. But they've been missing for hours. I thought one of them had had an accident. But what if…'

'What if *what*?'

'I don't want to alarm you, Faye, but what if they're being held against their will?' In the gloom, Tom's expression is a mixture of horror and sympathy.

'Dylan!' I yell through the glass. 'Jake!'

We both fall silent, cocking our heads to listen. But there's no sound from within.

'What should we do?' I cry. 'Shall we break in?'

'No.' Tom steps back from the window. 'I've got a better idea.'

CHAPTER EIGHTEEN

THEN

Lainy dumps her few sticks of driftwood on the growing pile of kindling and wonders if that's enough or if she should go off and search for more. Everyone's spent the past twenty minutes gathering wood from the beach and cliffs under orders from Cath, who thinks she's in charge.

'Why are we making a fire, anyway?' Kayla asks.

'It's a beach party!' Cath replies with a laugh, tugging at her micro-skirt to stop it riding up her thighs. 'Everyone knows whenever there's a beach party, you have to have a fire. It's tradition. And anyway, it'll brighten everything up and keep us all warm.'

'Maybe if she wore more clothes, she wouldn't be so cold,' Kayla mutters to Lainy, who giggles.

'I heard that, Kayla Smith.' Cath puts her hands on her hips and shakes her head indulgently. 'If you've got it, flaunt it, that's what I say. Anyway, fires are romantic.' She looks across at Mark and smirks. Mark clears his throat, embarrassed by Cath's forwardness.

Kayla nudges Lainy. 'Looks like Cath's after Mark,' she whispers.

'She can have him,' Lainy murmurs with a sigh of relief. 'He's been stuck to my side all night. It's doing my head in.' She doesn't mention that she wishes it was Owen who was stuck to her side. But she realises that that's probably never going to happen. Her dreams of Owen are going to stay just that – dreams. He still hasn't paid her any attention. He probably never will.

Lainy checks her watch and sees it's already 10.40. She and Jake promised their parents they'd be back by eleven, and it'll take them at least fifteen minutes to walk back up the cliff path. She glances down the beach. Jake is still sitting on the rocks with Rose. They've been cosied up all night. She knows her brother has a humungous crush on her, but Lainy assumed Rose was way out of Jake's league. Her brother's good looking, but he's also a bit awkward and tends to rub people up the wrong way. Mark's the only one who puts up with him – and that's only because they're both a bit… unsociable.

Jake will be annoyed if she interrupts him, but Lainy doesn't want to get into trouble with Mum and Dad. Not right at the start of the holidays. If she's late home tonight, they'll ground her forever and her life will be ruined.

Lainy decides that interrupting Jake and Rose will be better than being grounded, so she starts making her way over to the rocks. The sand is firm and dark beneath her shoes. Her cotton halterneck dress swishes as she walks. She spent so many hours working out what she would wear. So much emotional energy. For what? For someone who doesn't even realise she exists.

Rose looks up as she approaches, her freckled face bathed in moonlight. She waves at Lainy and nudges Jake with her elbow.

'Hey, Lainy.' Her smile is open and friendly.

'Hey,' Lainy replies, not really knowing what to say to the older girl. 'Jake, we better go. It's almost quarter to eleven.'

'You can't go yet,' Rose says, turning to Jake and wrinkling her nose. 'It's still really early.'

'We've got to be back by eleven,' Lainy says, realising Jake will be cross with her for making them sound like losers.

'That's because you're here,' Jake says. 'I'd be able to stay later if I didn't have to get you back home.'

Rose watches with amusement, and Lainy can tell that this amusement has irritated her brother. He's trying to act cool for Rose, but his image has been ruined by his little sister coming over and talking about his parents and his curfew. But what else was she supposed to do? She's not about to get in trouble because her brother wants to impress a girl. Jake scowls at Lainy and shakes his head.

She shrugs apologetically. 'So? You coming?'

'I'm gonna stay a bit longer,' Jake says nonchalantly, but Lainy notes the lines of irritation still etched across his forehead.

'Cool,' Rose says, giving his arm a light punch. 'We're having way too much fun for you to go home now, and anyway, there's something I really want to talk to you about.' Her cheeks flare red for a moment, the skin on her neck mottling.

'Lainy,' Jake says, 'can you stay for another half hour? We'll head back at quarter past, okay?'

Lainy shifts from one foot to the other. She feels for Jake, but she pictures her dad's disappointed features. Her mum's tight lips, arms folded across her chest. 'You stay if you like. I'm gonna go back now.'

'Lainy—'

'Sorry, but I'm going.'

He heaves out a sigh and gets to his feet, but Rose pulls him back down and gives him a meaningful stare. Jake licks his lips and turns back to Lainy. 'Sorry, Laines, I'm staying. But you can go, as long as you get Mark to walk you back.'

'I don't need Mark to—'

'Yes you do. You're not walking back up there on your own.'

'I'll be fine.'

'Lainy, I'm not joking.' Jake glares at her.

She drops her shoulders. 'Fine. I'll get Mark flipping Tamworth to walk me.' Lainy turns and walks back towards the others, who start cheering as the fire catches light. The scent of woodsmoke stings her nostrils, and she catches her breath as the flames whoosh upwards, licking around the tinder-dry driftwood and sending showers of sparks up into the night.

Someone turns the music up. It's as though the party is only just getting going now that she's leaving. As she approaches the fire, she spies Mark and Cath sitting close to one another. Cath is leaning in towards him, whispering in his ear, her hand on his knee. There's no way Lainy's interrupting whatever it is that's going on there. And she doesn't want Mark walking her home anyway. He might try something on – and that would be too hideous to even imagine.

Lainy alters her course and moves away from the fire, towards the darkness of the cliffs. She'll walk home on her own.

CHAPTER NINETEEN

NOW

Back at the entrance to the caravan park, Tom and I wait in his car, windows rolled down, the night air warm and sticky. A rhythmic thump of music has started up from the clubhouse, with the even louder drone of the DJ's voice booming through the speakers in an indecipherable monologue. Tom spoke to DS Nash on the phone ten minutes ago, and she said she'd be up at the site within the next quarter of an hour.

Tom texts Lainy to keep her in the loop, while I breathe deeply and try Jake's mobile yet again. As expected, it goes straight to voicemail. I leave another frantic message, and then I count the cars in the car park – anything to try to stop myself spinning out.

'I asked Lainy to ask Cath why she thinks Mark might have run off,' Tom says.

Irrationally, I'm annoyed that he's interrupted my car counting. It was helping me to stay calm. 'What did she say?'

'She said she'll give her a call.'

I pick at a loose thread on my crumpled trousers and then pull at it viciously, trying to snap it off. But instead it digs into my fingers, making a painful red line, refusing to break. I swear under my breath.

'Hey.' Tom puts a hand on my arm. 'We'll get to the bottom of all this. You know that, right? We'll find them.'

I nod and blink back a tear, glancing up as a car sweeps into the park, headlights blinding me for a moment. My breath catches and then my shoulders sag as I realise it's not a police car.

'I think that's them,' Tom says.

'Where?'

'Just pulled in. It's an unmarked car.'

'How do you know?'

'There.' He points to the front of the dark BMW at a blink-and-you'll-miss-it flash of blue lights.

The doors open and two plain-clothes officers get out of the car – DS Lisa Nash in her grey suit and a younger fair-haired man in jeans and a T-shirt.

I square my shoulders, slide out of the passenger side and cross the car park with Tom.

'Hello again,' Nash says. 'This is DC Paul Soames. You said you think your family might be in one of the caravans here?'

'We don't know,' I reply. 'It was just a bit odd. We came to speak to a man called Mark Tamworth, but he took one look at us and ran off.'

'And why did you want to speak to him?' Nash asks, her forehead wrinkling. 'Do you know him?'

'No,' I begin, 'but Lainy and I ran into her old schoolfriend earlier – Cath, her name is. We told her about Jake and Dylan going missing and she suggested we talk to her ex-husband – Mark Tamworth. Cath said he knows everything that goes on around here. So we thought it was worth a shot.'

Nash raises her eyebrows. 'So, you don't actually know Mark Tamworth, and he's nothing to do with you or your family?'

I realise how tenuous this is all sounding. I hope Nash doesn't think we're wasting her time. 'No, but—'

'We just thought it was suspicious that he ran off,' Tom interjects. 'And we didn't want to ignore it, just in case.'

'I was also going to say that although I don't know him, my husband was friends with him at school,' I add.

Nash purses her lips and then gives a little nod. 'You said on the phone that Mark Tamworth does the maintenance here?'

'Yes,' Tom replies.

'And he lives in the caravan you visited?'

'Yes.'

'Okay. I agree it is a bit odd that he ran. We haven't had any luck so far up on the cliffs, so let's see if we can get a key from reception and check this place out.'

Tom and I follow her and DC Soames into the low red-brick building in front of us. There's no one around, so Nash dings the little bell on the counter. After a few moments, a large woman in grey leggings and a Minnie Mouse sweatshirt huffs out of the back room, her eyes sweeping over the four of us.

'Sorry, we're full up,' she says, turning away.

'We're not customers.' Nash takes out her badge. 'I'm Detective Sergeant Nash, and this is DC Soames. And you are?'

'Oh. Right.' She turns back with a sullen frown. 'My name's Sandra Coles. I'm the site manager. Something wrong?'

'Have you got a moment, Ms Coles?'

She huffs again. 'Well, I'm having my dinner and trying to watch *Corrie* on catch-up, but I suppose it'll have to wait. You can call me Sandra.' She eyes me and Tom suspiciously then returns her gaze to Nash. 'How can I help?'

'Mark Tamworth,' Nash says. 'He does the maintenance here, correct?'

'Mark bloody Tamworth,' the woman mutters under her breath and rolls her eyes.

'Something the matter?' DS Nash asks.

Sandra Coles shakes her head.

'If there's something you're not telling us…' Nash prompts.

'It's nothing,' she says.

'It might not be nothing to us,' Nash says with an encouraging smile.

'It's just that Mark came to me a few days ago asking for this weekend off. I said, "You're having a laugh. It's one of our busiest weekends of the year." Anyway, he told me that if I didn't give him the time off, he'll quit. We had a right barney and I wanted to tell him to piss off and leave right then and there. But that would've landed me in the crapper, and he *is* good at his job. So I had no choice. I had to give him the time off, didn't I.' Sandra crosses her arms over her ample chest. 'I'm not happy about it. Not happy at all.'

'Do you know where he's gone?' Nash asks.

'No idea. I did ask, but he said it was personal. An emergency. For all I know, he might still be here. He didn't say he was actually going away. What's he done, anyway?'

'We don't know. But it would be very helpful if you could open the door to his caravan and let us take a look inside.'

'Just because you're the police, you can't go marching into his caravan. I know the law. Don't you need a search warrant?'

Nash stands firm. 'We have reasonable grounds to search. A father and son have gone missing. Look, it'll end up being a lot less hassle for you if you just open it up for us. Chances are they're not there anyway. But we need to check.'

'All right, calm down. It's no skin off my nose. A missing kid, you say? You think Mark's something to do with it?'

'Like I said, we don't know, but we need to establish that the father and son aren't being held against their will.'

'Fine, okay. I suppose my bangers and mash will have to go cold.'

'Sorry to disturb your dinner,' Nash says, 'but it is important.'

'Can't imagine Mark doing anything like that. He's got kids himself, you know…' She waits for someone to reply, but no one does. 'All right, let me get the spare set of keys.' Sandra puffs into the back room and reappears moments later with the keys and a torch. 'Okay, let's go.'

'How far is it?' Nash asks.

'About five minutes' walk. Who are these two anyway?' She jerks her head in our direction.

'They're helping us with our enquiries,' Soames says without elaborating.

While Soames walks ahead with Sandra, Nash walks at a slower pace with me and Tom, asking us again to go over exactly what happened with Mark Tamworth. Tom repeats what he said on the phone. She nods, but doesn't pass comment. We soon reach the street light at the end of Block C and turn down onto the dark path. Sandra turns on her torch and we follow the unsteady circle of light until we reach Tamworth's caravan.

DS Nash climbs the steps and knocks on the front door. We wait, but all is quiet. She raps again. 'Mark Tamworth, it's the police, please can you open the door?'

Silence.

Nash turns to Sandra and nods. Sandra huffs up the steps with her key, turns it in the lock and opens the door.

CHAPTER TWENTY

'Wait here,' DS Nash tells me and Tom.

I open my mouth to protest, but Tom puts a restraining hand on my arm. 'It's best to wait.'

I give a start as the lights flash on inside the caravan. Sandra is inside with the officers while Tom and I wait down on the path. I shiver despite the warmth of the night, the taste of this evening's spaghetti bolognese burning the back of my throat. I hope I'm not about to vomit.

'Do you think they're in there?' I'm talking just to take my mind off the rising sick feeling.

'I don't know. I guess we'll find out in a minute. It'll be okay. Do you need to sit down? You could sit on one of the steps.'

'No. No, I'm fine.' But my knees are like jelly. There are so many what-ifs spinning around in my brain that I just can't think straight. I grip onto the wooden railing at the bottom of the steps, its splintered surface rough against my fingers.

Seconds later, the officers emerge followed by Sandra.

'Well?' Tom asks.

Nash shakes her head. 'There's no one inside and no sign of anyone having been held here.'

I exhale and my brain clears a little. I hadn't ever truly thought they were inside the caravan, but it's a relief that they haven't found anything sinister. 'Sorry for jumping to conclusions.'

'Don't apologise,' Nash replies. 'When it comes to missing children, it's always worth exploring every avenue.'

'I thought the same thing as you, Faye,' Tom says. 'I guess it's desperation. Makes you clutch at every possibility.'

'But I still don't understand why Tamworth ran away.' I make a mental note to quiz Lainy about him later. Maybe she's holding something back about her past. I glance at Tom. Maybe he knows more than he's letting on, too. Or am I just being paranoid?

I realise DS Nash is still talking, so I try to concentrate. 'We'll get the CSIs to take a look in and around the caravan, just in case. In the meantime, we'll try Mr Tamworth's mobile number again and have a chat. See if we can find out why he ran off when you approached.'

'How likely is it that Mark Tamworth is something to do with Dylan and Jake's disappearance?' Tom asks the officers as we leave the caravan behind and make our way back towards reception.

'Hard to say,' Nash replies. 'But we'll keep all our lines of enquiry open for now.'

'He keeps it nice and tidy in there,' Sandra says grudgingly. 'I'll give him that. To be honest, I thought the place would be a mess.'

'He must be behind their disappearance,' Tom says. 'Why else would he have run off? No one runs off like that unless they've got a guilty conscience, something to hide. You need to find him.'

'Don't worry,' Soames says. 'We will.'

Nash's phone rings and she waves us on as she stops to take the call. I want to stay and eavesdrop, in case it's something to do with my family. But she turns her back to us and takes a few steps in the opposite direction. I slow my pace a little, but Tom puts his hand on the small of my back to keep me moving. What can her phone call be about? Is it to do with Jake and Dylan? Have they found them? My palms begin to sweat and there's a pulse in my throat that I've never felt before.

A few minutes later, we're back outside reception and Nash has finished her phone conversation. 'Can you get Mr Tamworth's mobile number from Sandra?' she asks Soames. 'I need to talk to Faye.'

The background thump of my heart immediately comes to the fore, loud and insistent, vibrating my body and throbbing in my ears. 'What is it?' I ask, coming to a standstill. 'Has there been some news? Have you found them?'

Sandra is staring at me, but Nash looks at Soames and jerks her head in the direction of reception.

'Can I get that number from you, Sandra?' Soames starts walking towards the building and she reluctantly follows, disappointed not to hear what the news is about. Once she's out of earshot, I turn back to face Nash.

'Well?' I ask.

'Let's sit over there.' She gestures to a cluster of faded wooden picnic tables in front of the clubhouse and I wonder what it is she has to tell me that warrants sitting down. It can't be good news, can it? 'It's nothing to necessarily worry about.' Nash is trying to put me at ease. But my brain is jumping from one terrifying conclusion to another.

Tom doesn't say anything. He just comes to my side, and we walk over to the tables with Nash. A moment later, Soames has joined us – minus Sandra – and we all take a seat at a table littered with discarded rubbish, empty plastic cups and dirty crockery.

'So?' Tom asks.

'Our guys have found a child's red baseball cap on the cliffs,' she says.

I inhale and clench my fists. 'Dylan's. It has to be Dylan's, doesn't it? What does that mean? Are they looking down on the cliffs now? Are they doing everything they can to find him? I want to go down and help!' I stand clumsily, my body swaying.

'Look, I know it's hard,' Nash says quietly, 'but try not to jump to any conclusions. The cap could have blown off his head and landed down there quite easily. It doesn't necessarily mean something bad has happened.'

'It's not windy. It hasn't been windy all day!' My voice borders on a shriek. 'How could it have blown down there?'

'It's a clifftop,' Nash says. 'All it takes is one stray gust.'

'Faye, this could be good,' Tom says. 'Hopefully, now that they've found Dyl's hat, they'll be closer to locating the two of them.'

'There must have been an accident,' I reply. 'Maybe Dylan went down there to get his hat back and then Jake was forced to go down and rescue him. They could have been swept out to sea! Are the coastguard looking in the water? Jake's a good swimmer, but it's been hours…'

'We're got everyone looking,' Nash says. 'The coastguard's on the water with lifeboats. We have officers combing the headland, and the air-sea rescue helicopters are sweeping the area. If your husband and son are there, we'll find them.'

'But it's dark. They might not—'

'They use all the latest tech,' Soames interrupts. 'Night vision, thermal imaging cameras, that kind of thing.'

'What if they're trapped in one of the caves?' Tom asks. 'Maybe they climbed down, but couldn't get back up, so they took shelter from the incoming tide in a cave.'

'Like I said,' Nash replies, 'if they're down there, we'll find them. Our guys are good at their jobs. They know what they're doing.'

'We should have reported them missing earlier!' I cry, turning to Tom. 'Why did we leave it so late? I'm so stupid. I should have called the police the minute I felt uneasy.'

'Don't beat yourself up, Faye. We didn't realise. We just thought they'd lost track of time.'

I stand and run a hand through my hair, then put both palms to my hot cheeks. This is all turning into something huge and awful. Something out of a nightmare. Images of Jake and Dylan's faces flash into my mind. Tom gets to his feet and turns to me. 'It'll be okay,' he says softly. But I know he's only saying it to calm me. He doesn't know what's actually happened. He's only speculating.

The officers stand. Nash walks around the table to me. 'If we could follow you back to your holiday home and get some items of clothing belonging to your husband and your son... for the sniffer dogs to get a good scent.'

Her words blur and I can't respond.

'Sure,' Tom replies for me.

'We'll also need to collect DNA from a razor or a comb, or maybe a toothbrush?'

'No problem,' my brother-in-law replies.

'Faye,' DS Nash says gently. 'I know this all seems overwhelming, but the chances are your husband and son will turn up right as rain. Nine times out of ten, the missing person turns up safe and well. Try to stay positive, okay?'

Trying to stay positive is all very well, but when you keep picturing your husband's face still and lifeless, and imagine your child scared and confused, it's hard to take that advice. I check my messages for the millionth time, but there's nothing new. As I slip my phone back into my bag, I realise my whole body is trembling. I'm shaking from head to toe. The stress is finally showing.

'Faye?' Tom reaches out to touch my shoulder.

I flinch backwards, knocking into the chair.

He drops his hand, and his face creases in concern. 'You're shaking. Maybe you should sit down.'

'I'm fine.' I clasp my hands together to try to stop them trembling. 'Let's go back to the house and sort out those items for the sniffer dogs. I just need to keep busy.' I turn to Nash. 'Are you going to get people to look for Mark Tamworth too?'

'Yes.'

'But are you going to look for him tonight? Because he could be in a car and miles away by now. He could be—'

'I promise you, we're going to do everything to get your family back.'

'It's just…' My voice cracks.

'Faye,' Nash says, her voice softening, 'I take my job very seriously. I will look for your son and husband using all the resources I have. Okay?'

I look down at my shoes.

'Okay?' she repeats.

'Okay.' I look back up at her unflinching gaze. 'Thank you.'

But the panic bubbling up inside my body is like molten lava in a volcano. My mind is scrambled and I can't think straight. I keep telling myself *It will be all right, it will be all right.* But do I honestly believe that?

No. I do not.

CHAPTER TWENTY-ONE

Jake's body zings with recklessness as Lainy walks away. He's already defied his parents by deciding to stay out past his curfew. He'd better make it count. Maybe this is just the push he needs to make his move on Rose. If he doesn't kiss her then he'll be grounded for nothing.

'Will you get into trouble for staying out late?' Rose twirls a few strands of hair around her finger and it's sexy as hell.

'Maybe.' Jake shrugs. He wants to tell her that she's worth getting into trouble for, but he's worried it will come off as corny. That she'll laugh at him.

'I didn't have you down as such a rebel.' Rose giggles and her eyes flash.

'Ha, I'm not. Not really. But I'm almost sixteen. Old enough to make my own decisions.'

'Aren't you sixteen yet?' Her eyes widen.

'My birthday's next month.'

'Aw, so you're the baby of the year!'

Jake isn't happy with her pronouncement. It's always annoyed him that he's the youngest of their year group. Especially as he feels like he's the most adult of them all. Most of his year behave like immature toddlers.

'Don't look like that,' Rose says. 'It's cute that you're the youngest. I was sixteen last year so I'm one of the oldest.

'Age doesn't mean anything. It's just a number.' He says it more sharply than he intended, but thankfully she doesn't take offence.

'That's deep.' Rose tilts her head.

Desperate to change the subject, Jake decides it's now or never. He shifts position so he's facing her. Heart pounding, palms sweating, he can't afford to overthink this. Jake fixes her with what he hopes is a meaningful gaze. 'I really like you, Rose.'

She doesn't reply, so Jake leans forward to kiss her, his whole body fizzing with anticipation.

But his lips don't meet hers. They find nothing but air. Rose has jerked back as though electrocuted, her eyes wide with surprise, and a brief flash of something else – revulsion. Jake's belly roils as though he's been kicked in his lower intestine. A sharp ache that precedes a whole jumbled mess of other emotions.

Rose quickly covers her shock with a fake laugh, like shattered glass.

'I'm… uh…' Jake stammers and then springs to his feet. 'I'm sorry. I'll go.'

But Rose is on her feet too, pulling at his arm. 'No, don't go. I'm sorry too. I didn't mean for… I'm sorry that you thought… Oh I'm so silly.'

'Honestly, it's no problem,' he says through tight lips, anger and humiliation flooding his veins. 'I got it wrong,' he grunts. 'I thought you liked me, but it's no big deal. I'll go. Save us both the awkwardness.'

'Stay,' she pleads. 'Please. It won't be awkward. Look, I'm flattered. We'll pretend it never happened. And anyway, I need to talk to you about something.'

'About what?' he asks brusquely. The last thing he wants to do is carry on talking to Rose after her rejection. It's painful to even look at her now. To imagine what she must be thinking. She's bound to tell her mates what happened. It'll be all round town this summer. He won't be able to show his face.

'Look, Jake,' she says seriously, her smile gone. 'I really thought we were just friends. I hope you'll keep on being my friend and things won't get weird between us.'

She sits back down on the rock and pushes her hair off her face. Hair that he will never touch, a face that he will never stroke, never kiss.

'Yeah. Friends. Sure.' He knows he sounds sullen. Sulky, even.

'Promise me.'

He flexes his fingers and stares out to sea, letting the gentle crash of the waves take him out of the present for just a moment.

'Jake?'

'What?' He turns back to her enquiring eyes. 'Oh. Yeah. Sure. I promise.'

'Good.' She smiles with relief and pats the rock next to her.

'I'm gonna go get another drink,' he says, suddenly desperate to escape. To forget tonight ever happened.

'I just need you for two more minutes,' she wheedles, 'and then I'll let you go.'

He sighs and sits back on the rock. 'What do you need me for?'

'*Well* –' her cheeks flush and she stares down into her lap – 'it's actually a bit awkward now.'

'So I'll go.' He makes to stand up again, but she pulls him back down.

'No, silly. Stay. There's something I wanted to talk to you about. But maybe I shouldn't.' Her cheeks flush.

Jake grits his teeth. 'It's fine, just tell me.' He actually doesn't care what it is she wants to say. He actually just wants to leave Rose Cassidy sitting on a rock and never see her again.

'Okay.' She gives another giggle. 'I'll just come out with it. The reason I wanted to talk to you, well, not the only reason, but... Oh, listen to me, I'm babbling.' She takes a breath. 'I wanted to ask your advice...'

'About what?'

'Well, you know Owen in our year, right?'

'Owen Pearson? Yeah, I know him.' Jake wonders what's she's asking about him for. Maybe she knows something about him. Something bad. Something from his past. That would be good. That would at least mean that tonight wasn't a total bust.

'I just wondered…' she begins, 'is there anyone he likes?'

'Likes?' Jake echoes stupidly.

'Yeah, you know. Likes, as in fancies?' Rose twists her fingers in her lap.

Jake isn't really concentrating on her words. His mind is still bloated with disappointment from her rejection of him.

'Jake?' She looks up at him with an embarrassed smile. 'Do you know if Owen fancies anyone?'

'No idea.' Jake doesn't mention the fact that he has a strong suspicion Owen fancies his sister.

Rose gives another awkward laugh. 'Because the thing is, I really like him, and I wondered if you might put in a good word, or maybe find out what he thinks about me?'

Jake's blood grows hot in his veins. Can Rose really be telling him that she fancies Owen bloody Pearson? Has she lost her mind? Doesn't she know what an absolute arrogant twat Pearson is? And how can she be confiding all this to him after he's just bared his soul to her? This is the ultimate humiliation.

It hits Jake that this is the only reason Rose has been talking to him this evening. Not because she likes him as a friend, but because she fancies Owen. He's been used.

Jake doesn't even trust himself to speak right now. Unsure what will come out of his mouth. He gets to his feet and walks away, footsteps stiff, like his muscles have been encased in lead.

'Jake? Jake, are you okay? Where are you going? Did you hear what I asked you? Are you going to talk to him for me?'

But Jake doesn't reply. Her voice has become an annoyance that he can't bear to listen to any more. This evening has been a total shitfest. He can't believe Rose likes that loser Owen Pearson. What a monumentally crap start to the holidays.

He heads towards the fire where everyone else seems to have gathered, their voices bright and brittle, echoing in his ears. He stops short as he notices that Mark is snogging someone. His *sister*? But no... it's not Lainy he's kissing – it's Cath. Mark is with Cath! Jake marches over to his friend and pulls him away from her.

'What are you doing? I thought you liked my sister? I thought you were walking her home?' His voice is rough, aggressive. He knows his anger is nothing to do with Mark, and everything to do with Rose liking Owen. But he can't help himself. He wants to start something. He wants to punch something. Or someone.

Mark obviously senses that Jake is seriously pissed off, because he raises his hands and takes a step back. 'Hey! What's your problem?'

'What's going on?' Cath cries. 'Jake?'

'My problem,' Jake says, 'is that you said you would keep an eye on Lainy, but you're sucking the face off this tart instead.'

'Fuck off, Townsend,' Cath cries. 'I'm not a tart.'

'Where is she, then? Where's Lainy?' Jake snarls. The fire crackles and spits, the heat from the flames warming one side of his face.

'I dunno,' Mark says. 'She went off. Look, she's not interested in me. That's not my fault.'

Jake balls his right fist. He wants to punch Mark so badly. His arm trembles with the desire to draw blood. But then he realises that his fourteen-year-old sister is somewhere up there on the dark cliff path on her own. His parents are going to kill him when they realise he's let her walk back alone. If he runs now, he might just catch up to her before she reaches home.

'Forget it.' Jake unclenches his fist. 'You're a waste of space, Tamworth. Thanks for nothing.'

Mark shakes his head, white-faced and shaken, while Cath stands by his side glowering.

Jake gives them both a dirty look before taking off, sprinting across the beach into the darkness, towards the cliff path.

CHAPTER TWENTY-TWO

NOW

Back at the house, Tom and I almost fall through the front door, suddenly exhausted after everything that's happened. Lainy greets us in the kitchen. She's sitting at the table with a glass of wine.

'Sorry,' she says, tapping the side of her glass. 'I know I probably shouldn't be drinking. I should be alert, but my brain was racing, and I needed something to calm me down.'

'You don't need to apologise.' I sit opposite her. 'You can definitely pour me a glass though.'

'Me too,' Tom adds. 'Are the girls okay?'

'Fine,' Lainy says, getting a couple more glasses out of the cupboard. 'They both went out like lights. All that fresh air.'

Tom sits too and we fill Lainy in on our visit to the Grey Dolphin.

'He ran off?' she says with a sceptical look on her face. 'Are you sure? Maybe he didn't see you and was heading somewhere else.'

'No,' Tom says, taking a large sip of his wine. 'He looked up, saw us, froze for a second and then legged it.'

'Yep.' I nod in agreement. 'That pretty much sums up what happened.'

'But that makes no sense,' she persists.

'Maybe he thought we were someone else,' I say, having just thought of it. 'He might owe money to somebody, or something like that.'

'I suppose so.'

'What was Mark like?' Tom asks. 'Back then.'

She shrugs and then inhales deeply. 'A bit of an oddball, if the truth be known. Not dangerous or anything. Just a bit creepy I suppose. But he was Jake's best friend, so I put up with him. Cath thought the sun shone out of his behind. Well, she did back then. Not so sure she's too fond of him these days. He might be completely different now. I haven't seen him since we were teens. We didn't keep in touch.'

'Did he keep in touch with Jake?'

'Not that I know of. Faye, you look absolutely done in. Are you hungry? You barely touched your dinner earlier.'

'No thanks, I couldn't eat a thing.'

'But you have to eat something. You'll collapse if you don't.'

'Maybe later.' The thought of putting food in my mouth makes me feel queasy. The wine is all I can handle.

'Lainy's right,' Tom says. 'You should eat. I'm going to make some toast. Want some?'

I shake my head. 'Maybe I'll just go up. Get some rest.'

'Good idea,' Tom says. 'You'll be no good to anyone if you don't take care of yourself. We'll wake you if we hear anything.'

I drain my glass, take my handbag and leave the kitchen, checking my texts as I trudge up the stairs. Although there are still five of us left in the house, it feels empty. And I feel completely alone.

I lied when I said I was going upstairs to sleep. How can I get any rest, let alone sleep? And I know they're only trying to help, but I can't cope with their well-meaning words. It must be as exhausting for my in-laws to keep thinking of different ways to reassure me as it is for me to accept their words of comfort.

My mind circles like a creature chasing its tail. I switch on the light, shut the bedroom door behind me and lean against it, closing my eyes for a moment. But it doesn't matter whether my eyes are open or closed, I still keep picturing Jake and Dylan's faces in my mind's eye. Faces that are either lifeless, or terrified. And I don't know which of the images is worse.

I open my eyes once more and let my gaze travel over the closed curtains, to the huge unmade bed. There's no way I'm climbing under the covers. I don't think I could even bring myself to lie on top of it. Instead, I sink down onto the floor with my back propped up against the door. I'll stay here until Tom and Lainy go to bed and then I'll creep back downstairs. Sit in the kitchen. Drink more wine.

The low rumble of their voices vibrates through the ceiling. I think about all the other people who have stayed in this house. Did they enjoy wonderful family holidays here? Or was this place a catalyst that changed their lives? Maybe the house is cursed. Maybe whoever stays here is destined to suffer bad luck and have evil befall them. I give myself a little shake. That red wine must be making me think foolish thoughts. There's nothing cursed about this house. The only thing cursed around here is me.

I don't know how long I've been sitting with my back to the door, only that I heard Tom and Lainy go to bed some time ago and my legs are numb from sitting in one spot. I should have brought more wine up with me. Perhaps it would have helped me to pass out.

I should get up. Do something. What good is sitting here if I can't sleep? But I stay rooted to the spot, unable to stir myself.

Sometime later I check my phone, surprised to see it's already 2 a.m. I must have zoned out for a while. Not sleep as such, but… something else. With a sudden burst of clarity, I realise that I can't sit here any longer. My mouth tastes sour and dry. I ease myself up and tiptoe to the bathroom to brush my teeth. I should probably have a shower, but the noise might wake Tom and Lainy and I don't have the energy for conversation right now. Instead, I creep downstairs, scribble a note to say I've gone for an early morning walk (only a slight stretching of the truth), and leave the house.

The air is warm but with a hint of freshness that acts like a wake-up call to my brain. I inhale a lungful of tangy sea air and start walking, unsure of where I'm headed. Uncaring of the direction I choose.

Putting one foot in front of the other, that's what I've been doing for the past couple of hours. After a short time walking along deserted residential cliff roads, I found myself up on the headland once more. I concentrate on the sound of my trainers on the gravel pathway. *Crunch, crunch, crunch.* Sometimes my foot hits an uneven patch – a stone or a grassy tussock – and the regularity of my footsteps is interrupted, breaking the steady rhythm.

It's still dark. Still the early hours of the morning. I force my eyes to widen, ignoring their scratchy tiredness, their urge to close. My brain races but I don't allow it to settle on anything. I push out all my thoughts. All I allow in there is the crunch of the gravel and the juddering whirr of the search helicopter sweeping the headland and making loops out to sea.

Search-and-rescue teams in high-vis jackets carry torches, sweeping the cliffs below and the woods above. The hiss and chatter of their radios permeates the night air. All these people out looking for my family. I keep my head down, unwilling to catch anyone's eye. In case they ask me who I am. What I'm doing. I simply concentrate on navigating the path in the weak moonlight. Just walking.

I check my phone again, but there are no messages. The time reads a little after 4 a.m. At least out here I'm not tossing and turning in bed, suffering from my night terrors. I suddenly realise the helicopter has gone. Perhaps to refuel, perhaps to search further along the coast. The whirring from above is replaced by the crash of the waves on the rocks. I stop for a moment and stare out at the dark ocean, at the ripples of reflected moonlight. Where is Dylan right now? Please let him not be scared. Please let him be okay. I wrench my gaze from the water and turn too quickly, catching my foot on a rock. I swear under my breath and feel a tear drip down my cheek.

Exhaustion overwhelms me. I sit on the rocky ground and drop my head into my hands. What have I done? Coming to Swanage was supposed to be something good. Instead, it's… well, it feels like the worst mistake of my life. This hollowness in my heart feels endless.

I can't stay here. I don't know what time the sun will rise, and I don't want to be up on the headland when it gets light. The dawn of a new day without my husband. Without my son. Besides, I should try to get at least an hour or two of sleep. Who am I kidding? I will never be able to sleep. Not until this is over. Until I can wrap my arms around my baby. I stand and turn, focus on the path ahead, and start walking back.

I don't keep track of how long the journey down off the headland takes, but as I finally put my key in the lock, I notice a faint, pink glow behind the house – dawn; although it's not yet light enough for the street lights to go off. I've been out all night. My body is stiff and slightly chilly, my face dry, eyelids drooping.

'Faye?' Tom stands in the hallway wearing pyjama bottoms and a T-shirt. He scratches his chest sleepily and yawns.

'Hi.' I step inside and close the door behind me, the darkness more absolute inside the house than out.

'What are you—'

'Just went out for an early morning walk. Didn't you see my note?' I don't want him to know I've been out all night. He and Lainy will only worry more.

'No, I didn't notice it. Still half asleep. Cup of tea?' he asks.

I was planning on going back upstairs, but his offer sounds good. 'Yes please. Any news?'

He shakes his head. 'I'm sure the search will be easier once it gets light.'

'I hope so.'

We head into the kitchen and I sit at the table while Tom puts the kettle on.

'Lainy still asleep?' I ask.

'Yeah, only just. She was tossing and turning most of the night. Mumbling in her sleep.'

'I'm glad she managed to doze off eventually. How about you? Did you get any shut-eye?'

'Yeah, a few hours. Want some toast?'

'Please.' Part of me feels guilty at the thought of eating. What kind of person must I be to think about breakfast at a time like this? It's just fuel, I tell myself. Fuel to get me through this horror.

Tom and I eat our toast and drink our tea in near silence, zoning out, lost in thought. I wonder what my life will be like from now on. Is this the beginning of the end, or will I be given another chance at happiness? What will today bring? I put the last crust in my mouth, chew without tasting and take the last sip of tea, getting to my feet. 'I'm going back to bed for a bit.'

'Good idea. It's only six o'clock. I'll wake you if there's any news.'

'Thanks, Tom. And thanks for being such a good friend. I appreciate it.'

'Don't be daft. You're family.'

I swallow, not trusting myself to speak. Instead, I raise my hand in a half-hearted wave and trudge up the stairs to bed. Maybe this time, after all that walking and sea air, I'll actually brave the bed and get some sleep.

It works.

The doorbell rouses me from a deep, dreamless slumber. I snap awake, remembering everything in a rush. Staring blearily around the empty bedroom. I can't believe I finally managed to nod off.

I throw back the covers, pull on my crumpled linen trousers and roll on some deodorant under my shirt, wondering who it might be at the door. Wondering what news today will bring. Wondering if the police might have found my family. My gut clenches with anxiety as I head downstairs.

CHAPTER TWENTY-THREE

He glances at his watch, conscious that he's been gone for a good while now. He needs to get a move on. The cereal aisle is bewildering, with boxes upon boxes of the stuff. All brightly coloured, most of them emblazoned with cartoon animals. He selects three different cartons at random and hopes at least one will be suitable.

The air-con inside the hypermarket is brutal – a thick chill that, after an initial few seconds of bliss, makes him wish he'd brought a sweatshirt.

He really should have grocery shopped beforehand, but there wasn't the time or opportunity. Never mind, it can't be helped. He'll only be gone for an hour max and it's too early in the day for him to be missed.

What else should he get? Pasta? Cheese, maybe. He tells himself to stop thinking so hard about it. Instead, he marches down a few aisles and dumps several random items into the trolley without giving them too much thought.

That will have to do.

Worst comes to the worst, a few days of nothing but milk and cereal won't kill him. It'll do… at least until everything is ready for the next stage of the plan.

CHAPTER TWENTY-FOUR

As I walk down the stairs, I hear women's voices.

Lainy is talking to someone in the hallway. She turns as I approach. 'Faye, how are you doing?'

'Hello, Faye.' It's Lainy's friend from the pub – Cath.

'Hi,' I croak.

'Just popped round to bring you some homemade chocolate cake and see if I can do anything to help out,' Cath says, placing a large cake tin on the hall table. Her sharp eyes sweep across me, no doubt taking in my dishevelled appearance.

I reach the bottom of the stairs and rub my eyes with my fingertips.

'You look rough, Faye,' Lainy says. 'Why don't you go back to bed?'

'I'm fine. We need to get back out there. Where's Tom?'

'Just gone to pick up some milk and stuff. He won't be long.'

'Look,' Cath says, adjusting her massive cleavage, 'why don't I take the kids off your hands today? They can come down the beach with my lot. You can concentrate on finding your family.'

'That's so kind of you, Cath,' Lainy says, 'but I can't expect you to—'

'Course you can! We go way back. You'd do the same for me, wouldn't you?'

'Yes, but… I don't… I mean… It's complicated.'

'What's complicated about it?' Cath arches an eyebrow.

'We haven't seen one another for years.'

'So? We practically grew up together. You saying you don't trust me with your kids, that it?' Cath narrows her eyes.

Lainy blanches. While their exchange is going on, I'm still at the bottom of the stairs wanting to retreat back to the bedroom, away from this unexpected social interaction. I don't have the energy for this kind of conversation. When I heard the doorbell, I thought it might have been the police. I know Cath is well-meaning and it's a generous offer, but I can't see Lainy and Tom saying yes to shipping the girls off with someone else.

'I think she's worried about taking advantage of your good nature,' I intervene.

Cath's features relax. 'Oh, no need to worry about that. I love kids. It's no bother at all.'

Lainy is obviously reluctant to let Cath look after the girls, and I can't say I blame her. But it doesn't look as though Cath is taking the hint.

'Honestly, Cath, it's lovely of you but we haven't seen one another for years,' Lainy says to Cath, glancing back at me with barely concealed panic. 'I can't expect you to go to so much trouble.'

'Course you can,' Cath replies. 'Our families have known one another since we were toddlers. We're practically family.'

'Yes, but—'

'And we went to the same school and knew all the same people.'

'Yes, I know but—'

'So let me help you out. You're obviously having a rough time. You need to find your brother and your nephew. It'll be easier without young children around. More fun for them too. And I'd be happy to have them for a few hours. Let me do this for you.'

'It's just… after what happened with Mark last night… Do you still have contact with him?' Lainy asks.

'What do you mean?' Cath frowns.

'I went to see him last night,' I say.

Lainy and Cath turn in my direction.

'Oh… good,' Cath says. 'Does he know anything? If not, I'm sure he'll keep his ear to the ground.'

'Well that's the thing,' I say, remembering the hunted expression he wore. 'He ran off before we got a chance to speak.'

'What do you mean he ran off?' Cath's frown deepens and she turns to look at Lainy.

'I wasn't there,' Lainy says. 'Faye went with my husband Tom to speak to him.'

'Mark was standing outside his caravan,' I explain, 'but when we called out to him, he took one look at us and ran.'

Cath puts her hands on her hips. 'That doesn't sound like Mark. He might be a waste of space, but he wouldn't run off like that. Not at all. He wears his heart on his sleeve. What you see is what you get. I always liked that about him. He's honest. Too honest sometimes.' She takes her mobile out of the fake black and gold Gucci bag on her shoulder and makes a call, putting the phone to her ear. 'Answerphone,' she mouths. 'Hey, Mark, it's me, Cath. Can you call me as soon as you get this message? What were you doing running off last night? I've got Lainy Townsend – you know, from school – here with me and she needs our help. Her brother Jake's gone missing with his little boy. Call me, okay.'

'So you see,' Lainy says, 'I wouldn't feel happy with my girls seeing Mark. Not after what went on last night.'

'I still don't understand why he ran,' Cath says. 'Unless, maybe he thought you were someone else.'

'Well, it was quite unsettling,' I reply, deciding not to tell her that we called the police, who then went on to search his caravan.

'That's why I'm not keen on Mark being around my girls,' Lainy says, flushing slightly.

'Well…' Cath folds her arms again. 'It sounds like a mix-up to me. But anyway, I don't exactly hang out with my ex. He sees the kids every other weekend and that's it. So if you're worried about

Mark, don't be. We don't have anything to do with each other. It'll just be me and my kids, okay? And anyway, I love children and I'd have to be pretty stupid to put a foot wrong with them while the police are sniffing around.'

'It's really kind of you, Cath, but just… let me think about it for a minute.'

'No worries, lovey. But just another thing to consider – it might be nicer for the girls to be away from the stress of what's going on. I mean, kids pick up on this stuff, don't they?'

Lainy exhales. 'It's just… I'm nervous to let them out of my sight. You know, after what's happened with Jake and Dylan.'

'Well of course you are!' Cath throws her arms around Lainy and gives her a hug. 'I'd be the same. I promise you I'll guard them with my life and I'll call you every hour.'

Lainy's shoulders slump. 'Okay. That sounds… good.'

'Are you sure, Lainy?' I ask, not wanting her to feel pressured.

'They'll be fine.' Cath glances across at me with a kind smile.

'All right. Thank you, Cath.'

'Good. So that's settled. My eldest, Emma, she's fourteen and she loves little ones. Your two will have a great time. You don't need to worry. I've got Samuel, who's ten, and Lucy, who's almost eight. They'll have a ball together.'

'Mummy, who's that lady?' Annabel comes out of the kitchen into the hallway, Poppy trailing behind her.

'Hello, sweetheart,' Cath says, slipping her phone back into her bag. 'I'm your Aunty Cath. Me and your mummy went to school together.'

'Did you?' Poppy and Annabel chorus, staring up at Lainy.

'We did,' Lainy says.

'Were you best friends?' Poppy asks.

'Well, Cath was in the year above me. In Uncle Jake's year.'

'Why isn't Uncle Jake here?' Poppy frowns. 'And Dylan? You said we'd be able to play with Dylan on the beach.'

'How would you like to come to the beach with me and my kids?' Cath asks them, diplomatically changing the subject. 'They're outside in the car right now. Want to come and meet them?'

Annabel clings to the back of Lainy's legs.

'It's a generous offer, Cath,' Lainy says, 'but it doesn't look as though they're up for it after all. Bit shy, you know how it is.'

'Do you like puppies?' Cath persists. 'We've got two little spaniels. You can come and stroke them if you like?'

'Can we, Mum?' Poppy cries. My eldest niece loves animals.

'*Two* puppies?' Annabel slides out from behind her mother.

Cath takes advantage of their interest and takes each of my nieces by the hand. 'Yep, two. Want to see?'

'Go on then,' Lainy says with a sigh. She turns to Cath. 'Are you absolutely sure about this?'

'Course I am, wouldn't have offered otherwise.'

'It would be helpful,' Lainy says, looking to me for approval. 'Then we'd all be free to… you know, look for Jake and Dylan.'

I nod and shrug. Cath seems good hearted, and, like she said, they know one another from way back.

Lainy turns back to Cath. 'Thank you.'

She nods. 'Right. That's finally sorted then.'

'Let me get a bag of beach things.' Lainy slides past me, up the stairs, while Cath leads my nieces outside. I watch everything as though I'm in a dream. Lack of sleep is making my brain feel as though it's stuffed with cotton wool.

Outside, Cath is chattering away to the girls. The front door lies open, shafts of bright, morning sunshine flooding the hallway. Squinting into the light, I make out two figures coming up the steps. My insides quiver. It's Detectives Nash and Soames.

Soames raps on the open door before catching sight of me on the stairs.

I unfreeze my body and walk stiffly down to greet them.

'Hello, Faye,' Nash says, her dark hair gleaming in the sunlight.

'Hello,' I croak.

'Can we come in? Have a quick chat?'

'Did you… Have you found them?' I clench my hands and my nails dig into my palms.

'Shall we go and sit down somewhere?' she says, not quite catching my eye.

Asking me to sit down isn't a good thing, is it? It's what you say when you have to tell somebody bad news. 'Okay,' I reply, my ears ringing with blood. 'Let's go into the kitchen.'

We sit around the table, which is still strewn with breakfast things. The polite person inside me knows I should offer them a drink, but I can't speak. Instead, I stare at Nash expectantly, dreading what she's about to tell me.

'Now,' she begins, 'I have some news which may not necessarily mean anything bad, but we do have to take it seriously.'

I nod to show I've heard her, fear gnawing at my insides.

'When we first started the search for your husband and son, we discovered some blood near the base of the cliffs.'

'Blood! What do you mean? Is it…? Are you saying that…? Why didn't you tell me this before?'

'We didn't want to tell you before we'd tested it. It could have been nothing to do with your family.'

'But now you think it is? Is that what you're saying? So have you? Tested it, I mean?' I get to my feet and run my hands through my hair. Then I make myself sit back down again and wait for Nash to reply.

'There's no cause for immediate alarm. We did an out-of-hours quick-turnaround DNA test, using the samples you provided from Jake and Dylan.'

'And?'

'It was a match for your husband.'

'No!'

'But you mustn't jump to conclusions.'

'How can you tell me not to jump to conclusions!' This is all becoming too real now. I can barely look at either of them, afraid the unmasked concern in their eyes will finish me.

Nash carries on talking. 'Like I said, it was a small amount of blood, and it could simply mean he's had a scrape or a cut.'

'But he's missing! You don't go missing because of a scrape or a cut!' I stand once more and walk over to the window. 'What about Dylan? Have you found his blood too? Is there anything else you're not telling me?'

'No, no, there's nothing else. Nothing in relation to your son. Which may mean that your husband is injured, but your son is fine. I know it's hard, but please try not to let your imagination run wild. It could be a good thing that we found the DNA. Now we know where to concentrate our search. We have people combing that particular area as we speak. We also have divers searching—'

'Divers!' I cry. 'You think—'

'We're being thorough, but there's every chance we'll locate them both alive and well.'

In my mind, I visualise Jake's blood staining the rocks, the rescue services clambering over the cliffs searching for my missing family. Divers swimming in the murky depths of the Channel. Then I try to picture what's going to happen next. But I can't. My mind is a dark chasm. Empty. Blank.

CHAPTER TWENTY-FIVE

THEN

She picks her way up the steep path, as watery moonlight splashes down between the trees. Echoing strains of music and laughter floating up on the warm night air. The whispered hush and sigh of the waves in tune with her disappointment. She wishes she'd had more courage this evening. Why hadn't she been brave enough to speak to Owen? All that build-up to tonight… for nothing.

Her long strides turns into angry stomps. She'll be fifteen next week; she's not a child any more. So why does she feel so hopelessly young? So pathetically immature? The path narrows, and she ducks to avoid an overhanging branch. Blinks back frustrated tears and pushes her hair out of her eyes. She takes a breath, the familiar scent of sea salt and pine needles going some way to dampen her annoyance with herself.

A snapping twig makes her stop and cock her head to the side. She knows it's probably just a wild animal out hunting. Nevertheless, her breath hitches and her heart pumps a little harder. She's watched all the scary movies with her friends. She's seen the vampires and the zombies and the evil spirits that suck out teenage girls' souls. But it's the dark human characters who scare her the most. The ones who really do exist.

Still frozen in place, she wills herself to move once more. Lengthens her strides and quickens her pace. Not quite running. But almost.

Another cracking twig, a shuffle from behind. Sweat prickles on her back. Thoughts of soft lips and missed opportunities are pushed from her mind. Now, all she wants to do is reach the top of the cliff. To get home and slam the door closed behind her. For her mum and dad to be angry that she's late back. For them to be furious that she walked home alone. For her to reassure them that she's fine. To roll her eyes and say, *It's okay, nothing happened.*

But now there's no mistaking the steady clomp of footsteps coming up the cliff path behind her. She reaches the stone steps and takes them two at a time, her wedge heels making a dull scrape and thud. The panic wanting to tear itself from her lips. She's only halfway up, and she won't be able to outrun whoever it is – not in these shoes. But there's no time to undo the straps and take them off.

Whoever it is, they're getting closer. She daren't turn around.

She times her next step wrong.

She trips.

Falls.

A hand reaches out to clasp her bare ankle.

Lainy screams into the darkness.

CHAPTER TWENTY-SIX

NOW

Back up on the headland a small cluster of people walk towards us. They're wearing high-vis jackets and they appear to be led by a woman holding a clipboard.

'Hello, I'm Ramona,' the woman says, her fair hair tied back off her face in a no-nonsense ponytail. I take in her cargo shorts, National Trust T-shirt and walking boots. Maybe she mistakenly thinks we're part of their hiking group.

'Hello,' Tom replies. 'I'm Tom.'

'Good to meet you.' Ramona thrusts out her hand, and they shake. Two women and a man hang back behind her. 'Have you come to join the search party? I'm coordinating.'

'Search party?' I repeat.

'Yes,' she says, turning her attention to me, a grave expression on her face. 'A man and his young son have gone missing up on the head. We're here volunteering, trying to find them.'

'That's very good of you,' Tom says. 'It's actually my brother-in-law and nephew you're searching for – Jake and Dylan. This is Jake's sister, Lainy. And Jake's wife, Faye.'

Ramona's eyes widen and she looks a little taken aback before recomposing her features. 'Oh my goodness. Well, I hope you don't think it's presumptuous of me to—'

'Presumptuous?' Tom says. 'No, of course not. We're grateful. We've come up here to carry on searching so the more of us there are looking, the better chance we'll have of finding them.'

Lainy and I murmur our thanks. I'm touched that total strangers would give up their time to help look for my family, but it also makes me feel uneasy. This whole situation is spiralling out of control. It feels surreal, like I'm watching everything from far away.

'Don't worry,' Ramona says briskly. 'We'll find them, I'm sure of it. Won't we?' She turns to her little group, who nod enthusiastically while tossing us sympathetic glances. 'There are thirty-two volunteers so far, but I've been told we have plenty more on the way. Word is gradually spreading. We're a tight-knit community. Unfortunately, we're only allowed to search on the designated pathways, as the caves and cliffs are too unsafe. But the professionals are scouring the out-of-bounds areas, so don't you worry.' Her gaze flits from me to Lainy while she says this, but lands back on Tom, who probably seems the most approachable.

'Where would you say is the best place for us to start?' Tom asks. 'Is there anywhere you haven't searched yet?'

Ramona purses her lips. 'Hmm. I'd say the woods up above the headland. I do realise the woods are further away, but we've scoured the pathways along here, right up to the lighthouse and beyond, and so far we've seen nothing.'

Tom nods pensively. 'It's a pity we can't go down on the cliffs, since we know that's where…' His voice trails off.

'Where *what*?' Ramona's voice sharpens.

I'm sure Tom was about to let slip about Jake's blood being found, but that information wouldn't be common knowledge, so I'm relieved he stopped himself in time.

'… Since we know that's where they'd most likely be,' Tom replies, recovering from his slip-up. 'You know – if one of them had a fall, it was probably on the cliffs.'

'Maybe…' Ramona looks at each of us in turn, and I get the impression she's scrutinising us. Like she's trying to work something out. But the moment passes and she's back to being brisk once again. 'Lisa, can you give them each a whistle.'

A nervous-looking lady reaches into the rucksack she's clutching and pulls out a handful of bright plastic whistles on cords. She becomes flustered trying to untangle them, but finally passes one to each of us with a nervous smile.

'Blow loudly on these if you find them, or if you come across anything suspicious,' Ramona instructs.

A blonde woman hands us each an energy bar, and a man gives us a small bottle of water.

'It's hot out, so you need to stay hydrated,' Ramona says. 'I'm a first aider, so any problems, please come and see me. We'll be staying here, greeting newcomers.'

'Good to know,' Tom says.

'Tom's a paramedic,' Lainy interjects.

'Oh.' Ramona pouts, then nods. 'Great. That's great. Very useful.'

'So, we'll make our way up to the woods?' Tom asks.

Ramona points up towards the cliffs. 'You can either follow the cliff path, and then take a right, or you can turn back and go past the castle and head into the woods that way.' She starts making notes on her clipboard.

'Thanks,' Tom says. 'And thank you for volunteering. It's hugely appreciated.'

'It's our pleasure,' the nervy lady says, giving me a sympathetic smile. 'At least it'll be cooler in the woods than out on the cliffs.'

We take our leave of the volunteers as they turn to approach some newcomers. I was only up here a few hours ago, but it feels so different now, in the daylight with all these people and the sun pounding down. We head up past the castle and I keep my head bowed as we slip past a group of tourists – or perhaps they're yet more volunteers. I adjust the brim of my hat and wipe the sweat from my top lip with the side of my forefinger.

'Are you okay?' Tom asks, stopping for a moment to look at me. 'You don't look too great. Did you get enough sleep? Maybe you should go back to the house and let me and Lainy continue the search this morning.'

'I'm fine.' But I don't even sound convincing to my own ears.

'And you must be so hot with those long sleeves and trousers,' he adds.

'Trust me, I need to cover up – my skin would not turn a pretty shade of tomato in this weather.' But my attempt at levity doesn't fool him.

'Maybe you could go back, have a cool shower and a rest. You could come and join us after lunch.'

While that sounds tempting, I know that it won't matter whether I'm resting at the house or out here searching. I'll still feel sick and terrified. I shake my head.

'At least sit down for a bit,' he continues. 'And have some water.'

'I'm fine.'

'But—'

'I said I'm fine!' I snap.

Tom's eyes widen and he clamps his mouth shut. Lainy puts a hand on my arm. I shake her off and turn away but a sob escapes before I can stop it.

'Oh, Faye,' Lainy says, throwing her arms around me. 'Don't worry, it'll be okay.'

'But what if it's not?' I gulp. 'What if it's *not* okay?'

'With all these people out searching, they'll be found in no time,' Tom says, recovering his cheer.

'I'm in a nightmare,' I sob. 'I don't know what's up and what's down. Everything feels wobbly and strange.'

'Of course it does,' Tom soothes. 'It's bound to feel weird.' He glances helplessly at Lainy.

I stumble over to a bench that's tucked away off the path, in the shade. They make to follow me, but I wave them off. 'Just leave me here while I get myself together. I'll be better in a bit,' I lie.

'I don't like to leave you,' Lainy says. 'Not while you're upset.'

'Honestly, I'll just sit here for five minutes or so. It's the heat… and talking to those people. Realising that people are giving up their day to search for my family. It's… overwhelming.' I spread my hands wide.

'I know.' Lainy gives me a small smile. 'Sit for a bit. We'll come back for you in ten minutes or so, okay?'

'Thank you.' I brush imaginary dirt from the bench and sit on the edge, feeling mild relief at the instant shade from a couple of leafy sycamores.

As the two of them walk away, towards the nearby woods, Tom says something crossly to Lainy, but I can't make out his quiet, low words. She snaps back at him, and their disagreement temporarily jolts me from my misery. They've already had one argument this morning.

When Tom found out that Cath took Poppy and Annabel, he asked Lainy if that was such a good idea. Her response was to lash out, so I retreated to my room until they'd both calmed down. My guess is that Lainy was already feeling bad about letting the girls go off with Cath, but she didn't want to admit that to Tom. Before coming up to the headland, we drove down to the beach to check up on them. Luckily, the girls were having an absolute ball, and didn't want to come away with us. Seeing them so happy (aside from fussing over whether they were wearing enough sun cream – Cath had already re-slathered them) Tom relented and said they could stay for the day. But now it seems Tom and Lainy are disagreeing about something again.

'I'm not hiding anything,' Lainy hisses. 'You're imagining things.'

My self-pity dissipates and my heart begins to thump loudly. *Tom thinks Lainy's hiding something?* I'll have to find out what he's talking about. Maybe it's nothing. Maybe they're simply talking about something personal. But what if it's not? What if Tom thinks she's hiding something about Jake and Dylan's disappearance? Should I go after them? Demand to know what they're arguing about? No. It's best if I speak to Lainy later. She's more likely to tell me if we're on our own.

Hours later, after another day of searching, Lainy, Tom and I decide to call it a day, pick up the girls, and head back to the house. We get into the sun-warmed car, all of us exhausted and lost in our own thoughts. As Tom starts up the engine a message pings on Lainy's mobile.

'It's Cath. She says the kids are on the bouncy castle and then they're going to have a barbecue on the beach so she's dropping the girls home in a couple of hours. Says they're tired but happy.'

'That's good,' Tom replies.

I'm grateful that he doesn't add anything about our fruitless day. That he doesn't say how it will soon be dark and with another day over there's less chance of a positive outcome. That he doesn't try to be chirpy and offer up platitudes. We've all had enough of those from the well-meaning volunteers. Instead, we travel back to the house in a dark fog of silence. I check my phone for the umpteenth time, but there are no messages.

'Actually,' Lainy says a few minutes later as we drive down Scar Point, 'do you think we could keep going and get Poppy and Annabel *now*?'

'I was thinking the same thing,' Tom replies.

'Oh good. It's been a long day for them and I'm missing them like crazy already.'

Tom nudges Lainy. She turns around to where I'm sitting in the back seat, her face a picture of remorse. 'Faye, I'm sorry. That was so insensitive of me.' She reaches out a hand and briefly squeezes my leg.

'Don't be silly.' I gulp down a wave of emotion. 'Of course you're missing them. Like you said, it's been a long day.'

Down in the town, the traffic is bumper to bumper as all the holidaymakers head home. Even so, as we crawl along the coast road we can see that the beach is still really busy. People swimming, packing up, or having picnic teas. There are even some people just arriving. Families deciding to have early evening barbeques, and sprawling groups of teenagers meeting their friends.

'Do you want to text Cath?' Tom says. 'Find out where they're sitting.'

'She said the kids are on the bouncy castle.' Lainy gazes out of the window, scanning the beach.

'There it is.' I point to a spot on the beach ahead where a giant yellow and blue inflatable structure rises up from the sand like a weird mirage.

It takes us another ten minutes to turn around, find a parking space and get a parking ticket, by which time I feel completely exhausted and spaced out. Nevertheless, I get out of the car with my in-laws, wincing against the heat of the late-afternoon sun.

We walk along the promenade, weaving through the bright crowds towards the squeals and screams of delight coming off the bouncy castle up ahead.

'There's Cath.' Tom points at a red-faced woman wearing a pink swimming costume and matching sarong.

Lainy stops dead, her body stiffening, her mouth falling open, then immediately clamping shut.

'What is it?' I ask, the back of my neck prickling.

'It's Cath,' she says. 'She's with *Kayla*.'

CHAPTER TWENTY-SEVEN

'Kayla?' Tom asks. 'You mean the woman from yesterday morning, in town?'

'What the hell is she doing here?' Lainy mutters, ignoring Tom's question.

'Are you okay?' Tom asks her. 'Want me to go and collect the girls from Cath while you wait here with Faye?'

But Lainy doesn't respond. Instead, she begins striding across the promenade and down onto the sand. Tom and I follow behind. From the corner of my eye I see him look at me quizzically, hoping I can give him answers, but I pretend I haven't noticed. Instead, I increase my pace to catch up to my sister-in-law.

The sand is soft and undulating, and it's hard to walk quickly, especially as there are so many people with deckchairs, parasols, windbreaks and beach tents in our path. It's like a miniature city down here. I briefly wonder whether I should take my shoes off, or whether the sand will be too hot.

Cath's face darkens for a moment as she spies Lainy. She leans down to say something to the petite, dark-haired woman I recognise from yesterday – Kayla. Then, Cath smiles a broad smile and waves at us. 'Lainy!'

But Lainy doesn't reply. She's still marching ahead of us, her shoulders set in a rigid line.

'Why is Lainy so worked up?' Tom asks. 'Lainy! Wait!'

'Didn't she say she fell out with Kayla when they were kids?'

'Yes, but that was years ago. They should have got over it by now.' He frowns.

'Obviously not. Look, there's Poppy coming down the slide.' I point to the inflatable where Poppy is squealing in delight. Next up is Annabel, holding hands with an older, blonde-haired girl. At least the kids seem happy.

Lainy has already reached Cath and Kayla. Her arms are folded, but I can't see her expression from behind. Cath opens her mouth to speak, but Lainy gets in first. 'Hi, I'm grateful to you for having them, Cath, but I didn't realise you'd be here with anyone else. I thought you said it would be just you and the children.'

'Oh.' Cath's smile falters. 'Well, it's only Kayla. You remember Kayla, from school?'

Kayla shifts uncomfortably, glances across at me and Tom and then drops her gaze to the sand.

'Yes, I remember Kayla. But she didn't seem that thrilled to see me in town yesterday. She had a real go at me. I thought you didn't even want me here in Swanage, Kayla?' Lainy throws her hands in the air. 'And yet now you're here at the beach hanging out with my children? What's all that about?'

Cath's face darkens. 'I don't know what's going on between you two, but I don't appreciate you coming here and having a go at me after I've looked after your kids all day – who are lovely by the way, but that's not the point!'

Lainy's back stiffens. 'Well, thank you, Cath, I'm grateful to you for looking after them. But *I* don't appreciate you letting them hang around with random people after you specifically said you would be here on your own with them.'

'Kayla isn't a random person!'

'Lainy…' Tom tries to take her arm, but she shakes him off.

'It wasn't planned!' Cath huffs. 'If you must know, Kayla just happened to be walking past with her two boys and I asked them to join us.'

'*Just happened* to be walking past?' Lainy shakes her head. 'That's a bit of a coincidence, isn't it, Kayla?'

'Not really,' Kayla mutters. 'It's a hot weekend in the summer holidays so I came down to the beach with my kids.'

Cath's face is beetroot now, and I can't help feeling a little sorry for the woman. It's not really her fault. Lainy's outburst is probably making no sense to her. 'Do you know what, Lainy? I wish I'd never bothered offering to have them for you. No good deed goes unpunished.'

Lainy turns to face the inflatable castle. 'Poppy! Annabel!'

'Mummy! Daddy! Aunty Faye!' The girls' faces light up as they catch sight of us.

'Did you see me slide down?' Annabel cries.

'Come on,' Lainy says. 'It's time to go!'

'But we've still got four more slides left,' Poppy wails. 'I only went down it once.'

'Sorry, we've got to go now.'

Tom turns to his wife. 'Surely you can let them have a litt—'

She cuts him off. 'I said, we're going.' She turns back to the girls. 'NOW!'

Several people stare our way, and Cath's face is like thunder. Kayla looks less certain of herself than she did yesterday. She almost looks as though she might cry. I want to support Lainy, but she looks like she'll bite the head off anyone who talks to her, so instead I tap Tom on the shoulder. 'Let's just take the girls and go.'

'Do you know what all this is about?' he murmurs. 'Because I'm at a bit of a loss.'

'We're all tired and worried. I guess she's just being protective. And it *was* Kayla who came over and starting yelling at Lainy yesterday. So it does seem a bit strange that she's here with your girls today.'

Tom shakes his head but decides to go along with Lainy. 'Okay, girls. Time to go!'

My nieces do as they're asked, but it's sad to see their previous joy squashed into disappointment. Not that I'm blaming Lainy. She's under pressure too, and she's had the added worry of being without the girls today. I think it must all be getting too much. For the millionth time, I wish we'd never arranged this trip. Our lives are imploding.

Once the girls step past the barrier, Lainy hugs them tightly and kisses their red cheeks. 'Okay, let's find your stuff and go back to the house.'

'Aren't we having a barbecue on the beach?' Poppy asks, her chin wobbling.

'We'll get pizza at home.'

'But—'

'Come on.' I take Poppy's hot little hand in mine. 'Listen to your mummy, let's get your stuff.'

We spend an uncomfortable five minutes gathering the girls' sandy belongings while Poppy and Annabel hug the two dogs – who are panting under a parasol – and say goodbye to their new friends, who seem a little confused by their sudden departure. Kayla has taken herself off somewhere else, and Cath stands tight-lipped, watching us without saying a word. Her arms folded across her chest.

Once all their things have been packed in their rucksack, Lainy leads the girls over to Cath. 'Say thank you to Cath for having you today.'

'Thank you, Cath,' the girls say quietly.

'You're very welcome,' she replies with a warm smile. But it's quickly replaced by a dark scowl for Lainy.

'Look,' Lainy says, as we're preparing to leave. 'I do appreciate you having the girls today. I really do. But you promised me it would just be you. And with everything that's been going on with Faye's family, I thought you'd understand that I'd be worried about them being with anyone else.'

'But you *know* Kayla!' Cath insists.

'Yes. I know a lot of people. But it doesn't mean I trust them with my children.'

'Fine. Let's not keep in touch then, eh?'

Lainy shakes her head and turns away with her daughters. Tom and I follow on behind. I give Cath a regretful glance. She shrugs her shoulders and shakes her head, turning away from us.

Back in the car, it takes an uncomfortable fifteen minutes to drive back up to Scar Point. Tom tries to ask Lainy why she got so angry with Cath, but she just apologises before saying she doesn't want to talk about it.

There's a space opposite the house on the other side of the road. Tom pulls into it in one fluid movement. My throat is tight, my chest hollow. Sitting in the back seat next to my sleepy nieces makes me realise how much I miss my boy. My baby. My Dylan. I try to picture his face and grow short of breath when his features won't come. But then I suddenly see him in my mind. Laughing at some silly joke he heard from one of his friends at school.

'Faye…'

I look up at a tap on the window.

'You coming in?' It's Lainy. She and Tom are already out of the car.

'Sorry,' I mouth, and unfasten my seatbelt. I climb out, my limbs stiff and heavy. I help the girls with their seatbelts and wait for them to slide out after me. We follow Tom and Lainy across the road and up the steps to the house.

I almost crash into Lainy's back as she stops abruptly next to Tom.

'What is it?' I ask.

Tom pushes at the front door, which swings open at the touch of his fingertips. The edge of the door next to the lock is splintered.

'All of you, go back to the car,' Tom says in a low voice. 'I think we've had a break-in.'

CHAPTER TWENTY-EIGHT

THEN

Lainy lands heavily on her knees, any pain dulled by the spikes of adrenaline speeding through her system. Her heart beats so loudly it's drowning out the thump of music from the party on the beach below. With a gasp and a sob, she realises she must fight off her attacker. He still has hold of her ankle.

'Get off me!' she cries, terrified and half sobbing, but knowing that she has to fight. She inhales deeply and kicks backwards, hard, with her free leg. Feels the sole of her shoe make contact with her attacker's face.

'Ow! Shit!'

Her ankle is suddenly free, and she makes the most of it, scrabbling to get upright.

'Lainy, what are you doing? It's me! Owen!'

She's on her feet now, panting hard, preparing to run, but his words suddenly cut through her fear. 'Owen?' Lainy pauses, turns her head, still not trusting that he really is who he says he is. 'Is that you?'

'Yes, it's me.' His voice sounds muffled and slow.

In the silver moonlight she sees that it really is Owen. He's crouching down, cupping his jaw with both hands. 'Are you... okay?'

'I think you might have broken my jaw.'

'No! I'm so sorry. Here, let me have a look.'

He stands and she gently takes his hands away from his face. 'Careful,' he says through gritted teeth.

'What were you doing chasing me up the cliff?' She examines his jaw but can't see anything amiss.

'I wasn't chasing you, I was trying to catch up to you. I was going to ask if I could walk you home.'

'I thought you were a murderer, or a rapist! Your jaw looks okay. It doesn't seem dislocated or anything. Are you able to move it?'

Owen tentatively tries to open his mouth, then move his jaw from side to side. 'Okay, maybe I was exaggerating. It feels all right now, just a bit sore. Sorry if I scared you back there with the whole coming-up-behind-you-in-the-dark thing.'

'That's okay. Sorry I kicked you in the face.' They grin at one another.

'So… can I walk you home?' he asks.

'Er, yes. That would be nice. Thanks. My brother was supposed to be walking me back, but he got sidetracked.'

'Yeah, I saw him hanging out with Rose.'

'I think he likes her,' Lainy says without thinking. Jake would kill her if he knew she'd told Owen that. Oh well, anyone with half a brain could work out that her brother likes Rose. He wasn't exactly subtle about it.

'I think you're right,' Owen says.

'But then again, everyone likes Rose.'

'Do they?' He pauses. 'I'm sure not everyone likes her. I bet some people like you too.'

Lainy's cheeks grow hot and she's glad it's dark so he can't see her blushing. Could one of those people be Owen? Or is that simply wishful thinking?

The path isn't made for two people to walk side by side – not if you want your own personal space, but Owen obviously doesn't care about that because he walks at Lainy's side. So close that their arms touch and she can feel the spark of electricity between them, making her go hot and cold at the same time. She's trying to think of something cool and funny to say, but all she can think of is his body next to hers, and the thumping of her heart.

Maybe tonight isn't turning out to be such a disaster after all.

Lainy realises they've already reached the clifftop. She's not far from home now. But suddenly home is the last place she wants to be.

'Stop here a minute,' Owen says, putting a hand on her arm.

'What? Why?' She's flustered, embarrassed. Everything she says sounds so immature. Standing at the cliff edge, Lainy is struck by how beautiful it is up here with the moon reflecting down on the water below, and all the lights sparkling in the black distance.

'I want to talk to you,' Owen replies with a teasing tone in his voice.

'Do you?' she replies, trying to keep her voice as light as his. But her throat feels tight, like it might close up. She wants Owen to tell her that he likes her. She wants him to kiss her. Why else would he have followed her up here?

Lainy can no longer feel the ground beneath her feet. She's focused on Owen's questioning smile. She can't believe that the boy she likes might actually like her back. This moment might just be the most perfect of her life so far. Owen leans forward an inch and she catches her breath.

His face flushes and she can tell he's feeling a little awkward. A little embarrassed. But this only makes her like him more.

He murmurs something to her... but then the sound of someone yelling makes them both jerk back like they've been scalded.

'What the fuck, Pearson!'

CHAPTER TWENTY-NINE

NOW

'What do you mean?' Lainy asks, putting her arms around the girls and ushering them back down the steps.

'I mean exactly what I said.' Tom takes a hesitant step into the hallway. 'The door's been forced open. Someone has broken into the house.'

'Broken in?' I echo stupidly. 'But who would… why would…' The hairs on the back of my neck stand up and I take a step back down, away from the door, ushering my nieces down with me. 'Whoever it is might still be in there. I'm calling the police.' I begin fumbling in my bag for my phone, panic making my fingers clumsy.

'What if it's something to do with Dylan and Jake going missing?' Tom asks. 'I'm going inside. Get back in the car, all of you.'

'Tom, no!' Lainy cries, reaching a hand out as though to stop him. But he's too far away from her. He's already moving away down the hall, peering into rooms as he goes.

She pulls out her phone and manages to get through to the police station before I do, so I end my call and listen while she gives out our details. Between us, we usher Poppy and Annabel back across the road and inside the car. I do my best to soothe away their questions with bland answers while Lainy continues talking to the police. She perches on the edge of the back seat, facing outwards onto the pavement, while I wait outside, resting my elbows on the roof of the car, keeping one eye on the house.

Tom told us to stay put, but what if he needs our help? Should I go back in there? My heart hammers as I straighten up and take a hesitant step away from Lainy. She's talking intently on the phone but looks up questioningly when she sees me moving away.

'Faye, wait!'

Just as she calls out to me, Tom peers out of the front door and beckons me over. He's shaking his head and his expression is grim.

'Hang on, Lainy. I'll be back in a second.' I glance up and down the street, jog across the road, and head back up the front steps. Tom ushers me into the hallway.

'There's no one downstairs,' Tom says in a low voice, 'but we've definitely had a break-in. The rooms have been trashed.'

My hand flies to my mouth. 'Did they take anything? Do you think whoever it was has gone now?'

In answer to my question, a reverberating thump from upstairs freezes my blood.

'Don't go up there,' I hiss. But it's too late. Tom is taking the stairs two at a time, uncaring that his thudding footsteps must be alerting the intruder to his approach.

'The police are on their way,' Lainy calls up the steps.

'What are you doing here?' I cry. 'What about the girls?'

'They're in the car. Is Tom okay?'

A crash sounds above our heads. 'What are you doing?' Tom's voice booms overhead.

A rough male voice replies, letting out a string of expletives. I'm momentarily relieved my nieces aren't in here to witness any of this. Or Dylan… but then my thoughts fly back to Tom and how much danger he might be in.

'Tom!' Lainy cries, heading for the stairs.

'Don't!' I grab her by the shoulders and pull her back as a figure appears at the top of the staircase. Lainy and I both squeal and reel backwards. But it's okay; it's Tom.

'Are you all right?' Lainy calls, rushing up to meet him. 'You're bleeding! Are you okay?'

'I'm fine, I'm absolutely fine.' As Tom makes his way down the stairs, I see that blood is beading across his eyelid and down his cheek, making a jagged line.

'You don't look fine.' Lainy reaches up to touch his head with her fingertips, but Tom jerks his head away.

'Where are the girls?' Tom cries.

'They're in the car with an audiobook. I locked them in for a moment. What happened? Who's up there?' Lainy and I gaze nervously up the stairs. 'Are they going to come after you? We should leave.'

There's banging and shouting coming from upstairs. The whole house judders. My body is tensed, ready to flee.

'He's shut in the bathroom for now,' Tom croaks. 'Bastard whacked me on the forehead.'

Lainy takes his hand and leads him out onto the front steps. 'Who is it? Who's up there? Are you sure you're okay?'

I follow them outside and glance across to the car, where Poppy and Annabel are sitting, their attention held captive by whatever story they're listening to, oblivious to the drama going on in the house.

Tom sits heavily on the third step. He's white as a ghost, his eyes wide and glassy. 'It's just one man. He was in Faye's room,' Tom says, looking up at me. 'He was going through your things.'

'In my room?' I wonder who it could possibly be. 'Who is he? Did you recognise him?'

The shouts from inside are becoming louder and he's crashing around so violently that the whole house seems to be vibrating.

Tom's words slip out of his mouth in a breathless jumble. 'I didn't get a look at him, he was wearing a baseball cap and it was pulled low over his face. When I opened the bedroom door, he walloped me on the head with a chair. I staggered back onto the landing and he followed me out there.'

'Shit,' Lainy gasps.

'It was a blur, but I somehow managed to tackle him and shove him into the bathroom. Then I used the chair to wedge the door closed. But from the sound of it, he could break down the door at any minute. We should get away from the house. Be with the girls.' He gets to his feet. 'Did you call the police?'

'They'll be here any minute,' Lainy says.

'This is all too much of a coincidence,' Tom mutters. 'He could be something to do with Jake and Dylan's disappearance.'

'Do you think so?' I ask.

'Don't *you?*'

'I don't know.'

Tom stands and closes the front door behind us, which means the intruder is now on his own inside the house. But if he breaks out of the bathroom, there's nothing to stop him barging his way out of the front door. Or maybe he'll slip out the back…

'Where are the police?' Lainy says, staring up the road and then down it. 'They said they'd be here any minute.'

On the edge of my hearing, I make out the distant wail of sirens getting louder. Seconds later, two marked police cars hurtle down the street and park over someone's driveway. The sirens stop, but the flashing lights continue, casting an erratic blue haze over the houses. I wonder if it's usual for two cars to show up at a burglary – perhaps it's because they think it could be something to do with Jake and Dylan's disappearance.

Two male officers make their way over to where we're now standing on the pavement. The older of the two nods at us. 'Lainy Ellis?'

'Yes, I made the call,' Lainy says. 'He's still in the house – the burglar or whoever he is.'

'You're hurt,' the officer says, staring at the drying blood on Tom's forehead.

'I'm fine.'

'Did you call for an ambulance?'

Tom gives a brief shake of the head. 'No, but I'm a paramedic, and like I said, I'm fine.'

'Still, you should get yourself checked out.'

Two more police officers join us on the pavement; one of them walks up to the house, crouches down and peers through the letter box. He straightens and returns to join us. 'There's yelling and banging coming from inside,' he says.

'The intruder hit me with a chair,' Tom explains, 'but I managed to trap him in the bathroom. He must still be in there, but I don't know for how much longer – he was doing his best to try to batter the door down.'

'Is he armed, do you know?' the older officer asks.

'Not that I'm aware of,' Tom replies. 'But he's pretty strong and very pissed off.'

The officer nods. 'Is there a back way out of the property?'

'There's a door to the garden from the kitchen,' Lainy says. 'But the garden walls are quite high.'

The first two officers head inside, the shouting and hammering from within easily heard from the street. I notice a couple of neighbours peering through their windows, and a few have come out of their houses to see what all the commotion is about. I try to avoid eye contact.

'Can you come away from the front door please, sir,' one of the remaining policemen asks Tom, who's tried to follow the first officers inside. This policeman's over six foot, and his uniform is stretched over his burly frame. He looks more like a wrestler than a police officer.

Tom does as he's asked and retreats back down the steps onto the dusty pavement.

'And can you all move away from the entrance,' the officer continues. 'Be better if you crossed the street, in case this guy decides to do a runner.'

We cross over the road to the car and then turn to face the house, our eyes trained on the open front door. My heart pounds as I wait for a glimpse of the person who broke in. *Could* he be something to do with Jake and Dylan? Surely it's more likely he's an opportunist?

It seems like only moments later that I make out dim shapes in the hallway. A police officer steps outside followed by a scowling dark-haired man wearing handcuffs, yelling abuse. The other officer follows behind.

Lainy and Tom instinctively move into the road, blocking the car windows with their bodies so the girls can't see what's going on outside the house. I join them. We have to flatten ourselves against the windows every time a car goes past.

The intruder has a wiry frame and a pinched-looking face beneath his baseball cap. My heart gives a jolt as I recognise him. 'I think that's…'

Tom finishes my sentence. '…the guy from the caravan park.'

'I know it was dark,' I say, 'but he has the same build and the same angry eyes.'

'Who do you mean?' Lainy asks.

'You know, the guy from last night when Faye and I went to the caravan park. He ran off when he saw us. What's his name…? Mark Tamworth.'

'Mark?' Lainy screws up her face and peers across at the guy until he's put into the police car and we can no longer see him clearly. 'I know it's been a few years since I last saw him, but that guy is definitely not Mark Tamworth.'

'You weren't there last night, Lainy. You didn't see him outside his caravan. That's him. That's Mark.'

'No, it isn't.' She frowns. 'His build is all wrong. His colouring is too dark, his features, *everything*. There's no way that's Mark Tamworth.'

'Okay, so it might not be Mark,' Tom says, 'but it's definitely the guy from last night. So if it's not Mark, what was that guy doing outside Tamworth's caravan? We need to let the police know.'

The older officer crosses the road to where we're standing. His eyes are fixed on me in an unreadable expression. My chest tightens. 'Faye Townsend?' he asks.

'Uh, yes, that's me. I'm Faye. What is it?'

'Would you mind coming down to the station with us?'

'What, *now*? What's this about? Is it to do with the break-in, or is it about my family? You know my family has gone missi—'

'Yes, we've all been working hard trying to find them for you. That's why we'd like to speak to you. We actually have some news in connection with their disappearance.'

Needles of dread stab my back. 'Can't you tell me the news now? Have you found them? Are they okay?'

'Please tell us you've found them,' Tom says.

'I'm not privy to the new information, I'm afraid. DS Nash just messaged me to ask you to come in. Sorry not to be more helpful, but I can give you a lift to the station if you like – not in the same car as matey boy over there, obviously.' He nods his head in the direction of the burglar, whoever he is.

'We'll come with you, Faye,' Tom says. 'I'll drive.'

'Tom,' Lainy says, with a sudden panicked look on her face, 'I don't want to bring the girls to the police station. But I don't want them inside the house, either. Not if it's in as bad a state as you say it is…'

'And you shouldn't be driving with that head injury, Tom,' I add.

'Why don't we take you there, Mrs Townsend?' the officer says.

I nod. 'Okay, thanks.'

'Lainy,' Tom says. 'You go with Faye. I'll stay here with the girls. Just wait here in the car with them for ten minutes or so while I try to tidy up at least one of the rooms. Is it okay to go inside the house, officer?'

'Yes, it's fine. Go on in. It's not pretty, but at least he didn't have the opportunity to run off with anything.'

'Thank you,' Tom says. 'And we appreciate you getting down here so quickly.'

'All part of the service.'

'Actually, thanks for the offer of a lift, officer, but I think I will drive.' I reach into my bag for my car keys, wanting a tiny piece of normality. Hoping the action of driving will shake away the quivering fear in my guts. Dreading what news they're about to give me.

CHAPTER THIRTY

His farmhouse is a little run-down these days, but it's still comfortable. The property is situated several miles down a private road. Consequently, when he's here, he feels like he's the only person alive in the world. Apart from today, that is.

Today is different.

He sits on the faded tapestry armchair absent-mindedly stroking Scout's head. He's not usually prone to dwelling on things, but today he just can't seem to help thinking about the past. About the present. And… well… yes, about the future too. He has always prided himself on his relaxed attitude to life. It helps that his work is mainly physical. Creative too, but there's a lot of manual labour. He likes it that way because it doesn't leave a lot of time for self-reflection. But, being here, waiting – it's just not good for him. His mind is skipping all over the place.

He stands suddenly and looks around the familiar room, trying to ignore the soft, sad sounds from upstairs. Perhaps he should set himself a task. There's plenty to do around the place – DIY jobs around the house, orchard maintenance, servicing his car or a hundred and one other things. Only, he doesn't feel like doing any of it. If he was alone it would be different. He could concentrate properly on whatever errand or job he set himself. But since he got back he just can't seem to settle to anything.

Well, it shouldn't be long now. A day or two at the most and he can get back to his life. Don't mix personal with professional. He's told himself that a million times. It never ends well. And the few times he's ignored his rule, it's always left him unsettled and questioning everything. Like now.

But he did make a promise. And he's never broken a promise yet.

CHAPTER THIRTY-ONE

After waiting with the girls in the car while Tom tidies the kitchen, Lainy and I cross the road and slide into Jake's Nissan. The drive to the police station goes by in a blur. Lainy directs me using the satnav on her phone, and I'm too busy concentrating on not crashing to have any kind of meaningful conversation. Anyway, what is there to say, other than us voicing all our fears? And there are too many fears to cover in one short car journey.

At the station, frustratingly, we're told by the desk officer that we'll have to wait ten minutes until DS Nash is free. Ten minutes may not sound like a long time, but when you're waiting for life-changing news it seems like forever. We sit next to one another on the hard seats in reception, but I can't keep still so I get up and wander over to the notice board, skim-read the information leaflets and then wander over to the vending machine and look at all the snacks, wondering if I'll ever regain my appetite. Anything to keep my mind occupied. To stop myself from breaking down.

I snap my head up as a figure comes into view. Catch my breath as I realise it's Nash, smart as ever in another of her light-grey suits. Or maybe it's the exact same one.

'Hello, Faye.'

'Hi.'

She turns to Lainy and gives a questioning smile.

'This is Lainy Ellis, my sister-in-law, Jake's sister,' I explain. 'Is it okay if she stays too?'

'Yes, that's fine. In fact, it's actually a good thing you're both here.'

'Oh, why's that?' Lainy asks as we follow Nash along the corridor.

'I'll tell you in a moment,' Nash replies.

We reach the small interview room I sat in previously, when I was here with Tom. It feels like days ago, but I realise with a shock that it was only yesterday. Lainy gives my arm an encouraging squeeze and we stare at one another briefly – an intense gaze that manages to convey all our unspoken thoughts.

'So, what's this about?' Lainy asks in her school-teacher voice. 'The officer said you had some news.'

'Please sit down,' Nash says, gesturing to the seats next to us. We do as she asks and then she sits opposite us, placing her bag on the floor and leaning her forearms on the wooden desk. 'Firstly, we'll be recording this interview, if that's okay with you?'

Lainy and I both agree.

'Just to explain,' Nash says, looking directly at both of us, 'this is a witness interview. And with these types of investigations where there's a missing child, we like to visually record as well as audio record. Is that okay?'

'Uh, yes, okay.' The thought of being videoed makes me a little uncomfortable, but of course I'll do it.

'Why do you need to visually record us?' Lainy asks.

'Mainly because we don't want to miss anything. Nodding, gestures, facial expressions. That type of thing. It's quite standard procedure. Nothing to worry about. Also a few simple words can be missed on a written statement or mumbled on audio. Later, these missing words could prove to be vital to help with the case. Does that make sense?'

Lainy nods.

'Okay then.' Nash reaches over to a side table and presses a button on a small black box. I glance around the room and notice a video camera fixed high up on the wall behind her, angled down towards me and Lainy.

'To put your mind at rest,' Nash says, 'as far as we're aware, no physical harm has befallen either your husband or your son.'

I exhale. '*What?* Really? How do you know? So… you've found them and they're okay?' I suddenly feel short of breath.

'Are they here?' Lainy's cheeks flush. 'Can we see them?'

'Unfortunately, it's not that simple,' Nash replies, pulling at the cuffs of her suit jacket. 'As you know, we've been out searching the area for your family…'

'Yes,' Lainy replies.

'But we've also been pursuing other lines of enquiry.'

'Other lines… I don't understand.' I wish she'd hurry up and just tell us what she knows. This waiting and second-guessing is torture. I'm literally biting my nails. And I never do that.

'Well –' Nash steeples her fingers – 'we circulated photos of your missing family to other police stations nationwide, but we've also been in contact with the French police and border authorities.'

I swallow and my heart begins to race. Sweat breaks out on my top lip. 'What are you saying?' I croak.

'This may come as a bit of a shock to you,' Nash says carefully, 'but the French authorities confirmed to us that both Jake and Dylan have been through the Port of Cherbourg.'

'What?!' I say. 'When?'

'Yesterday.'

'What are you talking about?' Lainy says, her mouth hanging open. 'There's obviously been some kind of mistake or mix-up. Jake wouldn't have taken Dylan to France. Not without telling Faye. No way. I'm his sister. I know him.'

'I'm afraid it's true. They used their passports in Poole and also at Cherbourg. I also have some security-tape footage that I'd like to show you. See if you can confirm whether or not it's them.' She reaches down to her bag and pulls out a slim black laptop, which she places on the table.

'This is crazy!' I reply. 'I'm sure when I see the footage I'll be able to tell you that it absolutely isn't them. What if... I don't know... what if someone faked their passports and they're pretending to be them? Maybe that's why the French authorities think they're in France.'

'That's a perfectly reasonable conclusion,' Nash replies. 'But it wouldn't explain why your husband and son are missing.'

'What about the intruder who broke into our holiday home?' Lainy asks suddenly, sitting up straighter in her chair. 'Maybe he's something to do with it? Maybe he's... I don't know... running some kind of passport scam.'

'You mean Mark Tamworth?' I add.

'It wasn't Mark,' Lainy replies.

'Can you bear with me a moment?' Nash says, getting to her feet and gathering up both the laptop and her bag. 'I'll be back shortly.'

'Where are you going? What about the footage you were going to show us?' I stand and run a hand through my hair, a thousand and one thoughts flying through my mind.

'Don't worry, I'll only be a few minutes.' She leaves the room abruptly, closing the door behind her.

I sit back down. My left leg is shaking and my hands feel numb.

'Where do you think she's going?' Lainy asks.

'I don't know.' I stare ahead at the cream wall, focusing on a thin crack in the plaster. There's so much more I want to discuss with Lainy, but I don't know where to start, and anyway, DS Nash will be back any moment and our conversation wouldn't exactly be private in here.

'So... they've got footage of them in Cherbourg,' Lainy says. 'That's...' But she tails off.

'That's what?' I prompt.

'Nothing. Never mind. Let's wait until we see it.'

I'm glad she's fallen silent. I need to think. To process what's happening. If this was a movie, I'd be hysterical about now, demanding answers, wailing, crying, yelling at people to find my family right now. But in real life, it's not like that at all. Instead, I feel closed down. Numb. I wonder if this is what it feels like to be on drugs. Detached from everything. Floating outside your body.

'Faye, whatever we—'

But I cut her off. 'You were right before – let's wait and see what shows up on the tape.'

'I was just going to say, whatever we find out today, whatever happens, I'm here for you. I'll always be your support, okay?'

My throat tightens. 'Oh, Lainy, please stop, you're going to make me cry. And I can't cry. Not in here.' I take her hand and hold it tightly. We sit like that for a few minutes more, deep in our own anxieties, until the door bursts open and Nash re-enters, bringing her vitality back into the sombre room. Lainy and I glance at one another with a look of support. I let go of her hand and focus on the detective.

'Okay,' Nash says, 'I've just spoken to the arresting officer. He's interviewing the man who broke into your house, and I'm able to clear something up for you. He's not Mark Tamworth.'

'I told you it wasn't him,' Lainy says to me.

'But it looked just like him! I swear to you, it's the same man I saw at the Grey Dolphin. He was standing outside his caravan. Tom agrees with me.'

'What I mean is…' Nash sits back down. 'The man you saw at the Dolphin is the same man who broke into your holiday house. But he's not Mr Tamworth. Mark Tamworth is currently in Cornwall at a music festival. He went there with his girlfriend a couple of days ago. He's still there now.'

'Oh.' I'm surprised by the news.

'That's why the thief ran off when you called out to him last night,' Nash explains. 'We think you must have startled him just as he was about to break into Mr Tamworth's caravan.'

It takes me a moment to digest this information. 'So who is he? This thief.'

'He's a local man wanted in connection with a string of recent house burglaries. He's predominantly been targeting holiday homes.'

'So, he's nothing to do with Jake and Dylan going missing?' Lainy asks.

'No. You probably saved Mark Tamworth from having his home burgled. We think the felon must have known Mr Tamworth was away.'

'Isn't it a bit of a coincidence that he burgled our house too?' Lainy asks.

'Yes and no,' Nash replies. 'He admitted he's been online looking at local holiday letting websites, working out which houses have holidaymakers staying in them, knowing that they'll generally bring a lot of cash with them for the week. That and the fact they'll also be out sightseeing or on the beach for most of the day, and eating out in the evenings, giving him long windows of opportunity.'

'So, he confessed?' Lainy asks.

'His backpack is stuffed with electronic devices, cash and alcohol, much of which is incriminating, so if anything of yours is missing, make a note of it and we should be able to get everything back to you eventually.'

I nod, but the last thing on my mind is stolen goods. I honestly couldn't care less if he's taken any of my stuff and I doubt I'll be checking through and reporting it. Not with everything else that's going on. I can't deny that I'm relieved the burglar is nothing to do with Jake and Dylan though. The man looked so shady, it made me shudder to think that he might have somehow had contact with my beautiful son.

'So if he's nothing to do with my missing family, can you show us this footage you were talking about?' I ask, impatient to steer the detective back to the subject of Dylan and Jake.

'Of course. I'm sorry to have left you hanging, but I just wanted to go and confirm that this guy was nothing to do with your husband and son.'

'Thanks,' Lainy says.

Nash slides her laptop out of her bag once again, opens it up and turns it towards us. She presses a few buttons on the keyboard and clicks a link on the screen. Lainy and I lean forward in our seats.

'This footage was caught on CCTV outside the ferry terminal in Cherbourg at 2.20 p.m. yesterday afternoon.'

The video is dark and grainy, but I instantly see the two figures as they walk out through the terminal's sliding doors. My heart jolts when I see Dylan. I hold my breath, remaining utterly still until the two of them move out of camera shot.

'Is that Jake and Dylan?' Nash asks as the video ends.

'Yes,' Lainy replies, glancing at me. 'Definitely.'

My throat seems to have closed up, so I nod my agreement.

'Dylan's face is clear enough, but Jake's face is angled downwards, because he's speaking on his mobile,' Nash says. 'I'll play it again and slow it down so you can really study the image. Make sure it's definitely him. Don't assume that, just because he's with Dylan, it's him.'

'Okay, but it is definitely him,' Lainy repeats. 'I'd know my brother anywhere.'

Nash taps the play icon and we watch them leaving the ferry building once more. Dylan looks happy. He gives a little skip as he exits the building. Probably thinks he's on some fantastic adventure. My heart twists. I wonder if he's asked about me. About where I am. I bite my lip to stop myself from crying.

'Are you okay?' Nash asks. 'Do you need a break? Tea? A glass of water?'

I shake my head and manage to force out a quiet, 'No, I'm fine.'

'It's Jake,' Lainy says again.

'And can you also confirm it's your husband, Faye?' She gives me a hard stare that makes me feel under pressure.

I nod. 'I think it's him. But can you run it one more time, just to be sure?' The main reason I want her to play it over is so that I can see my son again. It's hard to watch him there without me. But I'd watch it ten more times if I could.

Nash presses play again. I drink in the footage, feeling slightly less anxious now I see my son isn't upset – well, not at that point in time anyway. Lainy and I reconfirm that the two people are Jake and Dylan.

Nash seems satisfied with our answers this time. 'There's one further piece of footage that I'd like you to watch.' She double clicks another link. 'This clip was taken several minutes later in the ferry car park. But it might come as a bit of a shock to you, Faye. So please prepare yourself, if you can.'

I glance at Lainy, who gives me a worried stare in return.

Nash clears her throat and we turn our attention back to the laptop. Lainy and I watch as the man and boy walk across a busy car park to where a slim, fair-haired, attractive woman stands, talking into her mobile phone with one hand, and waving at them with the other. Her hair is pulled back off her face into a stylish chignon. She's wearing pale capri pants and a fitted short-sleeved top. The woman ends the call and smiles. Dylan's walk is less confident now. He slows right down and comes to a halt a few yards before they reach the woman.

'See here,' Nash says, 'Dylan seems hesitant to approach the woman. It looks like Jake is cajoling him to keep walking. Do you recognise her?'

Watching them both there with my son, I'm starting to feel physically sick. While Dylan stands, refusing to budge, the woman approaches and ignores my son while the man and woman kiss on the lips. Not just a peck, but a deep, passionate kiss. Both Lainy and I inhale. Hers is more of a gasp.

'I'm sorry, I know this must be hard to watch –' Nash gives me a sympathetic glance – 'but do you know her?'

'No,' I reply, my fingernails digging into my palms.

'So, I'm just trying to get this straight in my mind,' Lainy says, her voice now trembling. 'My brother hasn't had an accident on the cliffs, he has in fact run off to France with his fancy woman and taken my nephew with him?'

'It would appear so,' Nash replies.

'I'll kill him,' Lainy says through clenched teeth. 'I'll bloody well kill him.'

I know I should be yelling and screaming about my husband betraying me with another woman, but I can barely breathe. Seeing Dylan so unsure and hesitant on the CCTV cameras has brought home to me how much I miss my beautiful son. It's a physical ache in my gut. I need to go to him. I need my boy with me. Now.

CHAPTER THIRTY-TWO

THEN

Lainy and Owen step apart. Turn to see her brother striding furiously up the path. She recognises that look on his face. And with a sinking heart, she knows it's not a look that can be reasoned with.

Jake's eyes glitter, and his mouth settles into a hard line. 'Get away from my sister, you dick.'

'Jake, it's fine,' Lainy says. 'He was just—'

'Don't try to cover up for the sleazy wanker. I heard you scream, Lainy. He was trying to hurt you, wasn't he?' Jake takes a step forward and glares at Owen. 'I always knew there was something off about you, Pearson. Didn't I just tell you to get away from my sister? Are you deaf or what?'

'Jake!' Lainy pleads.

'Look, I wasn't doing anything wrong.' Owen holds his hands up in a gesture of surrender.

'Says you.'

'I just wanted to make sure Lainy got home safe, that's all.'

'Yeah, sure you were. You're just a Good Samaritan looking after poor little Lainy. You didn't run up here to try to get into her pants, did you?' Jake sneers.

Owen bristles at Jake's accusation. He drops his hands by his side and balls them into fists.

Lainy knows she should say something to defuse the situation, but the anger is pulsing off her brother in waves and she's scared that if she speaks, she'll only make things worse. The best way to deal with Jake when he's like this is to nod and agree with him until he's calm again. But it doesn't look like Owen is going to do that.

Owen scowls. 'You've got a screw loose, Townsend. Your sister told you she's fine. I've told you there's nothing wrong here, so what's your problem? Isn't your sister allowed to lead her own life?'

'She's only fourteen, did you know that?' Jake hisses.

'So? What's that got to do with anything?'

'She's fourteen and you're sixteen – that's wrong.'

'No, it's not. But anyway, I told you already, nothing's going on. And even if it was, why's that so bad?'

'Because she's my sister.'

'So, because she's your sister she can't do anything? That sounds fair.' Owen rolls his eyes.

Even though Lainy herself is trembling, she puts a calming hand on Owen's arm. He takes it in his and stands defiantly facing her brother. Despite the hostility of the situation, all Lainy can think about is the feel of her hand in Owen's. The fact that Owen Pearson is holding her hand. It's like a dream. But it's a false dream that's quickly falling out of her grasp.

'Get off her,' Jake warns, glaring at them both.

'Or what?'

'Jake, please…' Lainy says. 'Let's just go home, okay? Look, I'll come with you now. Owen's telling the truth. He was just going to walk me the rest of the way, but now you're here I'll go with you instead.'

Owen smirks at Jake. 'What are you doing up here anyway? I thought you were with Rose? Unless… Oh, I get it. I think I know why you're being so arsey – did Rose give you the brush-off? She did, didn't she?'

Lainy takes in a deep breath as Jake's expression darkens. Why did Owen have to stir things up? Doesn't he realise she's trying to calm the situation down? And why is he talking about Rose again? Everybody's always so interested in Rose.

'Ha! I'm right, aren't I?' Owen shakes his head. 'So, because Rose isn't up for it, you're taking it out on me.'

Lainy tugs on Owen's hand. If he's right and Rose really did reject Jake, it's no wonder her brother's in such a foul mood. 'Please, Owen, just leave it. Let's all just call it a night and go home, okay?'

'Fine,' Owen says, turning to Lainy. 'But I meant what I said before. And your brother isn't going to scare me off.'

Lainy's heart beats fast at his words. Blood rushes to her head. Her eyes flit from Jake to Owen.

Suddenly, Lainy is pushed sideways as Jake charges at Owen, shoving him onto the ground. She screams. 'Jake! Stop it! What are you doing?'

Owen's eyes are wide with shock, but he quickly springs back onto his feet. Now he's upright again, his eyes instantly narrow. 'What the hell?'

'I told you to keep away from my sister,' Jake pants. 'You weren't listening!'

'So, your solution is to shove me? Very mature, Jake.'

'Fuck off, Pearson.'

'Why are you such a weirdo?' Owen scowls.

'Stop it, both of you!' Lainy cries.

'What did you call me?' Jake snarls.

'I called you a weirdo.'

'Guys, if you don't stop this, I'm going to walk home on my own, okay? I'm not staying here to watch the two of you fight over nothing.'

'I'll just be a couple of seconds, Lainy,' Owen says. 'Your brother needs to hear a few home truths.'

'Oh yeah?' Jake replies. 'This should be interesting…'

'Look, Jake, no one likes you. They all think you're a freak. For some reason I've always stuck up for you. Always told them not to be so judgemental. But now I know they were right. You *are* a weirdo freak. And I feel sorry for Lainy having a brother as screwed-up as you.'

Jake roars and charges at Owen once more, getting him in a headlock. Lainy wants to intervene, but she's frozen in place, her limbs tingling. She stares wildly around, but the road and cliff path are deserted. She needs to decide what to do. And fast.

CHAPTER THIRTY-THREE

NOW

'Jake's having an affair,' I say quietly. 'He must have planned all this. He must have been planning it for ages.' I'm aware of DS Nash's eyes on me, scrutinising me. I think I must be in shock, because I'm saying things, but I feel barely any emotion. It's as though my mind and body have decided to go on strike.

'How could he do this?' Lainy cries, her outrage far noisier than mine. After a pause she adds, 'And how could Jake take Dylan? He knows the boy worships you, Faye. He'll be beside himself without his mum.'

'I know this must be incredibly upsetting for you both,' Nash says, 'but are you sure neither of you recognise the woman? I'll play it again, so you can have a really good look.'

'What about the woman's car?' Lainy snaps. 'Surely you must have got her number plate?'

'We've got footage of the car exiting the car park, but unfortunately the plates were covered in dirt. We think they might have been obscured deliberately. And it's doubly tricky to track them because the car she drove was a white Peugeot 208, which is one of the most popular cars in France. We only became aware of the footage a short while ago, which means they've already had at least a twenty-four-hour head start.'

Lainy and I watch the video again. I stare at the screen so hard that the image blurs, but I can honestly say I've never seen that woman before. Not to my knowledge.

'Well?' Nash asks, hopefully.

'Sorry,' I reply, 'I don't know her. But you must be able to find them. Now that you know where they are and now you have them on camera. I can't believe it. Jake must have *wanted* us to come to Swanage so he could do this. But how can that be, because I'm the one who organised the trip. Well, me and Tom.'

'At least we know they're okay,' Lainy says. 'Before we saw this video, we were worried they'd had an accident on the cliffs. Fallen into the sea. Drowned.'

'But that's what makes it so awful,' I reply. 'Jake must have known we'd think the worst. He must have known how terrified we'd be, thinking they'd both been in this tragic accident. That they'd been killed!' I get to my feet, wishing I could run out of here and never return. Every cell in my body is screaming at me to jump on the first ferry to France to be with my little boy. But I know I have to stay. I have to deal with this properly.

'If it's at all reassuring, we're working closely with the French authorities to find them. They've put out an alert and we've issued a warrant for Jake's arrest for child abduction.'

'Child abduction? It sounds so... I don't know... so *terrible*.'

Nash nods her agreement. 'The thing is, he booked a one-way ticket and there's no evidence to suggest he's returning. This, along with his clandestine behaviour, leaves us no other option.'

'I'm not disagreeing with you,' I say. 'I'm just trying to get my head around everything. Trying not to freak out.'

'I understand this is an awful lot to take in.'

'How could he do this?' I cry again, banging a fist on the table so it judders and vibrates.

DS Nash puts a hand out to steady the laptop. To stop it falling off the table. But she doesn't say anything to make me feel bad for my outburst.

'Sorry,' I whisper, shaking my head. 'It's just, I still can't believe it. It doesn't feel real. My husband is having an affair and he's abducted my son. *My baby.* He can't do that. He can't get away with it. You will find them, won't you? You have to!'

'We'll do our very best,' she says evenly. 'But as I'm sure you're aware, there are no border controls between France and its neighbours, so Interpol have also been informed.'

'Even if they stay in France, it's huge. They could hide out there for years,' I say.

'Not if they want to have a normal life.' Nash's eyes are filled with sympathy. 'Dylan will have to go to school, interact with people. It's difficult to stay hidden.'

'But not impossible?' I counter.

Nash gives a brief nod. 'No. Not impossible.'

'What about the blood on the cliffs? And you found Dylan's baseball cap up there too?'

'We believe Jake planted those, to make it look as though they'd had an accident.'

'But why? Why do that? Why not simply go off with *her*?' I ask. 'Why put us through such trauma?'

'To stop people looking for them,' Nash replies. 'If we all believed they'd had a fatal accident, we wouldn't be searching elsewhere for them. Maybe if he'd gone off with this woman on his own it would be different. But because he's taken your son without your permission, he's broken the law. He knew we'd come looking for him if we thought he'd abducted Dylan. It seems he attempted to fake their deaths to try to throw everyone off the scent.'

'But what about *me*?' I cry. 'To let me believe my own son had died… it's so cruel. How could he do it? I thought he loved me.'

'I know this is hard, but it's not all bad news.'

'How do you figure that?' Lainy asks bitterly.

'Well,' Nash replies, 'for a start, he didn't bank on us checking with the port authorities. So now we know he's alive, but he doesn't know we know. That gives us a slight advantage.'

'Although they could be anywhere by now.' I lean back in my chair, inhaling deeply.

'The warrant we've issued is a European arrest warrant. Child abduction is covered under the Hague Convention and the European Convention, so we get a lot of help from our EU allies. Without this it would be a lot harder, believe me.'

'That's something, I suppose,' Lainy says.

'Can you tell me about the organisation of the holiday?' Nash asks. 'You said earlier that it was you who arranged the holiday, not your husband. So when did he first find out about the trip?'

'Not until the day we arrived – last Wednesday. It was supposed to be a birthday surprise. Ha, some surprise.'

'Any chance he could have discovered your plans earlier and not made you aware?'

I pause for a moment. 'I suppose it's possible. But he seemed miserable to be here. He was so moody. Made me feel guilty for organising it. It was his suggestion to go back home.'

'Maybe he was edgy because he knew what he was about to do,' Lainy says. 'Guilty conscience.'

'What if…' I tail off.

'What?' Nash prompts.

'Well, it's probably nothing, but before I booked the holiday, Jake told me how much he missed the sea. That's what prompted me to book it in the first place. What if he was nudging me into doing what he wanted? He knows I love arranging surprises.' I shake my head in disbelief. 'I still can't believe it! What the hell was he thinking, taking Dylan away? Did he think my own son wouldn't miss me? That he'd forget me?'

No one replies. I hear the sound of a clock ticking. It seems to grow louder until it fills my ears and I can hear nothing else. Tick, tick, TICK, TICK.

'Faye. Faye...' I realise Lainy is shaking my shoulder gently. 'Are you okay? Do you need to lie down?'

I stare at her, confused for a moment, until I remember why we're here. 'Sorry. Sorry, I'm just trying to get my head around this. Is the woman French?' I ask DS Nash.

'We don't know who she is, or what nationality. Has your husband visited France before?'

'We've been on a couple of camping trips over there.' I cast my mind back. 'One just after Dylan was born, and another a couple of years later.'

'Does Jake speak French?'

'A bit. He's not fluent or anything.'

'We'll need to search your holiday home, and also your actual home. He may have left some accidental clue about where he's headed. You're from London, right?'

'Yes.'

'And in your previous statement, you said that your husband grew up here in Swanage.' She turns to Lainy. 'So does that mean you also grew up here?'

'Yes. We moved to London with our family when I was fifteen.'

'Could the woman in the video be someone from your childhood? Someone you grew up with? Did Jake have a childhood sweetheart from around here?'

Blood rushes to Lainy's cheeks.

'Can I take it from your expression that a name springs to mind?' Nash asks.

'Well,' Lainy says, shifting in her seat, 'there was this one girl he liked. But it was years ago and I'm almost certain they never kept in touch. I think she broke his heart back then.'

'Do you recall her name?'

'Rose.'

'And do you have a last name?'

'I think it began with an S. Or maybe… Cassidy. Yes, that's it. Rose Cassidy.'

'He never mentioned anyone called Rose to me,' I say.

'Everyone was in love with Rose back then. Well, almost everybody,' Lainy mutters.

'Lainy, do you think the woman in the video could be this Rose Cassidy?' Nash asks.

'Let me watch it again?'

Nash presses play and we both watch.

'I don't know… she does have fair hair, but it's probably dyed. Rose had this long, reddish-blonde hair back then. But it was almost twenty years ago, and it's hard to tell from such a poor-quality image.'

'Of course,' Nash says with a tinge of disappointment. 'We'll try to get in touch with Rose anyway. Rule her in or out. In the meantime, if you could both have a think. See if there's anyone who you think this woman could be. Even if it's a long shot, I'd like to know, okay?'

'Okay,' Lainy says. Her face has returned to looking pale and tired. Her eyes dark smudges.

'I think that's it for now,' Nash says. 'We'll assign a family liaison officer to your case to keep you informed of what's going on. Likewise, if anything else occurs to you, no matter how seemingly trivial, please do let them know as soon as possible.'

'So that's it?' I ask. 'We have to leave now, and just… what? *Wait?*'

'I know it seems difficult. But we'll be working hard to find them.' She gets to her feet to signal the interview is over.

I stand too and stare into Nash's eyes. 'You will get Dylan back for me, won't you, because… because I couldn't bear a life without him.' I grit my teeth to stop myself crying.

'I'll do everything in my power,' she promises, gently propelling me and Lainy out the door.

CHAPTER THIRTY-FOUR

Lainy and I arrive back at the house. It's dark, but there are still a few people walking into town, enjoying a Saturday night out, dressed up, chatting and laughing, oblivious to our personal nightmare. This evening at the police station has taken it out of me. I feel wrung out. Hollow. But I can't afford to collapse. I need to refuel and keep going. Stay strong. We walk up the front steps to the silent, looming house. It seems as though it's stooping, leering, watching us. I fumble to unlock the door, but the key doesn't want to fit in the lock.

'What's wrong?' Lainy asks.

'Tom must have called the owner to arrange a locksmith – because of the break-in. I can't get the key to work.' I turn the door knob, not expecting it to move. But, strangely, the door is on the catch and it swings open.

'How did you—'

'It wasn't locked.' A feeling of foreboding washes over me as I step over the threshold. Cloaked in darkness, the hall swallows us up. I press the light switch, but nothing happens. I press it a few more times. Still nothing.

'Lights not working?' Lainy asks.

'No.' I open the door to the front room and try the light in there, but that's not working either.

'Tom!' Lainy walks hesitantly through the hall. 'Tom!'

'Maybe he's upstairs with the girls?' I spend a moment or two finding the torch on my phone and then we make our way through the gloom into the kitchen. It's equally dark in here and equally empty.

'Tom!' Lainy yells. I detect panic in her voice. 'I'm going upstairs to look for him. See if the girls are okay.'

'I'll try his mobile,' I reply. 'We can't have had another break-in, surely.'

Lainy leaves the room and I'm alone, the light from my phone casting strange shadows. I hear Lainy calling out to her husband. I hold my breath, expecting the worst. After everything that's happened, I can't help my imagination running wild. I find Tom's number and am about to press call when I notice something shift ahead of me.

A black shadow on the far wall of the kitchen begins to move and I take a step backwards, crashing into a kitchen cupboard and dropping my phone. *What the hell?* I realise it's a door in the wall. It's opening. I scream.

A man's voice grunts. 'Who's there?'

'LAINY!' I somehow manage to yell as the man walks towards me. He's between me and the door to the hall, but maybe I can make it out of the back door – if I can unlock it in time. But I'm paralysed by fear. Is this another burglary? Or something more sinister? What about Poppy and Annabel? Please, God, let them be okay.

'Faye! Faye is that you?' Lainy's voice calls from upstairs.

But now the man is saying something and then he seems to disappear again.

Suddenly, bright light floods the room. I put a hand up to my eyes and squint. The door in the wall opens again and I squeal as a man walks out. And then I realise who it is.

'Oh my goodness. Tom! I thought you were another burglar! Or worse!'

'Same here,' Tom says, his breaths uneven. 'You scared the shit out of me.'

'What were you doing? I didn't even notice that door before.'

'All the lights went out on the ground floor. I found the electric box in this walk-in larder. I went in there, but I couldn't see a thing. The door kept closing on me. Eventually, I managed to flip the switch and the lights came back on. I'm so sorry I scared you.'

'Didn't you hear me and Lainy calling out to you? And did you know the front door was on the latch?'

'Was it? The owner's brother must have left it like that. I stupidly didn't check.'

'The owner's brother?' I'm not sure what Tom's talking about, but I don't have the opportunity to quiz him further.

'Faye, are you okay?' Lainy calls. 'Was that you screaming?' She bursts into the kitchen, her face drained of blood. 'Tom!'

I explain what just happened with Tom seeming to appear out of the wall and we all hug one another in relief. Then we sit at the kitchen table, a little breathless and shaken, but grateful it wasn't anything more frightening than a tripped switch.

'How were the girls?' Lainy asks, her face drawn and tired.

'They're fine. Absolutely knackered and full of questions about the police cars that were here earlier, but I managed to fob them off. Told them the police came to check if we were having a nice holiday!'

'And they believed you?' Lainy raises an eyebrow.

'Not sure. But I didn't want them having nightmares about burglars.'

'Good thinking. I looked in on them when I was upstairs, but they're fast asleep.'

'They zonked out as soon as their heads hit the pillows.'

'All that fresh air. I see you did some more tidying up.' Lainy glances around the room.

'As much as I could.' Tom shakes his head. 'It was ridiculous. I can't believe that one burglar was able to create so much mess. There was smashed crockery and glass everywhere. I swept it up and threw it away. I also contacted the owner and let her know we were broken into. Luckily, she was fine about it – shocked but very sympathetic. She sent her brother round to fix the door earlier. What about the police? How did you get on at the station? Have they got any news?'

Lainy and I look at one another.

'What?' Tom says. 'What happened?'

My mind starts to close down at the thought of relaying the whole story. Thankfully, Lainy launches into a detailed description of everything we discovered. About Jake taking Dylan. And about the footage of him meeting up with an unknown woman.

'You're joking! I don't believe it.' Tom's eyes narrow and then fill with concern. 'Are you okay, Faye?' He reaches out across the table to me and squeezes my arm. 'Stupid question.' He shakes his head. 'Jake with another woman? He must be mad. And he's taken Dylan? How could he? Was it planned? Are the police sure that's what happened? I mean, maybe there's another explanation…'

'It was pretty conclusive,' Lainy says.

'But what about the blood on the rocks?'

'The police think he planted it there to throw us off the scent. Make it look like he and Dylan had an accident.'

'I'm sorry, I know he's your brother, Lainy, but that's despicable. Putting you guys through all this heartache so he could go off with another woman.' Tom shakes his head again, in disbelief this time. Keeps looking from me to Lainy and back again. 'Shit, Faye. What are you going to do?'

'The UK police are working with the French authorities and Interpol,' Lainy says, answering for me. 'They're going to try to find them.'

'I should think so! It's outrageous. What the hell does Jake think he's playing at? Have you tried his mobile?'

'Constantly,' I say, looking at the screen again. 'But he probably hasn't even taken it with him. I mean, if you're doing a runner, you're not going to take your phone with you, unless you're really stupid. I bet he's ditched it somewhere.'

'What about those phone-locater apps?' Tom suggests.

'He doesn't have one,' I reply.

'I'm sure the police could locate his phone without an app, but I guess they've already tried that? He's probably lobbed it into the sea anyway.'

I shake my head. 'You're probably right.'

Lainy's body goes suddenly taut, her eyes widen. 'What was *that*?'

'What was *what*?' Tom replies.

'Shh, listen…'

We cock our heads and do as she asks. It sounds like a key in the front door.

I grip the table.

'Is that…' Tom gets to his feet and Lainy and I follow suit.

All kinds of possibilities race through my mind. *Jake? Dylan?*

'Hello?' It's a woman's voice.

'Who's there?' Tom barks, his voice gruffer than usual. He marches into the hall.

'Hello, it's me. Yasmin!'

Beyond Tom, I make out the perfectly coiffed figure of Yasmin Belmont, the holiday-home owner. I'm irritated that she's let herself into the house without knocking. But then I guess she was probably worried after the break-in.

Tom greets her, but Lainy and I throw one another a pointed look. I can tell Lainy is as irritated as I am by her casual entrance.

Yasmin doesn't seem to pick up on our annoyance and follows us through to the kitchen. 'Well, it doesn't look too bad in here.' She casts a critical eye over the room.

'That's because my husband spent all evening cleaning up.'

'You did?' Yasmin places a hand on Tom's arm. 'What a hero. And you said you trapped the burglar in the bathroom? Such quick thinking.'

I can almost hear Lainy's eyes rolling at this blatant flirtation.

'Most of the plates and glasses were smashed.' Tom takes a small step away, so her hand slides off his arm. 'But I bagged them up and put them outside. The police made a report if you need to claim on insurance.'

'Hmm, I'll take a look around the house, if it's okay with you.'

'That's fine,' Tom says, 'but do you mind not going into the room with the bunk beds? The girls are sleeping.'

'Oh.' Yasmin's face falls. 'I was hoping to check over *all* the rooms.'

'Uh…' Tom looks at Lainy to help him out.

'You can look at the other rooms. But, like my husband said, the girls are asleep, and I really would rather they weren't disturbed. You can come back tomorrow and check that room if you like.'

Yasmin raises her beautifully manicured hands. 'Of course, of course. Not a problem.' She turns to me. 'And what about your delightful little boy? Is he also asleep? Or is he somewhere with your husband?'

My throat tightens and I can't seem to make my mouth work.

'They're not here at the moment,' Tom replies.

'Fine. I'll go and check the other rooms then. Is there any obvious damage? Or was it just broken crockery?'

'The bathroom door.' Tom gives an apologetic shrug. 'I'm afraid he kicked the whole thing in. It's come off its hinges.'

Yasmin tuts. 'That's all I need. And what a terrible thing for you to go through on your holiday.' She leaves us in the hall and goes up to inspect the damage. Once she's upstairs, the three of us return to the kitchen.

'Don't you think it's a bit off that she let herself into the house without ringing the doorbell?' Lainy asks. 'I mean, I know it's her house, but we've paid for it this week.'

I nod. 'I was thinking the same thing, but I suppose it is unusual circumstances.'

'She's probably not thinking straight,' Tom says. 'I mean, it must be a shock to find out your house has just been broken into.'

'I suppose,' Lainy replies. 'And you'd have thought she'd know about Jake and Dylan going missing. The news seems to be all over town.'

'Not necessarily.' Tom sits down at the table and leans back in his chair. 'She doesn't look like the gossipy type.'

Lainy raises an eyebrow. 'How do you know what a gossipy type is?'

'Maybe one of us should go up there with her.' I take a step towards the hall. 'In case she wakes the girls.'

'Good idea.' Lainy sidles past me. 'I'll go.'

I sit opposite Tom and steeple my fingers, resting my chin on them, trying to make sense of everything that's happened this evening. But I can't seem to get things straight in my head. I can't work out if any of it is connected, or whether it's just bad luck and coincidence that we were broken into.

'You okay?' Tom asks.

'Not really.'

'Is there anything I can do? Can I at least make you some food? A sandwich or something?'

My stomach growls despite my lack of appetite, and I know I'm going to have to keep my strength up over the next few days. 'That would be great... if you don't mind.'

'Good.' Tom stands. 'I'll make us all one. Lainy's probably hungry too.'

'Okay,' I say with purpose, getting to my feet. 'I'll be back downstairs in a bit.'

'Going for a rest?'

'No, not yet. I'm actually going to pack.'

'Really?' Tom stands and walks over to the fridge, making a start on our supper. 'Don't you want to stay on for a few more days, see what the detective and her team discover? Although, I

can understand that you'd probably rather be home than here –
especially after the burglary. Talking of which, I haven't got around
to cleaning up the mess in our bedrooms yet, so—'

'I'm not packing to go home, Tom.'

'Sorry, not quite with you.'

'I'm going over to France,' I say. 'To find Dylan.'

There's silence. Tom gives me a look like I've lost the plot. 'Uh,
Faye, I don't think that's such a—'

'I know what you're going to say, but it's not up for debate.'
I square my shoulders. 'I'm booking the first ferry out of Poole
and then I'm gone.'

CHAPTER THIRTY-FIVE

THEN

Lainy's whole body is shaking and her head has gone swimmy, as though she might faint. It all happened so quickly. One minute, Owen and Jake were grappling one another, neither one having the advantage. But now… now Owen has gone over the edge of the cliff.

Lainy sinks heavily onto the ground and watches as Owen's dark shape bounces down the cliffside with a series of sickening thumps and cries, until he lands on a rocky outcrop at an unnatural angle and is silent. She gives a shocked moan.

'What the hell?' Someone else's voice startles her further. Lainy jerks her head around to see Kayla standing at the top of the path. 'Was that…? Did you just…?

'Kayla,' Lainy sobs. 'I think he's dead!'

'What happened?' Kayla cries. 'Was that Owen I saw at the edge of the cliff? Lainy! Why did you push him?'

'Me?' Lainy looks at Kayla with mounting fear. 'You think *I* pushed him? No, you've got it wrong, Kayla. It was my—'

'But I saw you!' Kayla cries. 'He was at the edge of the cliff and you pushed him. Don't deny it, Lainy. I saw you!'

'What?!' Lainy looks from Kayla to Jake, waiting for her brother to speak. But he remains silent. 'No.' She grows cold. 'No!'

'Lainy, what's going on?' Kayla cries. 'Why the hell did you push Owen? Is he okay?' She strides towards the edge, but Jake blocks her path. 'Owen!' she yells. 'Owen!'

'Hang on a minute.' Jake shoots Lainy a warning look before turning back to Kayla, his face suddenly a mask of distress. 'It was awful, Kayla. Owen… he attacked my sister. I had to pull him off her and then she… and then she…' Jake breaks down and covers his face.

Lainy listens to her brother's lie without contradicting him. Jake is saying that Owen attacked her. Why is he saying that?

While Jake is feigning grief, Kayla slips around him to reach the cliff edge. She sinks to her knees next to Lainy and peers down. Lainy stares again in horror at Owen's broken body below, bathed in moonlight, his stare glassy and unseeing. She realises she's panting. The night air suddenly too thick to breathe.

'We need to call an ambulance!' Kayla cries, looking around wildly.

'Kayla,' Jake says, crouching by her side, and putting a hand on her shoulder. 'I don't think an ambulance will do any good.'

'You mean…'

'He's dead,' Lainy whispers. 'He means Owen's dead!' Her voice rises to a wail. 'You killed him, Jake!'

Jake jumps to his feet and takes his sister's arm, pulling her upright. 'Shout a little louder, why don't you? I don't think they quite heard you in France.'

'Sorry! I'm sorry, but it's true. You did kill him. It's your fault. If you hadn't come along… If you hadn't charged at him like that…' Lainy can't believe that only moments ago Owen was here. Alive. She was holding his warm hand in hers. She was so unbelievably happy. Happier than she's ever been in her life. And now… now… 'It's true!' she repeats. 'You pushed him, just because Rose doesn't like you—'

'What do you mean? No they won't. We'll be fine as long as we tell the truth.'

'That's naive. Wishful thinking. In fact –' Jake glances around worriedly – 'we need to get away from here before it's too late and someone comes along and sees us.' He gestures to them to follow him, but Lainy finds she can't move, and Kayla remains standing by her side.

'We can't not call the police,' Kayla says. 'Tell him, Lainy. Tell your brother we need to report this. It'll be okay. We'll just tell them the truth. We'll tell them exactly what you told me, and they'll totally understand that it was an accident. No one will blame you, Lainy. Not once they hear what he tried to do to you.'

'And that's the other thing,' Jake says.

'What other thing?' Kayla asks.

'Do we really want to do that to Owen's parents? Bad enough he's dead. For them to find out that he's a rapist … what would that do to his mum and dad? No. It's better that we walk away and let them think it was just a terrible accident.'

Lainy's palms are sweating and she's getting chills all over her body. She doesn't know what to do. If she contradicts her brother, it will make him look bad and he could get in serious trouble – aside from what he might do to her. But if she goes along with his lie then Kayla will think that she, Lainy, killed Owen and the thought of that makes her want to vomit.

She and Kayla are both still frozen in place. Lainy feels ill at the thought of Owen's parents thinking their son was capable of doing those awful things. To hear that about your own child – it would almost be worse than losing him. Especially as none of it's true. But if the police find out about their involvement, the truth is bound to come out and she or Jake could go to jail. Or worse, Jake will stick to his story and it will be Lainy's word against Jake's. And with Kayla's version of events, Lainy would be the person everyone blamed. She could be convicted of murder!

'Listen to me, both of you!' Jake hisses. 'If we tell the police the truth, then do you really think they'll believe us?'

Kayla frowns. 'But—'

'No, Kayla! I'm serious. This isn't a game. This is Lainy's life. Do you think she should be punished for defending herself? Because that's what will happen. Whether or not it was self-defence, she still killed him, and she could go to prison. For life. Do you want that to happen to an innocent girl, Kayla? Could you live with the knowledge that you'd ruined Lainy's life?'

'Oh my God.' Kayla is sobbing now, tears and black mascara streaking down her face. 'What should we do?'

Lainy shivers. She listens to the conversation as if looking down from a great height. She can't believe they're both discussing her like this. Making out she's a murderer, when all she did was fancy a boy. How can Jake have made up those lies about Owen attacking her? Maybe she should speak out, protest her innocence again. Lainy gazes at her brother pleadingly, but he gives her such a chilling look that she's unable to open her dry mouth to contradict him again. Terrified of what he might do. Bile slides up her throat. Lainy is shocked at her brother's cool composure, but now she's praying that Kayla accepts Jake's version of events, because she's not sure what her brother will do if Kayla doesn't. This isn't the first time her brother has frightened her.

Usually, he's fine. Just gets on with his life and leaves Lainy alone. But there have been a couple of instances in the past where Jake's anger has exploded to the point that she was terrified of what he might do next. Like last year, when Lainy pointed out that the back door had been unlocked all afternoon while they were out. Jake had left the house after everyone else, so he got the blame. As a punishment, their parents grounded him the following day, which meant he had to miss out on a trip to the cinema with his mates. Instead of taking the blame for something he'd done, he came into Lainy's room and blamed her for grassing him up. He said if she ever landed him in it again, she would regret it. He didn't shout, or yell. He wasn't violent. But the look in his eyes was cold and dark – worse than any screaming match – and she'd had nightmares all that week.

The memory of that version of her brother comes back to her now. Lainy turns to Kayla. 'We should probably do as Jake says,' she says dully.

Jake gives a single approving nod. 'And you, Kayla... do you agree? Or do you want your name to be splashed all over the papers? Your face to be on TV? The police to arrest you as an accessory to murder.'

'Murder? But I wasn't even here. I only came up the path a second before it happened.'

'Exactly!' Jake says. 'So, is it fair that you should have to go through a nightmare in court and probably prison when it's simply a case of bad timing?'

Kayla turns to Lainy. 'What do you think, Lainy? Do you agree with Jake, or do you want to call the police?'

'I... I don't know. Jake's my brother...'

'Lainy's in shock,' Jake says to Kayla, talking about her as though she isn't even here. 'She was almost raped. Do you want to add a whole load of extra grief on top of that, Kayla? Lainy will have to go through hell, along with the rest of us. Do you want that?'

'No, of course not,' she replies hesitantly.

Before she has a chance to continue talking, Jake latches on to her reply like a drowning man clings to a lifebuoy.

'Exactly,' he says, exhaling. 'Because you know I'm talking sense. You know it would ruin our lives. You're right to put your friends first.'

'But—'

'But nothing,' Jake says. 'You've already given your word. And you know it's the right thing to do. For everyone. We can't bring Owen back, what's done is done, so what good is punishing ourselves? How is that going to help anyone? It won't help us. It won't help Owen's family. And it certainly won't help Owen. Now let's get out of here before someone sees us and it's too late.'

Lainy and Kayla hurriedly follow Jake along the dark road. Lainy casting glances over her shoulder as they walk away. The image of Owen lying down there in the ravine burnt into her retinas.

Jake seems totally relaxed now, striding along as though he hasn't just sold out his own sister. As though Owen isn't lying dead a few feet away from them. As though he hasn't a care in the world.

CHAPTER THIRTY-SIX

NOW

Before Tom can say any more about me leaving for France, Lainy and Yasmin come back down the stairs and into the kitchen.

'Everything okay?' I ask, pleased at the interruption to Tom's questioning.

Yasmin shakes her head. 'Not really, but what can I do?' She sighs, seeming less sure of herself than earlier. 'I'm sorry if the break-in has ruined your holiday. At least they caught the man who did it and no one was hurt.'

'Except for Tom,' Lainy says.

'You were hurt?' Yasmin looks over at him. 'Oh, I see. That gash on your forehead... was that caused by—'

'It's fine.' Tom waves away her concern.

'The guy whacked him over the head with a chair,' Lainy says.

'My goodness! That's terrible.' Yasmin's face falls. 'I can't do anything about that, but I can send a cleaner over here tomorrow to get the place properly cleaned. Will ten a.m. be okay?'

'You don't have to do that,' Tom says.

'Of course I do. I didn't realise the other rooms would be so... awful.'

'Tom cleaned up the kitchen, but we didn't have time to get to the rest of the house.'

'Thank you, Tom. Well, I'll let you all get back to your evening. Please call if there's anything else I can do.'

'We will,' Lainy replies. 'You grew up around here, didn't you?'

Yasmin gives her a sharp look. 'My family live here, but I went to a boarding school. I did spend my summers here, though. How do you know that? I thought you were from London.'

'We moved to London when I was a teenager. But my brother and I grew up here. I thought I recognised you.'

'I was always really jealous of you local kids.' Yasmin gives a wistful smile. 'I would see you all in big groups on the beach, or walking around Swanage, and I wished I could join in. Summer holidays were the worst. I always got so bored.'

'But I was jealous of *you*,' Lainy said. 'You always seemed so glamorous, being driven around in your lovely car.'

'Ha! With my lovely jailer, you mean.'

'Jailer?' I interrupt.

'My driver, Donny. My father gave him strict instructions not to let me out of his sight. So I was stuck with this six-foot-four babysitter driving me around until I was sixteen. It was so frustrating. Not to mention humiliating.'

'If I'd known, I would have invited you to join me and my friends,' Lainy says.

'Thank you, but my father probably wouldn't have permitted it. Ah well, it was a long time ago.' Yasmin gives an elegant shrug. 'Anyway, I've kept you too long. I really must go.'

Lainy and Tom see her out before returning to the kitchen.

'I can't believe she was jealous of us,' Lainy muses.

'Lainy…' Tom's voice is abrupt, making Lainy look up sharply. 'Faye says she's going to France. To look for Dylan.'

Lainy stares from Tom to me but doesn't reply.

'Faye,' Tom says gently, in a voice you might use on a wounded animal, 'do you honestly think it's such a good idea?'

I walk towards the kitchen door, preparing to leave the room. 'Yes. I think it's my only option.'

'But...' He splays his hands wide. 'Lainy, back me up here.'

She doesn't reply straight away. Her face is pale and her eyes are red-rimmed with bruised circles beneath. She looks ill. I dread to think how I compare. 'I think...' she begins, 'I think if I were Faye I would do exactly the same thing.'

I throw her a look of gratitude.

'But it's crazy. To just go over there with no information about where they are. Have you even brought your passport with you?'

'Shit.' I run a hand across my forehead. 'It's at home in the kitchen drawer. Jake must have brought his and Dylan's with him.'

'You could get it couriered here.' Lainy sits at the table and rubs the back of her neck.

'Good idea. My neighbours have a spare key. I'll ask them to go into the house and send it to me. When they hear what's happened, I'm sure they'll do it, no problem.'

'It's Sunday tomorrow,' Tom says.

'You can get stuff couriered at the weekend.' Lainy turns to me. 'It'll be expensive though.'

'Look, Faye...' Tom leans back against the kitchen counter. 'I know you think you'd be doing something useful by going over there, but you have absolutely nothing to go on. They could be anywhere in France by now. They could even have left the country, be in Spain, Germany, anywhere... it would be like looking for a needle in a haystack.'

'Tom! Give Faye a break.'

'Sorry, but I seem to be the only person talking sense here. And anyway, I'm sure the police won't want her to leave the UK.' He turns back to me, his expression sympathetic, but also firm. 'They'll want you to stay put to answer any questions, surely. Why don't you come and sit back down, have something to eat, and we can talk it through properly.'

'Tom,' I say wearily, 'I know you're only looking out for me, but at least over there I'd be doing something proactive – showing people his photo, going to petrol stations and cafés and asking around. What am I supposed to do here? Other than wait for news that might never come. My bastard husband took my child. I'm not going to sit around moping. I'm going to go and look for him. And it might take me days, weeks, months, whatever, but I *am* going to get my boy back. I'll hire a private investigator if I need to. Anyway, even if I don't manage to find him on my own, at least I'll be close by when the police do. Then, I can go to him straight away without having to book ferry tickets and everything.'

Tom's shoulders slump and he exhales a long, slow breath. 'Okay. You're right. It's not logical. But if it were my child, I'd probably do exactly the same thing.'

'Thank you for understanding.'

'I'm just worried about you going over there on your own. I wish Lainy and I could come. But we've got the girls…'

I wave his generosity away. 'You've both…' My voice breaks and I take a deep breath. 'You've both been amazing. You've been there for me like no one else has ever been there for me. I'm so grateful to you guys for all your support.'

Lainy scrapes her chair back and envelopes me in a warm hug. Tom joins in and we all have to sniff back our tears.

'I'm so sorry about my brother,' Lainy says. 'Truly I am. I'm ashamed to be related to him.'

'It's not your fault. Just because he's your brother, you're not responsible for what he does.'

'I know, but I still feel so guilty. Like it *is* partly my fault. I should have warned you off him years ago.'

'You didn't know! And do you think I'd have listened? I was totally besotted by him when we got together. Passionately in love – more fool me. Anyway, without Jake I would never have had my beautiful Dylan, so at least something really good and amazing has come out of it.'

Lainy nods, tears flowing freely down her cheeks now.

Tom puts an arm around his wife, and she leans her head on his shoulder.

'Anyway…' I take a steadying breath. 'Enough crying. I'm going to pack a bag, come back down for my sandwich, and then I'm going to try and book a ferry crossing.' I set my mouth into a determined line. 'I'm going to get my son.'

CHAPTER THIRTY-SEVEN

Chambourcy, France

He sighs as he juices a couple of lemons from the garden and adds a teaspoon of honey to alleviate some of the sharpness. If it was for himself, Louis wouldn't add any honey – he prefers the natural tang of the lemons. But it might be a bit much for the boy. Next, he adds a couple of ice cubes to the glass and gives it a stir with the long spoon, enjoying the clink of metal on ice and glass.

Louis gazes out through the tall windows at the orchard that has been in his family for generations. This place is in his blood, but he considers himself just as much English as French. His grandpère *would turn in his grave to hear such a thing. Louis' parents crossed the Channel when he was just a toddler, and he grew up just outside Swanage in Dorset, where he had an uneventful but peaceful childhood.*

Sadly, his own parents both passed away some years earlier, and when his grandfather died a couple of years ago, Louis was the only surviving relative. It's fair to say that he has a love–hate relationship with the place. He enjoys his life in Dorset but feels a responsibility to keep the orchard in the family – despite being the very last of his line. A situation that's unlikely to change, as he doesn't consider himself the settling-down-with-a-family type. So, Louis finds himself travelling often between England and France, caught in between two countries, unable to untangle himself from either.

He places the glass on a tray and opens a packet of butter biscuits. Louis knows he'll be in serious trouble if anyone finds out what he's done. But it's nothing he hasn't done before. And he didn't have much of a choice. Not really.

The boy is crying again, and it breaks his heart. It really does. But at least he won't be crying for much longer.

CHAPTER THIRTY-EIGHT

THEN

Without discussing it, Jake and Lainy begin walking the extra half mile back to Kayla's house.

'Look, I'm fine to walk back on my own,' Kayla insists. 'My place is totally out of your way.'

'It's fine,' Jake says. 'We don't mind.'

'Honestly, I'd rather be on my own.'

'After what's just happened?' Jake replies. 'It's dark and it's late and you must be shaken up. Of course we'll walk you home. And Pearson isn't the only nutter out there. We need to make sure you're safe.'

Lainy knows that this is just Jake's way of ensuring Kayla doesn't change her mind and go to the police station instead. Although, there's nothing to stop her doing that afterwards.

'Well…' Kayla frowns. 'If you're sure?'

'Totally,' Jake replies.

But Lainy can see that Kayla is uncomfortable. She's walking a little way off to the side and her face is taut, her head bent, hands wrapped around her body as she strides along.

After their initial shocking discussion back at the clifftop, none of them really knows what to say. There's too much to take in. Too much disbelief and horror.

Their footsteps ring out on the dark pavement. Beneath the street lamps, their shadows lengthen and shrink. At this moment, Lainy wishes she was a shadow that could shrink into nothing.

'Is it Kingshill Crescent?' Jake asks. 'Your road?'

'Next one along. Blakedene. Not far now.'

Kayla lives with her mum in a little council house in a cul-de-sac on the edge of town. Lainy remembers going there once for a playdate when she was much younger. Their mums had sat and chatted in the kitchen over cups of tea. But the playdate had never been reciprocated at Lainy's house, and so that was the end of it. They never really had the opportunity to become proper friends.

They finally reach the entrance to her narrow road and Kayla says she's fine to go the rest of the way.

'That's okay. We'll walk down with you,' Jake says in a voice that no one would argue with.

Kayla shrugs and they all continue trudging along the silent pavement.

'So,' Jake says, his voice clipped, 'are we all agreed that this stays between the three of us?'

Kayla keeps walking.

'Because if you've got any doubts, tell me now.'

Lainy wills Kayla to reply. To agree with her brother.

'Kayla?' Jake prompts.

'I already told you I wouldn't say anything.' She scowls. But Lainy doesn't think it's an angry scowl. More a nervous, worried scowl. It's probably the exact same expression that's on her own face right now.

'Good,' Jake says. 'So, if you're happy to keep quiet, then you won't mind swearing on your mum's life.'

'No!' Kayla stops and glares at him. 'I would never do that.'

'The thing is,' Jake says carefully, 'I need to know that we don't have to worry about you. This is my sister's life we're talking about here. And I can't have it ruined because of a sex attacker like Owen Pearson.'

Lainy flinches.

'Look,' Kayla hisses. 'I promise I won't say anything to anyone. To be honest, I never want to think about what I saw ever again, let alone speak about it. It was horrible… hearing about what Owen tried to do to you, Lainy. And then seeing him like that on the rocks. It's like something out of a nightmare.' Her voice cracks. 'I wish I'd never gone to the party in the first place.'

Lainy throws her arms around Kayla and they hug one another tightly, briefly before pulling back. Lainy sniffs hard as tears prick at her eyelids. But she can't cry. Not yet. Jake won't like it. Instead, she squares her shoulders, turns and continues walking down Kayla's road. The other two quickly catch up.

'If anyone asks, we'll say we walked you home because you weren't feeling well,' Jake says.

'Okay.' Kayla's voice is terse, impatient.

'We'll say you felt sick.'

'*Okay.*'

'It might be an idea if you tell your mum the same thing when you get in. You could just mention it. You know: *Hey mum, I'm not feeling too great, but Jake and Lainy Townsend walked me home.*'

Kayla gives Jake a withering look. 'I'm not an idiot. I know what to say.'

'Sorry.' Jake raises his hands. 'Just trying to—'

'Yeah, I know. Don't worry, all right. I won't say anything stupid.'

'Thanks. I'm just looking out for my sister. She's been through enough tonight.'

'Okay, well, this is me.' Kayla comes to a halt outside a yellow-brick terrace with a tiny, well-tended front garden. 'I hope you're okay, Lainy. But please, can we not talk about this again? Ever.'

Lainy nods. She feels exactly the same way. In fact, she'd be happy if she never saw Kayla Smith again.

'Good night, Kayla,' Jake says, fixing her with a stare. But she's already turned away and is rummaging in her pocket for a key.

Lainy turns and begins walking back, her heart thudding painfully against her ribcage, nervous about the conversation her brother will inevitably want to have now that Kayla has gone. Jake catches her up and she decides to be the first to talk.

'Why did you lie about Owen attacking me?'

'Isn't it obvious?' Jake exhales noisily.

'I suppose.'

'I mean, do you think she'd have kept quiet if we'd told the truth?' He's walking faster now. Almost too fast for Lainy to keep up.

'I don't know,' Lainy replies, almost jogging to match his long strides.

'Yes you do, Lainy. Don't be naive. You might be young, but you're not stupid. Well, not *all* the time. Why the hell were you walking back with Pearson, anyway? He's a wanker. Sorry, *was* a wanker.'

Lainy grits her teeth, but she knows better than to defend Owen to her brother. Not after what's just happened.

'He came after me. Wanted to walk me home.' She doesn't see the point in telling Jake what Owen said to her. That would only make him madder.

'If you'd walked home with Mark, like I'd asked you to, this would never have happened.'

'Yeah, well, Mark was with Cath.' Lainy doesn't add that it was supposed to be *Jake* who walked her home, but instead he was trying to impress Rose. She doesn't think that would go down too well either.

'What a fucking nightmare.' Jake runs a hand across the top of his head and quickens his pace even more.

Lainy can't get Owen's lifeless face out of her mind. She wonders if she ever will. She wonders if this evening will ruin the rest of her life. If she'll ever be able to feel normal again. Because right now, she feels as though there's a swarm of wasps in her head, buzzing and stinging and hurling themselves against her skull. To try to distract herself, she thinks about her parents, about how it's way past her and Jake's curfew and if they don't get home soon, her dad will end up calling the police and then questions will be asked about what time they left the party, and why they're so late and where they've been and who they saw. And Lainy realises that she won't be able to lie convincingly. That she'll ruin everything and end up in jail for the rest of her life. And her parents will be devastated and shamed. She gulps back a sob.

'Don't lose it, Lainy,' Jake barks, slowing a little.

'But—'

'No buts. You need to keep it together and be normal. If we get home and you're acting all weird, you'll ruin it.'

'I… I don't think I can keep it together. I don't feel well.'

Jake stops abruptly and grips her shoulders. Turns her roughly to face him. 'Look at me, Lainy.'

She raises her head as the tears streak down her face and under her chin. They slide down her neck and beneath her dress. Tears that feel as though they will never stop.

'Your name is Lainy Townsend,' Jake says slowly, enunciating every syllable. 'You went to a party. We're late back because Kayla wasn't feeling well, so we said we'd walk her home. That's it. That's all that happened tonight.'

'But how can I—'

'But nothing! Your name is?'

'What?'

'Tell me your name.'

'My name is…' Lainy wipes a hand across her nose. 'My name is Lainy Townsend.'

'And where were you tonight?'

'At… at a party.'

'And why were you late home?'

'Because…' Owen's face flashes into her mind.

'Because?' Jake's eyes bore into hers.

She takes a breath. 'Because Kayla felt ill, so we walked her home.'

'Good.' Jake starts walking again, this time at a slower pace.

Lainy makes her legs move after him, but they're heavy, like lumps of rock. And all she wants to do now is curl up in bed, go to sleep and never wake up. 'Jake?'

'What?'

'I don't think I can stay here.'

'What are you talking about?'

'In Swanage. I don't want to stay here any more. How can I go back to school and face everyone? Someone out there will find Owen soon, and then everyone will be talking about it and—'

'It'll be fine,' Jake says impatiently. 'They'll think it was an accident.'

Lainy doesn't want to anger her brother further, but she needs to get this sorted. 'What about if we move away?'

'What are you talking about?'

'Is there a way we can get Mum and Dad to move away from Swanage?'

'What do *you* think?'

'There must be a way. If we all went somewhere else, then I could forget what happened. But if I have to stay here and see where it happened. See Kayla. Owen's parents…'

'For Christ's sake, Lainy, keep your voice down!'

'We need to leave Swanage. If you can't think of way to convince Mum and Dad, then I'll leave on my own.' Lainy knows she's sounding hysterical now. She knows her brother is losing patience with her. But there's no way she can stay here in this place where this terrible, dark secret will gnaw away at her. Destroy her from the inside out. No way.

'Don't be so stupid,' Jake hisses. 'We are not leaving Swanage. If we left now, we'd look guilty as hell. No. We just need to carry on as normal.'

But Lainy knows she can't stay here. The thought of it makes her feel ill. She'll find a way. She will make it happen. Because the alternative is… there is no alternative. Not that she can see.

CHAPTER THIRTY-NINE

NOW

We drive off the small chain-link ferry onto the Sandbanks penin-
sula, leaving the Isle of Purbeck behind us. Tom's car bumps over the
metal exit ramp, joining the slow-moving crawl of traffic, mainly
made up of 4x4s, convertibles and performance cars. I'm grateful
to my brother-in-law for driving me to Poole today. I would have
taken Jake's Nissan and driven myself, but the only cross-Channel
ferry tickets I could find online were for foot passengers. I guess all
the vehicle spaces were sold out. After all, it is peak holiday season,
and the Poole to Cherbourg ferry is a popular route.

I know Tom is still not entirely happy with my decision to
travel to France, but at least he's no longer giving me a hard time
about it. I've decided not to tell DS Nash until I'm actually over
there. I can't risk her trying to stop me. Once I'm in France, I'll
leave her a message – explain that, as a mother, I need to be over
there. Surely they can't object to that?

Lainy and the children stayed back at the holiday house. She
and Tom are driving home to London tomorrow, taking Jake's car
back with them. I've arranged to pick up another car once I reach
France. Thankfully my schoolgirl French isn't too bad. I went on a
couple of exchanges during school where I lived with a host family
for a few weeks – they were enough to become semi-fluent. But
that was quite a few years ago now, so I'm probably a little rusty.

The roads are busy, so I stay quiet and let Tom concentrate on driving. We snake around residential roads that hide waterfront properties behind security gates, glimpsing modern glass edifices, pastel-coloured mansions and a few remaining traditional arts-and-crafts houses. Soon, the road widens, revealing a sapphire harbour on our left, and a string of contemporary townhouses and apartments on our right.

But all this glamour and beauty barely registers. My mind is filled with thoughts of the journey ahead. And of my son. Is Dylan all right? Is he worried? Upset? Is he missing me? All these questions are pointless, because I won't know the answer until I see him. Until I'm able to hold my little boy in my arms and tell him that everything is going to be all right. That I love him and won't let anybody take him away again.

Dylan and I have always been a team. From a young age, I would call him my little koala, as he would cling tightly to me, his head on my shoulder, never wanting to let go. I would have to peel his arms off my body to put him down to eat or sleep. He'd always choose to stay close to me rather than play with his toys or with his friends. Thankfully, his dependence has lessened as he's grown, but he still prefers my company to anyone else's. I've always had to work hard to encourage his friendships at school – inviting his classmates round for playdates and organising fun activities to try to get him to socialise more. That's why this separation is doubly hard. Thinking of him somewhere out there, without me, having to interact with strangers, breaks my heart. That's why I have this physical ache, as though a limb is missing. Why I'm desperate to get on that ferry.

I swallow the lump in my throat, but it comes straight back. I try to let the scenery distract me once more, but I don't feel as though this place we're driving through is even real. It's like a film spooling past in technicolour.

'You okay?' Tom stops at a set of traffic lights. 'You've been very quiet.'

'I'm fine.'

'You know, you can change your mind. If you're having second thoughts.'

'I'm not.'

'No, but if you are. If you do. We can brainstorm this thing together. Work out an alternative plan. Something less… uncertain. Something that doesn't involve you going to a foreign country with no real plan.' The lights change and we start moving once again. 'Just because you booked a ticket, doesn't mean you have to use it. And I know Lainy's really worried about you. We both are.'

'Thanks, Tom. I appreciate what you're saying, but I still want to do this. I *have* to.'

'It's just… you seem so…'

'So *what*?'

'I don't know. So sad. So alone.'

I don't need this. I can't have Tom being nice to me. Being kind. If he carries on showering me in sympathy, I'll fall apart. And that will be no good at all. I need to stay strong and focused. I take a deep breath and force a lightness into my voice. 'Tom, you make me sound like a helpless stray puppy! I might be going over there on my own, but I'm not *alone*. I have you and Lainy and the girls' support, don't I?'

'Of course.'

'Well then. And my French isn't too bad. I've been over there before.' The light tone I'm aiming for is fading. Replaced by a high-pitched wobble. So I clamp my mouth shut, afraid to betray how I'm really feeling.

'Okay. You're right.' He sighs. 'I won't hassle you any more. Just promise me you'll keep us posted. Call me and Lainy regularly. Let us know how you're doing.'

'I promise.'

We're already leaving Sandbanks behind and reaching a more built-up part of town with complicated road junctions and multiple lanes. Tom swears as he takes a wrong turn and we have to double back and do a couple more loops around the roundabout until we spot the exit to Poole Harbour.

After we cross the lifting bridge, the road narrows and we come to an older area with brick warehouses and workers' cottages lining the roads. Little pubs on each corner that look like they've been here for centuries. I realise that Dylan must have come this way too, and the thought both comforts and terrifies me in equal measure. I wonder what he thought of the bridge. Was he excited to drive across it, or was he upset and confused? This wondering is driving me crazy. I need to stop it.

Tom follows the signs to the ferry terminal and we soon reach a vast car park. 'I'll park here and get us a ticket.'

'No, that's fine. Just drop me at the terminal building.'

'What? No. I'll come in with you.'

'Look, Tom, I'd rather you didn't.'

Tom puts a hand to his heart. 'You've wounded me. I know I'm only the annoying brother-in-law, but I didn't realise you couldn't wait to ditch me.'

'Don't be daft. I just... I don't want this to turn into an emotional goodbye. It was bad enough this morning with Lainy. Both of us blubbing like two-year-olds.'

Tom pulls up onto the double yellows for a moment, two wheels on the narrow pavement. He switches his hazards on and turns to me.

I hold up a hand. 'Don't ask me if I'm sure I'm doing the right thing again, Tom. Please.'

His body deflates. 'Fine. Have it your way. But I'm sure the police will find Jake and Dylan soon, and then you and Dyls can come home together.'

'Thank you. Now, where's the terminal? These places are always so confusing.'

'I saw a drop-off sign back there.' Tom performs an illegal three-point turn and two minutes later I find myself standing outside the ferry building under the blistering morning sun, my suitcase at my feet, waving goodbye to Tom. Wondering when I'll next see him. But as his car turns the corner and disappears out of sight, a strange sense of relief overwhelms me. I was scared to do this. To come here on my own and leave behind the support network of Tom and Lainy. But now that it's just me, I feel a surge of strength infuse my bones. A strength I never knew I possessed. I pull out the handle of my suitcase and wheel it into the terminal building.

The queues are endless, and the noise levels are insane – echoing chatter and kids' cries blending with the muffled tannoy system announcements. But I don't let the wait bother me. Instead, I think about mine and Dyls' reunion. About how good it will feel. I don't think about Jake. And if he does pop into my head, I shove him out.

Eventually, boarding pass in hand, I make my way through the conveyor-belt system until finally I walk up the gangplank and board the ferry. I booked myself a seat, but before I go and settle myself in, I think I'll go up on deck and get some air. I need it after the drive and the air-conditioned terminal.

Although the ferry is full to capacity, I manage to find a spot that isn't too busy. Most of the passengers have made their way to the seaward side. But I'm on the land side, leaning against the railing, gazing towards Poole as a welcome breeze ruffles my hair and cools my skin.

I stare at this warm, southern edge of England that I'm leaving behind – my familiar, native country, with its English road signs and British pubs. Its right-hand drive cars and unique sense of humour. I soak it all in, wondering how long it'll be until I return. If indeed I'll ever return. And what that day will look like.

But these unknown worries aren't helpful. I need to focus on one day at a time. That's all. One day at a time.

CHAPTER FORTY

THREE MONTHS EARLIER

A tall stranger chases me through the rainy streets, but my legs are stiff and heavy, full of pins and needles so that I can't run properly. The stranger's feet thud against wet pavement. He's gaining on me and all I can do is stagger in slow motion, as though I'm caught in concrete. Terror grips my chest and squeezes. Sweat drips into my eyes. I know I won't be able to outrun him so instead I cross the deserted street and start banging on a wooden door that looks like it belongs to the apartment above.

I scream and yell for someone, *anyone*, to open up and let me in. The stranger is almost upon me. With my left hand I pound on the wood, and with my right hand I push the doorbell. Leaving my finger on it so that the ringing is continuous, becoming louder and louder. But I know it's no use. It's dark. It's late. No one is going to answer the door. No one will save me.

With a gasp, I sit up and open my eyes, my heart speeding like a juggernaut over a cattle grid. The details of the dream have disappeared, but the sense of terror still drenches me. My body is damp with sweat, my mouth dry, my ears ringing. And then I realise that the ringing is, in fact, my doorbell. It's dark in the room, so I reach out and switch on my bedside light and glance at my alarm clock – almost four in the afternoon. Discovering what time it is only makes me feel more disorientated, the blackout blinds making it seem like the middle of the night. My temples still pound from the headache I was trying to sleep off, the ringing doorbell not helping matters. Shakily, I slip out of bed and creep over to the window, lift the blinds and peer down to the street below. It's gloomy and drizzly outside – the recent aftermath of a storm.

The doorbell rings again. Through the blurry rain, I make out the top of a red umbrella. I'm not expecting any visitors. Maybe I should just ignore them. I'm sure whoever it is will soon give up and go away. And then the umbrella tilts back and I find myself staring down at a bedraggled-looking woman. It's Lainy. She's seen me. I give a short wave to let her know I've seen her too and let the curtains fall closed once more.

I sigh and move away from the window. I love her to bits, but she does have this annoying habit of dropping round unannounced. And as I work from home, it's tricky to tell her that I'm busy without sounding rude. Today, she's caught me in my pyjamas, which is even worse. She'll think I'm so lazy. I grab my dressing gown off the chair and pull it around me, tying the cord tightly. In the wardrobe mirror, I check out my reflection and wince. I'm going to have to resort to dark glasses.

I make my way down the dark staircase, reluctant to put on the hall light. Maybe Lainy will see I'm in my pyjamas and leave. I cross the small hall and pull open the front door, the scent of wind and rain making me realise how sealed off from the world I've been recently. I spy Lainy's retreating back down the front path, her umbrella bobbing above her.

'Lainy!'

She turns and I see that beneath her raincoat my sister-in-law is dressed in her teacher clothes – a smart print dress, with a green cardigan. She beams at me, and then frowns as she takes in my sorry appearance. 'Faye, hi! Sorry to disturb you. I wasn't sure if you were going to come down.'

'No, yes, of course I was. I was just having a rest. Bit of a headache, hence the sunglasses.' I'm trying and failing to sound upbeat.

Lainy walks back up the path towards me. 'Thought you'd gone all rock star on me.'

'Ha, I wish,' I reply, hearing the utter weariness in my voice. I really need to brighten up a bit.

Lainy leans in to give me a hug, but instinctively I cringe away from her, regretting it immediately. Lainy frowns. 'What? Do I smell or something?'

'No, of course not. Come in.' I mentally kick myself. Why did I invite her in? Now I'll have to offer her a drink and she'll want to talk, when all I want to do is crawl back into bed. Even the thought of another nightmare won't deter me from closing my eyes.

Lainy follows me into the gloomy hallway. 'I'm not stopping, just popped in to pick up my cake tins.'

I exhale with relief. 'Oh, yes. Sorry, I should've returned those ages ago. Come through, I'll get them for you.'

'It's the school cake sale next week and I really can't get away with shop-bought cakes. Not again.' She pulls a face.

'No one will know the difference, surely.'

'You'd be surprised,' Lainy drawls.

I'm not even sure how I'm managing to have a normal conversation; my head feels as though it's about to split into pieces. We walk into the kitchen. I'm too out of sorts to feel embarrassed by the state of it. The little room is dank and cold, the odour of stale food hanging in the air.

'Sorry to hear you're not feeling too good.' Lainy tilts her head. 'Can I nip out and get you anything?'

'Thanks, but I'll be fine,' I lie. 'A twenty-minute nap should sort me out.'

'Where's Dyls?'

'Playdate with the infamous Rafael Di Martino.'

'Oh, wow, he's in with the cool crowd.'

'I know. It's all he's been talking about this week. His mum's having three of them over and I don't have to pick them up for another couple of hours. I hope he's having a good time.' I drag a stool across the floor, wincing at the loud scrape, and clamber up onto it to reach the high cupboard where I'm hoping I'll find Lainy's cake tins.

'Careful,' she warns as the stool rocks precariously under me. 'It's a bit dark in here. Can you even see what you're doing?'

As I spy the tins and ease them out from beneath a couple of baking trays, Lainy opens the venetian blind to let more light in, and comes over to steady the stool as I pass down the tins.

'You really shouldn't be balancing on the stool like that, you could break your neck.'

'You worry too much.' I gingerly climb down.

'I'll get out of your hair and let you rest. Thanks for these.' She waves the cake tins at me, just as my sunglasses slip down my nose. Lainy gasps, her mouth hanging open. 'Your eye!'

I push my glasses back up onto my nose, but I can tell it's too late. She's already seen.

'What happened?'

'Fell off a stool?' I give a bitter laugh, knowing she won't believe me.

'Faye! Seriously, what happened? You have a black eye!'

I shake my head, feeling the weight of everything pushing me down. I realise too late that I should have ignored the doorbell. I should have stayed in bed. No, what I should have done is returned Lainy's cake tins ages ago. 'Let's just leave it at the fall explanation. It's easier than the alternative.'

Lainy swallows. 'Faye…'

'I'm fine, honestly.' Maybe it's not too late to fob her off. I give a forced laugh. 'It's embarrassing. The kitchen cupboard door swung open and the corner got me in the eye. Such a clumsy idiot.'

But her expression darkens. 'He's hurting you, isn't he?'

My stomach drops. 'What? What are you talking about?' I turn away and start to move the stool back to its original position, unwilling to let my sister-in-law see my face. Unwilling to let her see the truth written there.

'Faye, you don't have to pretend. Not with me.'

I stare out of the window through the slats of the blind to the courtyard garden, where the rain is beginning to hammer down.

'Faye, talk to me. It's Jake, isn't it? He did that to you.'

I shake my head, denying it, but I know my eyes are telling a different story.

'Oh God, is he hurting Dylan, too?'

I turn robotically to look at my sister-in-law, numbness filling my brain, replacing the sharp headache. 'He hasn't hurt Dylan,' I whisper with a surge of dread. 'Not yet.'

'Oh Faye, no.' Lainy's forehead creases and her eyes fill with concern. 'Why didn't you tell me? How long has it been going on?'

I shrug, unwilling to do the maths.

'Weeks? Months?'

I remain silent.

'Not *years*? I don't believe this.' Lainy wraps her arms around herself. I'm thankful she doesn't wrap them around *me*. 'You need to tell me what's been happening, Faye.'

Still I don't reply.

'Come into the lounge.' Lainy puts the cake tins on the counter and gently takes my hand, her fingers cold and damp against my warm, clammy skin. She leads me through to the little living room and sits me down on one of the battered leather sofas. 'I'm going to make you a cup of tea, and then we're going to talk about this.'

'I can't,' I stammer, panic filling my veins.

'Just stay there. I'll be back in a minute.'

Lainy heads out of the room, leaving me alone. I feel as though I've stepped out of my body, unable to believe she guessed what's been happening. How did she know? Most people would have accepted my story, wouldn't they? Jake is her brother. Why would she jump to the conclusion that he's been hurting me? Why would she believe *me* over *him*?

Back in the lounge, she shoves some paperwork aside and places one of the mugs on the side table next to me. Somewhere, deep inside my brain, I realise that I must have gone into shock or something. I'm sitting exactly where she left me, motionless, staring straight ahead.

'Drink your tea,' she says gently. 'I put sugar in it.'

I manage to nod absently but I can't seem to make any move towards it. Lainy sighs and sits opposite on the smaller sofa. She blows on her drink, then sets it on the coffee table. I realise she wants me to open up about Jake. She's probably wondering how to ask the question. I suddenly realise that I can sit here in silence, or I can unburden myself. She's already guessed what's been going on, so what have I got to lose? Before I can stop myself, I begin to talk.

'When Jake and I first got together, it was magical.' I sink back into the sofa. Thinking back to those early days, it's like it happened to somebody else. Jake was a different person back then. Or maybe he wasn't – maybe he was just a good actor. 'We were so in love, I couldn't bear to be away from him for a minute. And he felt the same about me. He really did. He used to call me his Pre-Raphaelite princess – corny, I know, but he adored me. Back then, I had no idea of the man behind the mask.' I give a little shudder, my throat closing up. But I can't stop now. I swallow and force myself to continue.

'I should have realised something wasn't right, because he always wanted to take charge of everything. At the time, I thought it was simply Jake being romantic and masterful. Hah. What a fool I was. I graduated from art college with so many opportunities to show my work. I was excited to begin my career. Looking back, I can see the ways that Jake subtly undermined my confidence and made it seem like it was my idea to give it all up. I think I lied to myself that it was what I wanted – to help him with his business and become a mother at such a young age. I'm still lying to myself today. It's what I always do. I suppose it helps me to accept my reality. Don't get me wrong – I adore Dylan. In fact, he's my only reason for living. But back then, all I wanted was to be an artist. And I never had the chance to even try for that dream.'

'How did I not see any of this?' Lainy mutters.

I look up, almost startled to realise she's still there. 'How *could* you see any of it? Jake's an expert at showing the world only what he *wants* them to see.'

'But why did you stay with him for so long? Once you found out what he was like?'

She doesn't understand. She doesn't know what it's like to be in my shoes. 'I didn't find out what he was like in one shocking revelation – it was a slow thing. The odd barbed comment here, a few little guilt trips there. I always felt like it was *my* fault he got angry. Not his. And anyway...' I put a hand to my belly, remembering. 'I fell pregnant with Dylan within that first year of being with Jake – we were bound together after that. I was nervous about telling him my news, but I needn't have been. He was ecstatic. We were both so excited to be parents. He proposed. I said yes. It was a whirlwind romance. Well, you know all that. You seemed pleased for us at the time.'

Lainy shakes her head. 'I'm so sorry. You always seemed so happy together.'

'No need to say sorry – it's not your fault.' I give Lainy what I hope is a reassuring smile. I can't blame her for her brother's behaviour. 'Anyway, after that first year of marriage, Jake became even more controlling. I can just about deal with that aspect of his personality. But these days it's his unpredictability that... well, it terrifies me. I don't know what will set him off. I have no idea what he'll do from one hour to the next.' My heart starts thumping again at the image of his scowling face. Or worse, at his smiling face – the smile that's not quite a sneer. The one that means he's enjoying himself.

'And you really never thought of leaving?'

I stare at her. A stare of frustration. At her utter lack of comprehension. But it's not her fault. 'Lainy, leaving is all I think of. I *dream* of it. I imagine this mythical life where I'm free. But every time I think of the *when* and the *how*, it all becomes impossible. Especially when I imagine what he would do to me. Every night I wake up drenched in a cold sweat with everything going round and round in my head. All the impossibilities of my life. What if I leave and he gets custody of Dylan? What if no one believes me? What if he *kills* me?' I know I'm sounding more and more hysterical now. My fingers are shaking, and my breathing is shallow. Everything I've bottled up over the years is pouring out in a torrent. I'm not even considering the consequences. The very thought of those consequences terrifies me.

'Well now you have *me*. I believe you.'

'Thank you.' My shoulders drop and I push my fingertips into my forehead, not sure if it's relief I'm feeling or deep, deep regret. 'I wasn't sure if you'd take my side. If you'd think I was making it up.'

'Let me look at your eye.' Lainy gets to her feet. 'Do you need to see a doctor?'

'My eye's okay.' I barely feel any discomfort from the results of last night's punch to my face. There's too much else to worry about. I decide that Lainy may as well see it all… 'It's not just my eye. There's more.'

'What do you mean?' Lainy stares in mounting horror as I untie my dressing gown. I'm wearing vest-top pyjamas underneath. I slip the robe off my shoulders and let it puddle around me on the sofa, revealing my arms. They're zebra-like – my pale white skin circled with black and purple bruising where he likes to grab me. To squeeze and pull, and yank and push.

Lainy chokes and puts a hand to her throat. 'Jesus! Why didn't you tell me before?' she stutters. 'Why didn't you tell anyone?'

'I told you, I didn't think you'd believe me. He's your brother. I thought you'd be more likely to take his side than mine. I thought you two were close. What Jake's been doing to me… he keeps that side of him so well hidden. There's far worse than this underneath my pyjamas but I don't want to show you. I don't want to show anyone.' My pulse throbs. Acid burns my throat. What will this revelation mean for me and Dylan? I realise I haven't thought this through properly. I was still half asleep when Lainy called round. Not in my right mind. Not thinking straight.

I quickly tug my dressing gown over my shoulders. 'It never used to be this bad. He could go for months without losing his temper. I knew how to manage him. How to keep everything calm and on an even keel. But now he's becoming more violent more often, and I know it's nothing I'm doing to wind him up. I think he might be having worries at work.' Panic floods my veins. 'You won't say anything, will you? Don't tell anyone. Not even Tom. Promise me.'

'Faye, we have to get you out of here. We have to tell the police.'

'No! Lainy, please. Listen to me. I knew I shouldn't have shown you. It was a moment of madness. Please, please forget I ever showed you this. I'm so stupid. Why did I say anything? Listen to me…' I glare at my sister-in-law, shivers beginning to wrack my body. 'He cannot know that I've told you. He'll kill me. And I mean he'll really kill me.' My head swims at the thought of it.

Lainy opens her mouth to disagree, but then snaps it shut again. She sits back down. 'What do you want to do?'

I bow my head. Twist my hands in my lap. Grateful that Lainy isn't insistent. Isn't being a do-gooder without fully grasping the situation. But now she's started speaking again, saying all the wrong things…

'Why don't you pack a bag now and come home with me? We'll pick Dylan up on the way.'

I snap my head up and fix her with a hard stare. 'I can't do that. He'll find me. He'll take Dylan. You really don't understand what he's like. You have no idea.'

'I'm so sorry, Faye. If I'd known what he was doing…'

'It's not your fault.'

'But I've always known he had a temper.'

'That's an understatement,' I whisper.

'I know you think you can't, but you absolutely have to get away from Jake.' Lainy's face takes on a haunted look – a look I've never seen on her before. 'There's something you don't know. Something I need to tell you… something I haven't spoken about to anyone.'

I shake my head. 'If you know what he's really like, then you know how difficult it would be to get away from him. If I take his son, he'll… I don't know. I don't even want to think about it.'

'I know, Faye. I can't believe this nightmare hasn't gone away. I can't believe he's still the same as he was back then. I really thought he'd changed.'

'He was like this *before*?' I jerk my head up at a sound from the hallway. At the click of a key in a lock.

Time seems to slow down.

Lainy's words cut through my fear. 'Is that…?'

'Oh no!' I freeze. 'It's Jake. He's home early!'

CHAPTER FORTY-ONE

With trembling fingers, I hurry to fix my sunglasses in place and slip my arms back through my dressing gown, tying it securely at the front. 'Don't say anything,' I hiss, praying that Lainy won't give anything away. Wondering if she can act as convincingly as her brother. I take a deep breath, desperate to regain control of my emotions.

'Don't worry,' Lainy reassures me. 'I just dropped round to pick up some cake tins, that's all, okay?'

I nod vehemently, grateful that she understands what's needed. 'Cake tins. Right. Stay calm. Act naturally.'

'Faye!' Jake's voice booms through the hallway, sending my pulse spinning.

'In here!' I call out brightly.

Jake's head appears around the door, his eyes twinkling. But this is to be expected. He's always his best possible self the day after one of his violent episodes. He steps into the room, an enormous bouquet of flowers in his arms. His expression falters a little when he sees Lainy, but he soon masks it with a smile. 'Hey, Laines, didn't expect to see you today.'

She stands and they kiss awkwardly on the cheek. 'Just came round to pick up some cake tins, but poor Faye has got a bit of a headache. Nice flowers.'

'Wow, they're beautiful.' I hope my smile looks genuine enough.

'Beautiful flowers for a beautiful woman,' Jake says, leaning down to kiss me.

I kiss him back, my body rebelling, but my mind forcing my lips into submission.

'Ah, poor you. Sorry you're feeling a bit rough. I've actually got to go straight back out – I'm meeting with a new client.'

The relief I feel at his words – knowing he's not staying – is like a tangible thing. I hope Jake doesn't notice it. I get to my feet, desperate to be away from his scrutiny for a few moments. 'No worries. I'll go and put these in water. They're so lovely.'

'How's things with you, Lainy?' Jake asks as I slip past him, taking the flowers with me.

'Oh, you know, same old.' I eavesdrop on their conversation as I walk slowly down the hall, trying to get my breathing under control.

'And how are Tom and the girls?'

'They're good. What's this meeting you've got?'

'Shit, I'd better love you and leave you. Don't want to be late. Traffic's terrible. I just wanted to see how Faye was doing. Her headache started this morning, poor thing. Maybe you should leave her to rest up, Lainy. Socialising will only make her head feel worse.'

'Sure.' Lainy's voice sounds fake and forced. I hope Jake doesn't notice anything amiss. 'I'll just finish my cuppa, and then I'll be off.'

I rush into the kitchen, grab a vase from the cupboard, fill it with water and dump the flowers in without trimming the ends or pouring in the sachet of plant food. I take another moment to compose myself before returning to the lounge and placing the vase on a side table.

Years of practice has taught me not to jerk back as Jake strokes the side of my face and kisses me on the lips. Necessity has made me a passable actress.

'I'll leave you two to it. It's all right for some,' Jake says good-naturedly, 'lazing around on a weekday.'

I notice Lainy gritting her teeth and I pray she doesn't blow it. Not when we're so nearly close to him leaving again. If she decides to let on that she knows what he's done, it won't end well for either of us. 'Have a good meeting,' she says instead.

I let out a breath.

'Thanks, Laines. You and Tom will have to come over for dinner soon.'

'Sounds good.'

Finally, he leaves, closing the front door quietly behind him. And it's as though the whole house lets out a sigh, a loosening of tendons and sinews that were wound up tightly only moments ago.

'How can you live like this?' Lainy demands, running a hand through her rain-damp hair. 'The fear I just felt when his key was turning in the door…'

'He was coming home to apologise.' I gesture to the flowers on the table. 'He feels guilty after last night. But the guilt won't last. He'll be angry again soon enough.'

'Then you mustn't stay here.'

'Before he came home, you were going to tell me what he was like, back then.' I have to get her to change the subject. I sit back down on the sofa, tucking my legs up under me and crossing my arms tightly around my body to try to quell the trembling that has returned with a vengeance. I slowly rock back and forth like there's a baby in my arms I'm trying to soothe. I find the motion helps me to stay calmer.

Lainy shifts in her seat, doubt etched across her face. Like she's changed her mind about telling me.

'Lainy?' I prompt.

'When I was fourteen,' Lainy begins, 'a boy I fancied walked me home from a beach party. And I know he fancied me back. His name was Owen Pearson.' She catches her breath. 'And he was the most gorgeous, funny, sweet person.' Lainy closes her eyes for a second, as though remembering. 'But my brother… he caught up to us at the top of the cliff path. He accused Owen of assaulting me. It was all a load of rubbish, of course, but Jake had just been humiliated by a girl he fancied and was taking it out on Owen. I tried to tell Jake that he was mistaken. That Owen hadn't done anything wrong. But my brother wouldn't listen. For some reason he seemed to hate Owen. He wanted a fight. It was awful. And…'

'And?' I get the sense that this is no ordinary story. That what she tells me here, today, will be equal to my own earlier revelation.

'Jake charged at Owen. They were grappling, but not actually fighting, just kind of locked together. I didn't know what to do. I couldn't call anyone for help – not all of us kids had mobile phones back then, me and Jake included.'

I nod my agreement and encouragement.

'Anyway, Owen managed to kick Jake in the shins hard enough so that he let him go. They broke apart, and I thought that was it. I thought they'd stomp off in separate directions. Go home and calm down. But…'

'What?' I ask, my heart in my throat.

'Jake… he pushed Owen. We were on the clifftop.' Lainy stops.

I break the silence, daring to hazard a guess. 'Did Jake… did he push him off the cliff?'

Lainy bites her lip and nods. 'Owen went over, but it was okay, because he still had a hand hold on the edge of the cliff. I could see his fingers gripping on, and the desperation in his eyes. I reached down to give him my hand and pull him up, but before I could grab him, Jake…' Lainy's voice catches. 'Jake used the toe of his trainer to loosen Owen's grip. He stamped on his fingers until he had to let go.' A tear slides down Lainy's cheek and she smudges it away. 'It was terrible.'

'He killed him?' I ask in a whisper. Shocked but not shocked. After all, I know the man she's talking about.

'I saw Owen fall,' Lainy says. 'He bounced down the ravine and then was freefalling part of the way. I thought he'd still be all right. That a tree or bush would break his fall. But he slammed into a rock. Landed on his back at a weird angle. The moon was so bright that I could see his eyes, staring, and the dark pool of blood that was spreading.'

'Oh no!' I'm waiting for her to go on, but Lainy's face is rigid. Her mind obviously fixed on a place that's as haunting for her now as it ever was. 'Lainy? Are you okay?' I get up and sit next to her.

Lainy gives herself a little shake. 'Sorry. I'm so sorry. I was remembering…'

'It's okay. It must have been shocking. You were still only a child really. Fourteen is no age.'

'When I think about Owen's face after he fell… it was blank. Like he wasn't there any more. It was so unbelievable to me that he was gone. That he would never laugh and tease and joke again. That I would never again get to know the feel of my hand in his. It was so… *final*.'

'What did you do?'

'That's the thing. I didn't have time to do anything, because just at that moment, Kayla appeared at the top of the cliff path.'

'Kayla?'

'Yes, a friend from Jake's year. She saw Owen fall, but when she saw me reach out to save him, she thought I was pushing him.'

'What?!'

'I wanted to tell her that it was Jake who pushed him, but before I could open my mouth, Jake was agreeing with her. He said it was me!'

'And she believed him?'

Lainy nods. 'I should have told Kayla the truth, but I didn't want Jake to go to prison. He was my brother; he *is* my brother. But I see now that prison would have been the best place for him.

It's where he belongs. There isn't a day goes by when I don't think about poor Owen.'

We sit in silence for a moment. Lainy's breath is ragged, as though she's been running. 'You know, just before my brother came along that night, Owen told me he liked me. I was so happy. So besotted. It was the best moment of my life… until it wasn't any more.'

'I'm so sorry, Lainy.' I lean into my sister-in-law, take her hands and squeeze them.

She sits up and stares at me for a moment. 'You don't seem shocked by what I've told you.'

'I am,' I reply. 'It is shocking. But we're talking about Jake, so I'm also not surprised. But –' my voice catches – 'most of all, I'm just tired and overwhelmed and I want it all to end.'

Lainy nods.

'Sometimes –' I lower my voice – 'when it's really bad, I wish Jake would just get it over with and kill me. But then I wouldn't be here for Dylan. And I couldn't bear the thought of that. I couldn't leave my baby.'

'Oh, Faye! I understand. I've had a lifetime of Jake and I think I've always been scared of him. At first it was a small fear. Like being afraid that he would shout at me if I did something to annoy him. But after that terrible night I realised that he was capable of so much more. And even if he didn't always show me his dark side, I still knew it was there.'

'Did you tell the police what happened?' I ask.

'I wanted to report it, but events happened so quickly. Things got confused. I was only fourteen. Like you said – still a child really. Afterwards, Jake told me that if I ever told anyone the truth, he would turn me over to the police and now he had a witness who would back him up.'

'He said that?'

Lainy nods. 'He was quite clear about it.'

'What about the girl, Kayla? Couldn't you have told her what really happened? Surely you could have gone to her afterwards and explained.'

'Jake twisted the whole thing into a clever lie. He told Kayla that Owen had tried to rape me and that the reason I pushed him was to defend myself. He made it sound so rational and believable. He played on her sympathy. Told her that if she went to the police she would be ruining my life. So Kayla agreed to keep our secret. I was worried that if I told her the truth, she would go to the police and then we'd all be arrested. But anyway, I didn't have the courage to contradict him. I didn't know what to do for the best. All I could think about was that Owen was dead.

'After that night, Jake was nice as pie to me. I rarely saw that dark side of him after that. I sometimes think I imagined it all. That it only happened in my head. But now – seeing you like this, seeing what he's done to you – I know it was all true. I know he really is that awful person. And I'm so, so sorry I didn't realise.' Lainy's chin wobbles, but she doesn't cry. I can tell she's trying to be strong – for me.

'What happened to Owen?' I ask. 'Did they find him?'

Lainy bites her lip and nods. 'The inquest ruled that it was death by misadventure. They found alcohol in his bloodstream. They concluded that he must have accidentally lost his footing and gone over the edge. It was all seen as some terrible, tragic accident. No one was suspected of anything untoward.'

'So you all just got on with your lives,' I murmur.

'Jake seemed to have no trouble getting on with his life. It took me years to feel anything approaching normal. But Faye, that was then. This is now. And right now we have to get you away from him.'

'I can't.'

'Look, what if I went to the police now,' Lainy persists. 'I could tell them about Owen. Tell them about what Jake did back then. Maybe they'd arrest him?'

'But you already said that Kayla thinks you pushed him over. With Kayla's and Jake's word against yours, it would end up with you being arrested and Jake getting away with it. And then he'd be angry with you too. He'd be furious.'

'Why can't we just show the police your bruises?'

'If I could guarantee that the police would keep me and Dylan safe from him, then I would go to them in a heartbeat. But Jake has already said that if I contact them, he'll never let me get away with it. He says he'll kill me and take Dylan. And if he can't do it personally, he knows people who will do it for him. And I believe him. I can't take any chances. Not with Dylan's life.' My voice is quavering now and I feel physically sick at the thought of what he would do if he knew I was even discussing him like this.

'You could move away with Dylan. Hide. I'd help you.'

'For the rest of our lives? Where would we go? How would we live?'

'There has to be a way.' Lainy taps her fingers together. 'We need to think outside the box. We need to come up with a plan.'

'Believe me, I've considered every option.' I hug my knees to my chest.

But Lainy's gaze hardens. 'Not *every* option,' she says.

CHAPTER FORTY-TWO

NOW

Chambourcy, France

Carrying the tray of fresh lemonade and biscuits, Louis walks up the creaky wooden stairs, the stiff soles of his boots squeaking with every step. He crosses the landing and knocks on the door at the end, three sharp raps.

The muffled sobs from within suddenly stop.

'Hello!' Louis calls out, trying to tone down his gruff Dorset accent. 'Can I come in? I've got some nice cool lemonade for you, and a snack.'

Silence.

Louis pushes the handle down with his elbow and opens the door.

On the floor beside a metal-framed single bed sits seven-year-old Dylan. His eyes are red, his face white and puffy from a night of crying his eyes out.

'Hey, still feeling sad?' Louis says with a tilt of his head. 'I brought you something to eat.'

Dylan sniffs. 'I want to g-g-go home. I want my mummy. And where's my daddy?'

'I'm sorry, Dylan. We spoke about that already, didn't we?'

'B-b-but—'

'And do you remember what I told you before?'

Dylan bows his head and clenches his fists.

'Sorry, lad, but your daddy's not coming.'

CHAPTER FORTY-THREE

The road is sweeping and unfamiliar. A road that's taking me away from my past and all its horrors. The scenery to my left and right is flat and green and wide, bordered by neatly clipped hedgerows. Ahead lies nothing but grey road and thick forest, all bathed in a warm, late-summer glow.

I haven't been able to call ahead, so I'm not sure what to expect. And, if I'm honest, I'm ever so slightly terrified. Lainy said that I'm over the worst. That things will only be good from now on. I'm not sure I believe that. But I've decided to take each day as it comes. To try not to look too hard into the future.

Much like the road, my car – a left-hand-drive navy Renault Clio – feels unfamiliar. But I already love it. It already feels like mine. The forest that lay ahead for so many miles is fast approaching, and now the fields are being swallowed up by trees, tall and green but with a crisp curl of yellow here and there. A nod towards the arrival of autumn. The season of change.

The road narrows, and every now and then, I flash past intriguing walls with high wooden gates and private roads leading off to hidden dwellings. According to the directions I found in the glove box, it won't be long until I arrive at my destination. Just a couple more kilometres.

I reach a charming hamlet situated at a crossroads – stone buildings with grey or green shutters, a couple of pretty restaurants, a farm shop. I consult the directions and take a right where the road leads me back into the forest. I'm getting close now, so I slow down and keep my eyes peeled for the turning. My stomach flutters as I pass the first landmark – a cream farmhouse with blue shutters on my left… then a field of ponies… and a stand of three oak trees on my right. Luckily there are no cars behind me as I slow almost to a crawl. And here it is! On my left, an innocuous dirt track. This has to be the one. Despite there being no one around, I indicate left and nose the Clio onto the track.

My inclination is to zoom to the end as fast as I can, but I have to take it easy because this little car is not made for a pitted road like this. I'm jolting around all over the place, my teeth and bones rattling. As I follow the track, it feels like it's taking forever, my hands aching from gripping the steering wheel so tightly.

And now, suddenly, the forest thins out and I'm driving through a lush, green orchard with fairy-tale red and green apples hanging from the trees like something out of a child's colouring book. A stream meanders off into the distance, a rippling blue ribbon. Up ahead, nestled in a shallow dip, sits a handsome stone farmhouse with the obligatory wooden shutters, a slate roof and tall chimneys.

Despite my quivering insides, my heart lifts ever so slightly. I never expected anything as beautiful as this.

As I approach the house, the road evens out and brings me to a gravel drive. The tyres hiss and crunch across its surface. A dog barks and a child cries out in the distance.

I unclench my hands from the wheel, turn off the engine and get out of the car just as the front door to the house swings open.

'Faye, you made it!'

'Hi.' I push my sunglasses up onto my head and walk across the drive to meet him. We kiss on the cheek. He gives me a hug and, despite his reassuring familiarity, I feel my anxiety levels creep up again. So much has happened since we last saw one another. 'Sorry I'm late,' I say. 'Hope you weren't worried I wouldn't come. It didn't happen exactly as I thought. I had trouble getting my passport… Anyway, is he here? Is he okay? I've been going out of my mind with worry, imagining all sorts.'

'Hey, no need to worry. Everything's fine. Come in.' As always, he's laid-back, composed.

I follow him through to a cool, wood-panelled hallway. He and I have known one another for years. We went to the same art college. I studied fine art, while he studied sculpture. He ended up becoming a stonemason (among other things). Said it was good for his soul, chipping away at rocks all day, creating beauty. I don't know how he manages to do everything he does – the stonemasonry, looking after an orchard, and the other thing… I guess he must have help.

'Where is he?' I ask, looking around at all the doors leading off the entrance hall. 'I thought I heard him outside. Sorry, but I need to see him.'

'Of course. He's out the back with Scout.'

'Who?'

'Scout, my sheepdog.'

'Oh, right. I didn't know you had a dog.' I pause. 'Was it… traumatic? Did you play him the video? Did he… see anything he shouldn't have?'

'No, nothing like that. Don't worry. It all went exactly as planned. He had one night of tears, a bit of homesickness the following morning. But since then he's been happy as anything. And now I can't prise him away from Scout. Last night, I broke my rule of no dogs upstairs to let Scout sleep in his room. I think you might have to get the lad a dog.'

'Oh, *Louis*. I can't thank you enough for looking after him. And for… the rest.'

'Well…'

'Oh, yes. I have your cash in the bottom of my suitcase. I can get it for you now if you—'

'No, no. Later is fine.'

During our college years, Louis and I shared a house with four other art students. The two of us were close – maybe because I'm such a good listener – but there was never anything more to our relationship than a deep friendship.

Louis always had such glamorous girlfriends and boyfriends, all of whom he told me about in intimate detail. I would always advise him and try to steer him down the right paths. I guess you could say I acted like his conscience. Although we're the same age, in some ways he seemed older, worldlier somehow. But I guess in other ways I was the sensible, grown-up one.

At first glance, Louis seems like an ordinary guy. But he's anything but. He has this magnetic aura about him that pulls you in. Makes everyone love him. Ultimately, I always thought he was a bit of a lost soul who needed looking after. Turns out, in the end, I needed him just as much as he needed me.

Looking back, I think the real reason we were drawn to each other was our lack of parents and siblings. Both his parents were dead. My mother was dead, and my father had been emotionally absent since that day, never coming to terms with it. While most of the other students went home to their families for weekends and holidays, Louis and I stayed behind in our student house together. We became one another's family. Like brother and sister.

It was during that final year at college that Louis – while drunk – confided in me what it was he did, aside from his college work. I don't think I believed him at the time. But when I looked back at the conversation, I realised he was probably telling the truth. The way he explained it to me was that he sorted out other people's problems. It sounded so innocuous. So... *helpful*. Of course, I asked him what sort of problems. Louis told me, 'Difficult problems. Problems that need to go away.'

I remember raising my eyebrows and laughing. He gave me an amused look and said that someone as lovely as me would most likely never have the sort of problems he dealt with. But if I did,

I should call him. I never even thought about it again. Not until Lainy suggested that we might need help with Jake. Even then, I was nervous about calling Louis up. Convinced I had the wrong end of the stick and was misremembering a conversation that happened so many years ago. That he would be shocked at my insinuations. But he wasn't shocked. Not at all. He said he was sorry about what I'd been subjected to over the years, and that of course it would be his pleasure to help.

After art college, Louis and I still kept in close contact for a few months – calling, texting and meeting up for drinks. But when I got together with Jake, there was no room in my life for other people. So we ended up not keeping in contact as much as we thought we would. To my shame, I let the friendship lapse. We gradually drifted apart. Of course, we liked the odd social media post and heard of one another through friends of friends. Occasionally, he'd message me or call to arrange a meet-up, and I loved those unexpected telephone chats. But as for meeting up in person – it simply never happened. It would have been impossible explaining to Jake why I was meeting up with another man – despite us only being friends.

'How was it getting through passport control?' I ask.

'No trouble at all,' Louis replies. 'You were right – Jake and I do look pretty similar. They didn't bat an eyelid.'

I exhale. 'Where's his passport now?'

'I destroyed it, like you wanted.'

'I still can't believe the police bought it. That they believed Jake abducted Dylan and ran off to be with another woman.'

'I told you it would be fine. Celia was outstanding as always,' Louis replies. 'Played her part for the CCTV cameras perfectly. She's back in her own country now.'

'Where's she from?'

'Probably best I don't say.'

I nod.

'And – I'm just checking – no one else knows, apart from Lainy?' Louis fixes me with a piercing stare.

'Of course not. I'm not daft.' In any case, there's no one else to tell – my mother is dead, and I haven't spoken to my father in years. I don't have any really good friends – none who would miss me terribly. Jake never allowed me to get close to anyone. He always discouraged friendships, finding fault with everyone I ever introduced him to. Making it obvious that he disapproved. It's something I'm nervous and excited about for the future – making new relationships away from the control of my husband.

'Louis…'

'What?'

'I wanted to ask… was it you?'

'Was what me?' he asks, although the tilt of his head suggests he knows exactly what I'm talking about.

'Outside the window. That first night?'

'Of course it was me. Who else would it be, lurking in dark places?' He smiles.

'You almost gave me a heart attack, you know that, right?'

'Apologies.' He puts a hand to his heart.

'And…' I chew at the inside of my cheek.

'What?'

'Can you tell me…'

He raises an eyebrow.

'Where did you… where's Jake now?' I'm scared of the answer, but I can't help asking the question.

'Look, Faye, like I said before, it's better if you don't know. You don't need to ask those questions. That's what you paid me for. Try to put it out of your mind. All you need to know is that he'll never hurt you again. Okay?'

It will be hard not to know where Jake is. To not know how Louis dealt with him. Every day I ask myself if I've done the right thing. If I could have done things differently. But when you're in the middle of a nightmare, frightened for your life, living in terror every day, you don't think straight. You don't act rationally. It took months to plan this and every one of those days was spent drowning in fear, trying to act as though nothing was wrong. Trying to present a calm exterior to my husband. I thought I would crumble and crack under the pressure. But I didn't. I managed to hold it together. Mainly because I had Lainy to talk to. She was my rock during everything. I still don't understand how two siblings can be so different.

My husband was a monster. I was scared for my life. And worse than that, I was terrified for Dylan's future. If I had tried to leave with my son, Jake would have fought me for custody. He was clever. He could have won. And even if there was the tiniest chance of that happening, I couldn't take the risk. Because if *I* wasn't in his life as a punch bag, then he would have taken it out on our son.

I follow Louis through to a charmingly rustic sitting room with a huge inglenook fireplace at one end. Through the open French doors, my heart swells as I catch a glimpse of Dylan running across a green lawn, throwing a tennis ball for a black and white collie dog. A part of me wonders if I'm a terrible person. If I'm actually as bad as my husband. After all, I've deprived my son of his father. I've done something that most people could never understand. But as I gaze at Dylan, I can't feel any remorse for my actions. I feel only relief. Relief that I'm not living in terror any longer. Relief that I've shielded Dylan from certain pain. Mine and Dylan's future may be uncertain, but at least it isn't one filled with fear and violence. At least I've saved my son from that.

Louis hangs back while I cross the room and stand in the doorway, shading my eyes against the sun. Watching. Drinking in the sight of my beautiful Dylan.

CHAPTER FORTY-FOUR

After a few moments, my son spots me. And for a split second he stands perfectly still on the lawn, like a picture from a bygone era.

'Mummy!' he yells and pelts towards me accompanied by his new four-legged friend.

I grin and run to meet him. 'Dyls!' I bend down and gather him into my arms, bury my nose into his neck, and inhale. This moment has been a long time coming. Although we were only parted for a few days, it feels like a lifetime.

He pulls away from me too soon, but his eyes are shining. 'Mummy. This is Scout. He's amazing. He can sit and lie down and high five. Can we get a dog? Where *were* you?'

'Oh, Dyls, I missed you so much!' My voice catches in my throat.

'Me too.' He rolls his eyes. 'Why did I have to go with Louis? I mean, he's nice and everything but I missed you.'

'I told you... because we're going to have an adventure and he's the one who helped to arrange it. Did you watch the video?' I gave Louis a recording to show my son. It was a video of me telling Dylan that it was safe to go with Louis. Telling him exactly what was going to happen, and that I would be coming soon to get him. It was a way to ensure that Dylan felt reassured. I'd spent so many years warning my child about not going off with strangers that I felt it was important for me to tell him Louis was a friend. I also made sure we met Louis beforehand, together.

We'd arranged to meet accidentally on purpose in an art gallery in Swanage, the night of Jake's birthday. I hadn't been keen, but Louis had insisted that if he was to take my son, then he wanted to meet him first – if only for a few minutes.

'You sounded funny on the video,' Dylan says, stroking Scout's ear.

'Funny?'

'Yes, like you were going to cry.'

'Oh.' I hadn't realised my emotions had shown up so strongly in my message to my son. I thought I'd covered them up so well. Obviously not.

'Where did Daddy go? He went down the cliff to get this beautiful lady's handbag – she dropped it down there – and then I couldn't see him any more. But it was okay, because Louis was there to look after me.'

'Let's talk about all that later. Why don't you show me some of Scout's tricks?'

'Oh. Okay. But, Mum, how long are we going to stay here? When are we going back home? Can we stay a bit longer? Because Louis said I can teach Scout some new tricks if I want.'

'Well, we can stay here for a little while, maybe a few weeks. But then we're going to a *new* home.'

'With Scout?' His eyes light up.

'No. Sorry, Dyls. Scout belongs to Louis.'

'With Daddy?'

'No, I'm afraid Daddy can't come. It's just going to be the two of us, okay?'

Dylan frowns for a moment, and my guts twist. Once again, I worry that I've made the wrong call. That I should have found another way.

'Is Daddy cross with us?'

'Why do you think that?'

'Because he's always cross with you. And… I…'

'You what?'

'I get scared when he shouts.'

My heart cracks. I pull him close again and kiss the top of his head. 'Daddy won't shout at you any more.'

'But what about you? Will he shout at *you?*'

'No, my gorgeous boy. He won't.'

'Promise.'

I take a breath to steady my voice. To inject some lightness into it. 'Pinky promise with chocolate buttons on top.'

Dylan smiles and his shoulders lose their tension. 'Can I show you some of Scout's tricks now?'

'Yes please. I can't wait to see them.'

'Okay.' Dylan strokes Scout's head and commands him to stay. He walks away and then calls him over. I watch as the sheepdog obeys all Dylan's excited commands, and I smile at Dylan's total concentration on his new friend, my heart so full of love that it's spilling over, running down my cheeks as tears. I try to wipe them away before he notices.

I don't know how our futures will pan out. I don't know whether Dylan will accept the lies I'm going to have to tell him. Lies to protect him from the fact that his father was violent. A murderer who was willing to frame his own sister. Although I realise that I too am now a murderer. I can't lie to myself about what I've done, even if I didn't carry out the act myself.

I wish I hadn't had to put Dylan through the trauma of going off with Louis, but it was the only way I could think of to protect him. And that's what all this has been about – protecting my child. I can't regret what's done. I can't let guilt eat me up or it will all have been for nothing. No. I can't dwell on the past. I have to look forward.

I vow with every fibre of my being to love my son and protect him for as long as there is breath in my body. Whatever happens, nothing will ever change that. It's a vow I will never break.

EPILOGUE

Closing the suitcase with a click, Lainy straightens up and feels her shoulders relax for the first time in years. She can't believe it's finally happened – she is free of her brother. For good. Her whole body feels light and unencumbered. Like she's just removed a crippling load from her back.

As planned, Faye has gone to France today to be reunited with Dylan. It won't be easy for the two of them at first, but Louis assured Faye that he could get them impeccable false documentation so that she and Dylan will be able to live abroad with no fear of anyone discovering what she's done. Faye said she would dye her glorious red hair a nondescript shade of brown. They'll lie low in France for a couple of months, and Faye plans to drive them east, find a small village where she can paint and maybe get some online commissions, and Dylan can integrate into a local school. Perhaps somewhere like Latvia or Hungary. She hadn't decided yet.

Lainy never told Tom what she and Faye planned. He wouldn't have understood. He's always been a straight shooter. He would have insisted on finding another way. But actually, that's what she loves about Tom – his solidity and goodness. He balances her out, and he's the best father to their girls. But in this situation with her brother there was no other way. Not for Faye and not for Lainy. And certainly not for someone like Jake.

Tom has taken the girls for one last swim in the sea before the four of them drive back home to London. Term starts again next week, and she still hasn't bought Poppy and Annabel's' new uniforms and stationery. Lainy's already getting that sinking back-to-school feeling. At least she tells herself that's what it is.

While Tom is out with the girls, Lainy said she'd stay at the house and finish packing up their things. The truth is, she needs the time to get her head straight. To be alone with her thoughts. To go over everything in her mind and let it settle.

It's been hard – pretending to her husband that she didn't know where Jake and Dylan were. Trying not to let anything slip. She and Faye agreed that they had to do everything they could to make it look like they knew nothing about their disappearance. They had to be convincingly shocked and upset. From joining in the searches, to leaving worried messages on Jake's phone. Even down to Faye leaving her passport at home. She couldn't do anything that made it look as though she had planned any of this.

But the strain of pretending has left her drained. The strain on Faye was even worse. Lainy knew how terribly conflicted she was about the whole thing. It was Lainy who had to keep her sister-in-law focused. Had to keep telling her she was doing the right thing. That she had no other option. And even now the hardest part is over, things are still going to be tricky for Faye.

She's gone to France without telling the authorities. And, okay, she is going to leave a message for DS Nash from France to let her know that she's gone to look for Dylan. But Lainy is sure they won't be happy about it. Maybe they'll even suspect her of something. By then, hopefully, Faye will be off the grid. She and Dylan will have new identities and a new life. They will be safe. And that's all Faye wanted for her son. A way to keep him safe. Lainy understands that maternal urge. She would face down the hounds of hell to keep her own daughters safe.

At first, the plan was simply to make it look as though Jake had run off with a woman, taking Dylan with him. But Louis said they had to be cleverer than that. They had to imagine they were Jake. Think about what he would do to get away with such a thing. If Jake were really planning to abduct his child and run off with a new woman, he would know that what he was doing was illegal – taking their child without the mother's consent. He would realise that the authorities would search for him. So Louis surmised that Jake would probably have faked his and his son's deaths to make it look like they'd had a tragic accident.

But, of course, with Louis ensuring they were caught on the CCTV cameras, the police would then discover that it was all a ruse. That Jake had tried to fool everyone and had in fact absconded to France. The authorities would come to the conclusion that Jake had purposely left Dylan's baseball cap and traces of his own blood on the headland, to ensure everyone believed he had died in order to cover up his departure and abduction of Dylan. Never knowing that the whole thing had been perfectly orchestrated by Louis.

In reality, there was no accidental death of Jake and Dylan. The blood on the rocks and Dylan's 'fake' baseball cap – that was simply staging on the cliff carried out by Louis. In fact, the blood on the rocks wasn't even Jake's. Faye and Lainy gave the police DNA on toothbrushes provided by Louis. Louis had obtained another father and son's DNA from an area outside Europe. Otherwise, with Dylan's DNA in the system, if he was ever to flag up on the system anywhere in the future, then all the alarm bells would start going off. This way, Dylan can start afresh with a new name and a new life and no risk of anyone connecting him back to his former life.

And of course, Jake didn't run off to France to be with his lover. There *was* no lover. Louis pretended to be Jake, using his passport to take Dylan across the Channel. He paid a beautiful 'work' colleague to meet them at the ferry port to act as Jake's lover. And Faye paid Louis to get rid of Jake. For good. The rest was done to throw the police off the scent. To prevent them looking elsewhere for possible suspects. To prevent them turning their suspicions on Faye and Lainy.

Louis told them that in delicate situations like this you could never be too careful. Never too thorough. He said that it's better to do *more* than you need, than not enough. Follow the logic through and leave no loose ends. Louis said it had served him well so far, and it was why he was confident of never getting caught. Lainy agrees with this logic. She likes the sound of Louis. Although she's never spoken to him personally, she's beyond grateful for what he's done for her and for Faye.

After Lainy initially came up with the idea to make her brother pay, Faye took quite a bit of convincing to get on board with the plan. After all, murder is not something you undertake lightly. But eventually, after another terrifying round with her husband's fists, Faye called round to see Lainy. She was in a terrible state – shaking and hysterical – and so she finally agreed to it. Faye had been friends with this Louis chap for years, and he was more than happy to oblige. And for a drastically reduced fee. Which is a good job, because otherwise they would never have been able to afford it.

Luckily, Faye had quite a bit of money stashed away from her cash-in-hand freelance sideline. Jake's control over her finances was the reason she set up this secret business in the first place – so she could earn her own spending money. And that money – saved carefully and secretly over the years – was the means she used to gain her freedom. So, ironically, his controlling behaviour gave Faye the means to ultimately escape him.

Lainy feels a little bad that she didn't tell Faye the whole truth about what happened all those years ago on the clifftop. But really, it makes no difference who pushed who. And the fact still remained that Jake was abusing Faye and he deserved to pay for that. And if getting rid of Jake also happened to tie in with Lainy's wishes, then that was simply an added bonus.

Because although most of what Lainy told Faye was the truth, she may have omitted a teeny tiny fact. Okay, maybe a couple of teeny tiny facts. The first of those facts being that back when they were teenagers, Owen did not at any time tell Lainy he liked her.

Just before she and Owen were interrupted by Jake at the top of the cliff path, Owen asked her something. Something that crushed Lainy's hopes. That made her feel small and irrelevant. He asked her if Rose was going out with her brother. Because, actually, Owen really liked Rose, but he didn't want to ask her out if she was already seeing Jake. Lainy had to pretend that she was fine with this revelation. She had to swallow down her grinding disappointment and look nonchalant. She had to act as though she was happy that he had chosen to confide in her. When inside she was twisting up and dying. Heartbroken.

She had been so excited after Owen had raced up the path to be with her. She had foolishly believed it was because he liked her. Because he really wanted to walk her home and be her boyfriend. But of course it wasn't that at all. Owen was using Lainy to find out if Rose was interested in Jake, because he'd seen the two of them spend all evening together. This was the first time Lainy had experienced the cold, sinking pain of unrequited love.

And it was more than she could handle.

So, when Owen had ended up breaking free from her brother's grip and had found himself standing on the edge of the ravine, it hadn't taken too much thought for Lainy to give him a good hard shove. Of course, she'd regretted it the second she'd done it. It was a moment of madness, a way to take back control of her emotions. She never imagined that her action would lead to his death. But she can't deny that in that instant, when her splayed hand pushed against his chest and she caught the utter surprise and shock on his face, she had enjoyed the power rushing through her bloodstream. The feeling of vengeance. She told herself it was her survival instinct kicking in. A way to banish the dark feelings that were threatening to drown her.

But then, afterwards, her brother had held it over her. He had saved her skin that night, telling Kayla that Lainy had acted in self-defence after Owen's supposed attempted rape. But Lainy knew that Jake wouldn't be able to leave it there. One day he would use it against her. And she couldn't let that happen. But unfortunately, a suitable situation to shut him up had never presented itself. Not until Jake's abuse of Faye had provided the perfect opportunity. And the best part was that Faye organised the whole thing. So that if the authorities ever discovered what had happened to Jake, none of it could be traced back to Lainy. It must have been fate. Serendipity or some such thing.

With a grunt, Lainy hauls the suitcase off the bed and starts lugging it down the stairs. She now realises that the one loose end in this whole sorry episode is Kayla – she's the only person left who saw what happened on the clifftop. She's like an unexploded bomb buried in the sand. Maybe she'll stay that way forever. But the chances are, that after their little altercation on the beach last week, she'll eventually go off with an almighty boom, destroying Lainy and Faye and everyone around her in the process. Lainy has to stop that from happening.

But that's going to take a little more thinking about.

A LETTER FROM SHALINI

Thank you so much for reading my eighth psychological thriller. I loved writing it and I especially enjoyed my day trips out to Swanage and Durlston Head to research this stunning stretch of coastline. I can highly recommend a holiday there if you ever get the chance. I'm sure it will be nothing like Faye and Lainy's experiences!

If you'd like to keep up to date with my latest releases, just sign up using the link below and I'll let you know when I have a new book coming out.

www.bookouture.com/shalini-boland

I'm always thrilled to get feedback about my books. Hearing your thoughts helps me to become a better writer, so it's very important to me. If you have the time, I'd be really grateful if you'd be kind enough to post a short review online or tell your friends about it. It also helps new readers to discover one of my books for the first time.

When I'm not busy making up conversations with fictional characters, I adore chatting to my real-life readers, so please feel free to get in touch via my Facebook page, through Twitter, Goodreads or my website.

Thanks so much!
Shalini x

shalinibolandauthor

@shaliniboland

4727364.shalini_boland

shaliniboland.co.uk

ACKNOWLEDGEMENTS

Thank you to my publisher, Natasha Harding, for all your flexibility, understanding, and for helping to make my stories the best that they can be. It's been a pleasure working with you on my latest novel.

Thanks also to the fabulous team at Bookouture: especially Ellen Gleeson, Peta Nightingale, Noelle Holton, Alexandra Holmes and Leodora Darlington, who are always SO lovely to work with. Thank you Natalie Butlin for your commercial expertise, and Alex Crow for your incredible marketing skills – my awe of you grows daily!

A huge thank you to publicity guru Kim Nash, an all-round fabulous person and superhero. And now an author too! Hope you don't mind me using your last name for my detective. I was trying to think of a good name, and yours just popped into my head!

Thank you to author and police officer Sammy H. K. Smith for advising on all the police-procedural aspects of my book, especially as you've had your hands full with your beautiful babies. As always, any mistakes and embellishments in procedure are my own.

Thank you to Fraser Crichton for your wonderful copy edits, as always. To Terry Harden, Julie Carey and Amara Gillo for beta reading – I always value your feedback and opinions. And to Becca Allen for your excellent proofreading skills.

Massive thanks to all my fellow Loungers in the Bookouture Lounge for your chat, advice, support and laughs. You really are the best of the best.

Thank you to all my readers who take the time to read, review or recommend my books. I'm so grateful for your unending support and it's been great getting to know you.

Finally, a kiss and a hug for my husband, Pete Boland. You truly are the love of my life. You're always there to advise and support me. And to force me out of the house for fresh air when I've taken root on the sofa with my laptop. It's been a strange year, but we're still here. xxx